The Body in the Bookshop
An Emerson Fox Mystery

Jennifer Shaw Wolf

Wolf Publishing

Chapter 1

Watermelon PhD

"And after I finished the academy, I spent three years bouncing around these little islands, not much going on, but I kept my head down and worked hard, always looking for the opportunity to advance..."

Emerson Fox picked up another chip from the bowl between them and dipped it carefully before leaning over the table to keep from dripping salsa on the cream-colored sweater she'd borrowed from her roommate, Ginny. The man sitting across from her continued as if this were a job interview. He'd spent the ten minutes since she'd introduced herself spouting off his credentials like he was reading his résumé. She'd taken in the first few words—he was from a small town, he'd gone to a state college, he was a cop, she'd known all this from his profile—and then her mind started to wander, as it always did. With his job, wavy dark hair and piercing blue eyes—probably where he got his name—Pierce Hamilton belonged in an old British mystery. Something by Agatha Christie, maybe. He'd be the young police inspector who was too smart to take advice from an old woman like Miss Marple.

Other than the fact that he was actually better looking in person than his profile picture, there was little in the reality of Pierce Hamilton that resembled the open, interesting, even funny guy she'd chatted with over the last five days; the one who'd persuaded her to leave the solitude of her apartment and take a ferry to Sharp Island, a tiny island in the San Juans off the coast of Washington.

She wondered what he was thinking now that they'd met in real life. Ginny had taken a more recent picture when she'd convinced Emmy to set up her profile on a dating app. This one included the extra fifteen pounds she'd acquired from the stress of her recent break up (nothing wrong with a few curves, Ginny had said) and her longer, browner hair now that no one was paying for her every other month visit to a high-end salon for a haircut and highlights. Her green eyes had stayed the same, albeit with the addition of a few stress smudges easily covered up with make-up.

Across the room, the waiter grinned at her as he flicked a damp white cloth over a recently vacated table. He appeared to be just a few years older than her. He had curly red hair, a white button-down shirt, and a black apron tied around his waist. He would be the flippant, down on his luck, young scoundrel in the story, the one everyone suspected. He'd have a sketchy alibi and a heart of gold. He'd end up with a young heiress he didn't deserve, but they'd still live happily ever after.

The clunk of muted metal against the hard tile floor drew her attention to an empty table in the corner. An old man leaned heavily on a cane as he stood. He'd be the perfect character for—

"Just got your degree, was that a master's program or a PhD or…" Pierce trailed off as Emmy looked at him blankly. She hadn't realized he'd stopped spouting his credentials and was asking for hers.

"A PhD?" Emmy repeated, trying to give the combination of letters some meaning, so he wouldn't know she hadn't been paying attention.

Pierce obviously took it as an answer. "That's impressive. It takes a lot of dedication to complete a doctorate program. I didn't go further than my bachelor's. What did you say you got your PhD in?"

Emmy took a long sip of the drink that had been placed in front of her, trying to decide whether it was worth it to admit the truth and correct her inadvertent lie. It had been so long since she'd been in the dating game that she couldn't judge whether there would be a second date or a third, or if they'd end up falling madly in love with each other and she'd have to confess the lie on their wedding night and he'd break things off, saying he could never tru— Something was off about her drink. She took another sip before she realized what it was.

"Watermelon!" she cried out.

"You have a PhD in watermelon?"

"No." Emmy reached across the table for his glass, knocking over the bowl of chips and dragging the sleeve of her roommate's sweater through the salsa. She took a couple of gulps of his plain lemon-lime soda, praying it would settle the storm in her stomach. It didn't. She stood, looking around frantically for the restroom. She was allergic to watermelon. Not in the "need an EpiPen and a ride in an ambulance" allergic, but "throw up all over the table, your date, and your roommate's cashmere sweater" allergic.

She spotted the bathroom and the old man making his way slowly toward it. She stood, covered her mouth and dashed toward the door. She plowed past the old man, knocking him against the wall. She was just inside the door when the chips and salsa, her date's lemon-lime soda, and the watermelon lemonade she definitely had *not* ordered spewed into the garbage can.

Chapter 2
The Professor

Emmy opened the bathroom door, just a crack, and peered out. She had this insane hope that the restaurant would be completely empty. It wasn't. If anything it was more full than it had been when she'd made her dramatic retreat. She tried to remember how the insidious watermelon-tainted liquid had ended up in front of her. She had a vague memory of her date saying, "I hope you don't mind, I was hungry, so I ordered drinks and appetizers already. I was told this is a house favorite."

She'd said she didn't mind. She hadn't smelled or tasted the watermelon in the drink until it had reached her stomach and the damage was done. Who puts watermelon in lemonade anyway?

She stood up straight, rolled up the sleeves of her roommate's cardigan to hide the stains and steeled herself to face her date and anyone else who had seen her spectacularly humiliating exit.

The table was empty.

Relief and disappointment washed over her. She didn't have to face the embarrassment of trying to explain where she'd gone and why, but she had to relinquish the exciting flutter of "what if" to the sinking weight of "not meant to be." Chatting with Pierce online had been a fun distraction. A couple of times she could almost imagine there was something between them. She wished Ginny hadn't talked her into the date. It was much easier to exchange witty banter over a phone than actually meet someone face to face.

As she got closer to the table, Emmy noticed a little piece of paper tucked under the salt shaker. At least he'd had the decency to leave a note.

She flipped over the paper to see what his excuse was for leaving. It took her a couple of heartbeats to realize it wasn't a note. It was the bill for the two drinks and the appetizer. In another heartbeat she realized that her date wasn't the only thing that was missing.

He'd taken her purse.

Growing more frantic and at least as red as the inside of a cut watermelon, Emmy searched around the table; maybe he'd tucked it under the seat so no one would take it. He was a cop, maybe he—

"Are you done with your meal?" The man who yelled at her from the cash register across the room wasn't the roguish redhead she'd seen earlier. This man was wide and tall and bald. He had a perpetual forehead that crinkled with nearly as much expression as his face. Both were angry. She guessed he was the restaurant manager.

Emmy swallowed hard and tried to meet his eyes as she walked over to the counter. This was just a big misunderstanding. Her date was a cop. How many times had he pointed that out? Cops don't steal purses. "Do you happen to see where my...where the man I was—"

"No one was sitting here, so we cleared the place. I can't hold the table when people get up and leave."

"But I didn't get the chance to eat anything. Well, except for a few chips and a little sip of my drink." She swallowed down the taste of watermelon, before it (and anything else) could rise up in her throat.

The man looked unsympathetic. "We don't charge by how much you consume. Somebody ordered the food, we left it on the table, and now somebody has to pay for it."

Emmy tried to keep her voice from wavering. "My purse is missing. Did anyone happen to—"

"Your purse is missing? As in you don't have any money to pay for your meal?" The man's voice was so loud that everyone in the restaurant turned to stare at her.

Emmy's mind raced. All she wanted to do was pay her bill and get out of here, but no purse meant no money. Maybe she could call her roommate. Ginny could pay via credit card over the phone and then Emmy could pay her back. But her phone was in the purse.

"Could I borrow your phone?" Emmy asked. "I need to—"

"We don't have a public phone," the man bellowed. "If you can't pay for your meal, I'm going to—"

"Don't be such a bully, Artie." The old man Emmy had knocked into the wall on her way to the bathroom hobbled over.

As he got closer, the larger man behind the counter appeared to shrink. He actually backed away as if he were afraid of the older man. He lowered his head in a kind of deference. "Professor."

"I'll pay for the young woman's meal," the old man—apparently, old professor—said, but he made no attempt to reach for a wallet.

"Thank you so much," Emmy blurted out. "I'll pay you back."

The old man chuckled, but it wasn't a kind chuckle, more of a "you're so far beneath me you could never hope to repay me" kind of laugh. He waved his hand. "No need. But there is something you can do for me." He held up his cane to show her a crack near the top, just below a carved dragon's head. "My cane was damaged when you hurled yourself at me just before you hurled up your dinner in the restroom." A faint smile creased his lips. "Walk with me back to my shop."

As he said it, Emmy understood two things: one, it wasn't a request, and two, this was a man who was used to having his orders followed without question.

Chapter 3

The Bookshop

The professor gripped Emmy's arm as they walked as if he needed it for balance, but his gait was steady even over the uneven cobblestones. Emmy looked around, taking in the old-fashioned charm she had been too nervous to notice when she first arrived on Sharp Island. The sidewalks were lined with gas lanterns with a hook below that held a colorful basket of flowers. The lights were just beginning to glow to life in the foggy mist that rolled off the ocean and enveloped the town. The air was damp and crisp at the same time. The first bites of fall chill made her shiver. This time of year always reminded Emmy of going back to school, probably because she had gone back to school this time every year for the last twenty-two years.

"What do you think of our little island?" the professor asked after a few moments of silence.

Emmy shook herself out of her trance and looked around her. "It's beautiful, but kind of a strange design. Are all the buildings connected?"

His eyes lit up as if he'd received permission to elaborate. "The main ones in town are. Sharp Island was once Fort Seabring, one of the most northwestern posts of the United States."

"Right," Emmy said, "and it was bought by newspaper mogul George Sharp nearly 100 years ago. He had the fort converted into a private mansion resort."

The professor seemed impressed. "You've read up on Sharp Island."

"A bit." Emmy didn't admit that she'd only looked up the history of the island after Pierce invited her on the date.

"Then perhaps you already know that it's evolved a bit over the years into a tourist destination. The main buildings, reminiscent of the old fort and later the grand mansion, are all connected to each other and circle a common courtyard or a literal town square in the middle."

Emmy nodded, but her thoughts had already strayed from the town back to her immediate problems. "Could I borrow your phone when we get to your bookstore? I need to report my purse stolen." Her mind was racing through the list of calls she needed to make to cancel her driver's license and credit cards. She was an expert at this. She'd gone through the missing purse drama too many times to count.

"Shop," the professor said.

"And maybe your computer?" she continued. She'd need to borrow money from Ginny to buy a ticket on the return ferry. She wasn't even sure when the next one sailed. The last one for the night left at nine-thirty. Ginny had made sure she knew that much, but without her phone she wasn't sure what time it was.

"No computers in the book*shop*." The professor emphasized the word as they stepped under a quaint wooden sign that read "Sharp's Bookshop."

"No computers?" Emmy stopped and looked at him with wide gray eyes. "How do you run a store without computers?"

The professor pulled out a ring of keys and sorted through them until he found a long brass key to open the door. "Shops were run for thousands of years before computers existed." He shook his head, muttering, "She always forgets," as he flipped the sign on the window from "Open" to "Closed." They stepped inside.

"Oh!" Emmy exclaimed. In a moment all the worries that had been racing through her mind about her bad date and her stolen purse and when the next ferry was coming were forgotten. The bookshop was amazing, beautiful, and huge, like her university library. No, more like a fairytale library—the kind of library that had enchanted Beauty into forgetting that she was being held captive by a Beast.

The professor released her arm as she moved into the center of the room, taking it all in. There was something familiar and comforting about the bookshop. The walls were covered in bookshelves that displayed every color and size of book imaginable. Comfortable reading chairs and dark wooden tables with antique lamps were tucked here and there in various nooks. There was a rock fireplace on the far wall flanked by two big wingback chairs. A fire burned inside. The room was cozy, the fire burning off the damp that was settling all around the island. A counter with an old-fashioned cash register by the door was the only hint that the bookshop was actually a store. It looked more like someone's private library.

"Do you like it?" The professor seemed to hold his breath for her answer.

"It's...amazing, perfect...just...wow."

The professor's eyes crinkled into what almost passed for a smile. "This was my grandmother's library. It was one of the first things my grandfather had built on the island when he bought the old fort."

Emmy stopped, mid-circle. "Your grandfather built this? Does that mean...he was...and you are?"

"Professor Edward Sharp." The professor bowed slightly. "But you haven't told me your name yet."

"Emmy. I mean Emerson Fox," Emmy answered.

"Emerson? Like the author?"

"I think so, my mom picked out my name, but I never got to ask her why. She died when I was six," Emmy said.

The professor looked sad. "It's a shame that you never knew her."

Emmy approached a photograph of the town's founder in a corner nook that said *History*. "Your grandfather was George Sharp?"

"Yes," Professor Sharp said.

"And all this is yours?"

"Yes."

"Wow." Emmy walked farther into the bookshop. She could barely take it all in, so many books, so many little knickknacks and lamps and tables and more books. She walked over to an ornate table by the fireplace. There was a leather-bound book lying there. The crimson ribbon held the place of whoever was reading the book. She opened the book and ran her finger down the page, reading out loud, "When a sensible woman has a serious question put to her, and evades it by a flippant answer, it is a sure sign, in ninety-nine cases out of a hundred, that she has something to conceal."

"Wise words." The professor saluted the passage with his teacup. "If you want to catch a woman in a lie, look for an indirect answer."

Emmy flipped to the cover. "*The Woman in White*, I love this book."

"You know Wilkie Collins?" Professor Sharp stopped in surprise. "I didn't think anyone your age could have read a book like this."

"I love a good mystery, it doesn't matter how old it is," Emmy said. "Although the way women were treated back then was horrible. Laura had inherited a lot of money from her father, but she had no freedom to spend it on her own after she married that horrible man."

"You have read it." Professor Sharp nodded with approval. "Good thing inheritances don't work that way anymore, eh? Marriage, on the other hand"—he clucked his tongue—"marriage can be an inescapable noose or the pathway to freedom."

"I wouldn't know about that," Emmy said. "I've never been married."

"But you've come close," the professor said. Before Emmy could ask how he knew that, he gestured to a wall adjacent to the fireplace. "If you like a good mystery, you might want to start here."

Emmy moved to the section he pointed out. A small wooden sign read *Mystery* and the entire wall was covered by her favorite mystery authors. Emmy slid her fingers over the smooth spines as she read the names Agatha Christie, Arthur Conan Doyle, Edgar Allen Poe, Daphne Du Maurier, Raymond Chandler.

She reached for one of her favorite Agatha Christie stories, *The Mousetrap.* "I saw this performed in London once. It was fantastic."

The professor put his hand over hers. "That one is to be unshelved only in case of emergency."

Emmy drew her hand back. "Oh, okay." She looked at the professor, but he didn't elaborate. She wondered if maybe he'd spent too many days alone with his books.

An old typewriter below the mystery shelf caught Emmy's eye. She ran her fingers over the keys.

"And that's very old," Professor Sharp said. "I'd prefer you didn't touch it."

"Sorry," Emmy said, stepping back from the shelf completely. She gestured to the bookshelves. "These seem fairly old too. Is this a used bookstore?"

"Bookshop," the professor corrected. "We sell new and used books. Many of these are from my private collection. I like to find and restore old books."

"Then they aren't for sale?" Emmy asked.

"Everything is for sale," he said. "If you know the right price or the correct currency."

Emmy thought that was a strange thing for him to say, but then again, everything about this was strange, from her purse disappearing, to him paying for her dinner and making her walk him home.

"Tea?" Professor Sharp was easing himself into one of the green wingback chairs when he pulled her out of her trance. He poured from a silver tea service set on a table beside his chair. "It's a special blend of licorice and chamomile only available locally from Ms. Lee's Teas."

"How is it here and ready for us?" Emmy's stomach flipped with anxiety. After her earlier experience, she was wary about drinking something someone else had chosen for her.

"My assistant, Victoria, always leaves a pot steeping for me before she gets off for the evening." He gestured to the chair across from him. "Try some. It will settle your stomach and your nerves. Then we can do something about your missing purse."

Emmy watched him take the first sips before she picked up the cup he'd pushed toward her. Her stomach still felt queasy and she could use something to get rid of the taste of watermelon and vomit that lingered in the back of her throat even after she had rinsed her mouth.

The tea was perfect—just the right temperature for sipping, sweet, but with a tinge of bitterness, the licorice coated and soothed her stomach. The constant stream of thoughts in her head slowed. She drained the cup and he poured her another one.

"You say you like mysteries?" he asked. "What have you read? Modern drivel, I suppose."

"I've read most of the authors you have on your shelf." Emmy gestured to the wall. "Some modern drivel maybe. Some you might like if you gave it a chance."

"Maybe." He appeared thoughtful. "You actually read books, then? Not just binge watch hours of Netbox?"

"You mean Netflix, and yes. I watch it sometimes, but I read a lot."

"That's good. There's so much about life you can learn from reading books. Even fiction. Especially fiction. In fact, I'd say the answers to everything can be found in books." He tented his fingers together under his chin and looked like he was studying her. "If you were called upon to solve an actual mystery, do you think you could do it?"

Emmy took another sip of tea and considered the question. "I like puzzles. I did an escape room with"—she stopped herself from mentioning her ex-fiancé's name—"with friends, and I was able to solve it. I have ADHD. It means I have a hard time focusing, but it also means I hyperfocus sometimes and catch details other people miss."

He nodded his approval. "That's an admirable quality. So few people actually pay attention these days." He pushed the silver tray toward her. "If your stomach is feeling better, you should try these." A circle of yellow and white cakes, dusted with icing sugar, covered the tray. "Anjuli's Patisserie, another local shop, makes the best petit fours you'll ever have."

Emmy reached for one, surprised that her stomach had settled enough to make the delicate cakes look appealing. A bump from behind the mystery shelf startled her. "Is someone else here?"

The professor's eyes crinkled with a genuine smile. "It's only a little bookshop mouse, eager for a few crumbs."

Emmy stared at the wall for a minute. She wasn't afraid of mice, but if it was a mouse, it had to be a big one.

"Don't worry, she won't come out while you're here." He moved his chair closer to hers. "But maybe we should keep our voices down, anyway." He looked around the bookshop warily. "The walls have ears, as they say."

"Right." Emmy glanced around her, wondering if her host was a touch paranoid.

He nodded at the tray of cakes. "The yellow ones are lemon and the white ones are almond. No watermelon here."

Emmy looked at him more closely. "How did you know—"

"I was there, in the restaurant, remember. And I'm sure your stomach is empty."

"Maybe just one," Emmy said, but three disappeared, chased down by another cup of tea and conversation about books. A clock above the fireplace chimed seven o'clock.

"I need to..." But she couldn't remember what she needed to do. Her limbs felt spongy, like the cake she had just eaten, and her mind had turned soft like the filling inside.

She stood, sensory details swirling in a kaleidoscope through her brain. Almond cake. Lemon icing. Licorice. Ferry. Purse. Books. Fireplace. It was too hard to stand. She sat heavily back in the chair.

"What is—" But her tongue was too thick to make the words come out. Then everything was bigger: the shelves, the chairs, the tables. For a second, Emmy felt like Alice in Wonderland.

"I think I've been here before," she said.

The professor's voice was an echo from far away. "You have. Many years ago."

Then she was on the floor.

The shop bell rang.

The professor leaned toward her. He put his finger to his lips. "Stay quiet. You'll be much safer."

Footsteps. Lavender. Another voice. "Are you sure?"

"Of course I'm sure."

A light behind the bookshelves. A shadow. Someone watching.

"Who?" But she couldn't tell if the question was on her lips or in her head. The voice was just out of reach. A faceless apparition.

"It has to be tonight?"

"What does delaying accomplish?" The professor was breathless, angry. He didn't like being questioned.

Paper rustling. "Done." A heavy sigh.

Her skin drooped off her bones as if every part of her was her face after the dentist. She wanted to say something, to let them know she was here, but she was hidden in her little nook. She shouldn't speak. The walls have ears. Her thoughts were fuzzy and dark. Her eyes were so heavy that she could only open them a tiny bit.

Books. Knife. Dragon.

Another voice. "Reminds me of Annie." No, not Annie, Maggie. "Reminds me of Maggie."

Broken cane. Paper tearing. Foghorn far away.

A thud on the floor.

"What are you—"

"Don't!"

"No! Not yet! I've only—"

Something cut through the air.

Thump.

"Why?"

A warm tang of copper. Stomach twisting. Eyes squeezed tight.

A blanket of soft, tea-scented fog.

Chapter 4
The Body

S creaming.

Emmy's eyes flew open. An acrid copper smell rose from somewhere beside her.

Her stomach roiled. Her body was stiff and sore. Her mind was cloudy. Her eyes were still heavy.

Screaming.

Someone was screaming. A nightmare. She reached to stand up, but caught a handful of books, pulling the stack onto the floor. Something slid out and sliced across her hand.

She opened her eyes. A thin knife with a green handle and...blood. Her hand was bleeding. No, the blood wasn't hers, at least not all hers.

She looked around. Where was she?

A rock fireplace, green chair legs, broken teacup, broken cane.

A body.

Another scream. This time hers.

"You're alive?" A woman was standing over her holding a phone. A dispatcher's voice came through.

"Have you checked either for a pulse?"

"The woman is alive, but Professor Sharp..."

Emmy scooted herself across the floor and away from the body without standing up. The old man from last night, Professor Sharp, lay with his back to her. His shirt and the rug around him were crimson.

Blood.

Emmy pushed herself to her knees, holding a hand over her mouth, looking frantically for a bathroom. There were two doors leading from the bookshop; she wouldn't make it to either of them.

She reached for a jade-colored garbage can and, for the second time in less than twelve hours, lost the contents of her stomach in front of a stranger.

When her stomach was completely empty, she looked up, making eye contact with the woman still gripping her phone. "Who are you?" The woman was pale and her voice was breathless. She wore a plaid skirt and sweater, her hair swept back into a bun with a clip shaped like a butterfly. She had to be at least sixty years old and wore no makeup except lipstick that was too red.

"Emerson. Emerson Fox," Emmy managed to choke out, knowing that her name meant nothing to the woman in front of her.

The woman kept her distance from Emmy and the body on the floor beside her. "What are you doing here?"

Emmy struggled to come up with an answer, but there was a gaping hole in her memory. She had no concept of what time it was or how she'd ended up on the floor—even less about how the man next to her had ended up that way. Heavy red drapes had been drawn over the windows of the bookshop, but the gray light coming between them made Emmy think it was morning.

Sirens wailed from somewhere far away.

"Is she hurt?" A dispatcher's voice came through the phone again. "I don't..."

Emmy looked at her hand. "I'm bleeding. I cut myself on..." But she couldn't see the knife anymore. There were only books on the floor. She pulled herself to her feet. "I'm okay."

The woman knelt beside her. "She thinks she's okay."

"Good. Both of you stay put. Don't touch anything. The police are on their way."

"Right," the woman said.

The door opened with a clatter of bells as a middle-aged man pushed his way inside. "Vicky, is everything all right? I thought I heard screaming." He moved a couple of steps forward. "Is that Professor Sharp? What the...? Who is she?"

Vicky. Right. Professor Sharp had said his assistant's name was Victoria. She must have come in for work.

"She said her name was Emerson." Victoria mindlessly re-stacked the fallen books.

"Like the author?" The two of them stared at Emerson as if she were a sideshow oddity who couldn't understand what they were saying.

"What's going on here?" A tall, slender woman in a white apron appeared at the door. "Was someone screaming?"

"Professor Sharp is dead," the man said. "Vicky found him and this woman on the floor together. But the woman isn't dead."

"Professor Sharp is dead?" The woman moved in for a closer look. "And where did she come from? Did she kill him?"

All three turned their gaze on Emmy, their eyes narrowed in suspicion.

"I didn't...I just..."

Before Emmy could finish, two more people pushed their way into the bookshop. This time it was a young couple, both blue-eyed and blond-haired. They could have been siblings, but the way the woman clung to his arm with one hand and her coffee cup with the other told Emmy they were most likely a couple.

"Party at the bookstore?" the man joked, and all eyes turned on him in disapproval. "What? Too early to make that joke?"

His wife gasped, "Is that... is he...?"

Two more people crowded the doorway: an older woman in a purple apron and a younger man wearing shorts, a tank top, and a baseball cap. They kept their distance, talking in loud, excited voices, and staring at Emmy for what felt like an eternity.

"Police! Let me through!" A voice shouted from behind the crowd. The sea of gawkers parted somewhat reluctantly to allow a tall man with broad shoulders and dark hair inside the bookshop. His eyes met Emmy's and his mouth fell open.

"You," Officer Pierce Hamilton and Emmy both said at the exact same moment.

She finished with, "Stole my purse."

Chapter 5
Thief

"We need to secure the room." An older woman came through the door. She wasn't wearing a uniform, but was obviously in control of this situation. She directed the crowd outside. Another cop started taking photos. Pierce and Emmy continued to stare at each other.

"Your purse?" Pierce said like he'd just comprehended what she'd said.

"I left it on the chair when I...went to the restroom. It was gone when I came back, and so were you," Emmy said.

Pierce appeared as shocked to see her as she was to see him. "I didn't see your purse. I got a call so I had to go. I left a note. I told the waiter to make sure you got it."

"He didn't give it to me. He was gone when I came back," Emmy said. "Without my purse I didn't have any money to pay for the food."

"I left money on the table to pay for dinner, with the note."

"That was gone too." Emmy wasn't sure whether to believe him or not. What she knew was absolutely unfathomable was that she was standing next to a murdered man, arguing with a police officer who she'd recently gone on a blind date with, about whether or not he'd taken her purse.

Pierce was also having a hard time with the situation, "How, how did you end up here?"

"Do you two know each other?" The woman police officer came back in. She stood between them.

Emmy said, "Yes."

Pierce said, "No."

Emmy added, "Not really."

Officer Hamilton looked embarrassed. "Chief Howe, this is Emerson Fox. We, uh, met last night over dinner."

"Not that I really had anything to eat," Emmy said quietly.

The woman shook her head. "That's something we'll have to sort out later. For now I need to know how you ended up here, and if you killed the man on the floor."

Her words sank into Emmy's chest like a dull knife. She looked down at her hands, covered in blood. Her face flushed hot. She had to sit down. Her knees buckled, but Pierce caught her before she hit the floor.

"Are you okay?" he asked as he directed her to a chair. There was something like terror in the way he looked at her.

Emmy swallowed to keep from vomiting on him. "I need to wash my hands. I don't do well with blood."

"I can't let you do that," Chief Howe said. She called the man taking pictures over. "I need swabs of this woman's hands. And take a picture of that cut on her palm. Can you tell me where that came from?"

Emmy held her hands up like she was surrendering. "I grabbed something sharp when I was trying to get up."

"Uh huh." Chief Howe looked at Pierce and then at the man taking pictures. "And where is it now?"

"I don't know." Emmy looked around, but there was nothing sharp on the floor. Her head was swimming again.

"How did you end up here?" Pierce asked again.

"I didn't have money to pay for my food, because you...because my purse was missing and the manager at the restaurant wasn't going to let me leave. That man, Professor Sharp, said he would pay for me and then he asked me to walk him home, because his cane was broken."

"How long ago was this?" the chief asked.

"I'm not sure," Emmy said.

"You're not sure?" the chief repeated.

"I don't know what time it is now. I fell asleep or..." Emmy remembered the tea, the petit fours, the fog in her brain. "I think I was drugged."

"Drugged?" The chief exchanged another look with Pierce. They clearly both thought she was lying, or crazy, maybe both.

"Professor Sharp was talking about books and about the island. I drank some tea and ate some of those cakes." She pointed to the scattered remains of the tea service and the food that had been so neatly arranged.

"I was so tired. My eyes wouldn't stay open." She closed her eyes, trying to remember. "Someone came in. They were talking about ... about me, I think. But I couldn't focus. And then someone else came in. There was a knife, a little dagger with a...a green handle. And a pile of books."

"Uh huh. And did you see the person's face?" the chief said skeptically.

"No. I only heard voices. I think I might have already been on the floor."

"You said you were drugged," Chief Howe said. "If you were drugged, how could you remember so much detail?"

"I have ADHD so I hyperfocus on things. Details, usually meaningless details, stand out to me. The important stuff is usually blocked out." Emmy laughed nervously. "I remember voices and a pile of books, a knife, and a name. But no faces." She glanced down at her hands and her stomach roiled again. The jade garbage can was too far away to reach.

"A name?" Pierce asked.

"Maggie?" Emmy said, but she wasn't sure.

"Who's Maggie?" Pierce asked.

Emmy searched her scattered thoughts. "I don't know."

"No faces, huh?" The woman shook her head. "Why did you kill Professor Sharp, Ms. Fox?"

Emmy set her chin and forced herself to look the chief in the eye. "I didn't kill him. I didn't even know him."

"You followed a stranger to his bookstore," the chief began.

"Bookshop," Emmy corrected. "He said it was a bookshop."

"Not that it matters, but you followed a stranger to a bookshop. Then you had high tea with him, he drugged you, and you woke up to find him dead? I'm sure you understand how unlikely your story sounds."

Emmy looked over at Pierce, but his mouth was set in a firm line. His eyes gave nothing away. "I know how it sounds, but that's what happened."

"And yet you have what is probably Professor Sharp's blood on your hands, a cut that could have been caused by the murder weapon, and you find yourself the only person in the room with a dead man."

"I'm not lying. I just met Professor Sharp. What possible motive could I have for killing him?"

"No! Let go of me! Let me see him!" A woman forced her way past the police officers at the door.

"I'm going to have to ask you to keep back, Mrs. Sharp." Pierce stepped in front of her.

"What did she do to him?" The woman pursed her obviously collagen-infused lips as she glared at Emmy. She had dyed platinum-blonde hair and a fresh face of full makeup, despite being dressed as if she was going to the gym. She clasped her hand to her heart and swooned. Pierce didn't even attempt to catch her, so she slid carefully to the floor.

"He's gone, isn't he?" The woman sobbed without tears from the floor. "Why would you do this, Emerson?"

Pierce looked at Emmy. She stared back at him in surprise. He turned back to the woman on the floor. "You know who she is?"

"Of course I know her." Venom and spit flew from the woman's mouth. "This is my father's niece. The one I knew was going to come back to try to take my inheritance."

Chapter 6
Red Handed

"His niece?" Pierce looked at Emmy, dumbfounded. "You're Professor Sharp's niece?"

Emmy stared at the woman in shock. "No. I'd never seen him before last night."

"You need to arrest her. Arrest her right now!" the woman shrieked.

"Madelyn, I understand this is all a huge shock, but if you could try to stay calm..." Chief Howe's frustrated attempt at a soothing voice made Emmy think this wasn't the first time she'd had to deal with the distraught woman.

"Stay calm? She killed my father!" Madelyn yelled loud enough for the crowd still gathered outside the bookshop to hear.

"Father-in-law," Chief Howe said under her breath. She turned to Pierce. "Officer Hamilton, maybe you should take these two someplace quieter, like the offices upstairs. I'll finish questioning them once I have the basics from forensics. Stay with them, but don't allow them to talk to each other. I'll be up as soon as I can."

"Come with me, ladies." Pierce led them to an alcove beside the fireplace, through a nearly hidden doorway and to a set of stairs that Emmy hadn't seen before. They led to the floor above the bookshop. There was a hall with four doors. He pushed against two of the doors before he found one that was unlocked.

It led into a sparsely furnished office—a big desk with a couple of chairs, a painting of the island behind it. On the desk there was a corded phone, a pen and a yellow legal pad, and a book that looked like it was being repaired.

"How could you?" Madelyn spat at Emmy as she flounced into a chair.

"You have me confused with someone else," Emmy answered as she sank into the other chair. She slid the chair across the wood floor and farther from the other woman. That had to be the explanation for all this. Everyone thought she was someone else. Maybe the professor thought she was someone else too. *She reminds me of Maggie.* But Emmy wasn't sure if he or the person who was with him had said that.

"I know exactly who you are and why you're here," Madelyn said.

Pierce had positioned himself between the two women. "Chief said you two aren't supposed to talk to each other."

Madelyn huffed and turned her head away. "Treat me like this when I've lost my dear father. You'll hear from my lawyer." She buried her face in her hands and proceeded to burst into dry tears that weren't likely to ruin her abundance of mascara.

After a few minutes of the dramatic show of emotion from across the room, Emmy looked at Pierce and asked quietly, "Can I wash my hands, please?"

He hesitated. "I guess they already took the swabs and the pictures. Yeah, go ahead. The second door next to this one is a bathroom."

She didn't question why he knew so much about the rooms above the bookshop. She got up and followed his instructions.

The water was ice cold when she turned it on. She let it run over her hands, rubbing them together without looking down at the reddish hue it left in the sink. She concentrated on the ornate bronze mirror, the black toilet, the gold-flecked tile and the three cherubs helpfully holding a hand towel and a roll of toilet paper.

She only looked down at the black basin when she was sure the blood had been washed away. She couldn't stand the sight of blood, an unfortunate fact she hadn't fully known until her second semester as a pathology major. Sure, she hadn't liked blood when she was a kid; she'd even passed out after one of her friends had wrecked on his bike and made a long bloody gash in his knee. Somehow, she thought her adult brain would have handled it better. She was at the top of her class, right up until she'd passed out during the first video of a bloody victim her professor had shown. Thus ending her dream of becoming a crime scene investigator.

She kept the water running long after it had run clear. She turned her hands over and stared at a long gash in her palm. Some of the blood had been hers, but not all of it. She dried her hands on a black towel strung between the two cherubs and then looked up at herself in the mirror.

She'd spent a lot of time on her hair and makeup before her date yesterday—curling her hair around her face, framing her eyes with smoky eyeliner, and picking the coral lipstick that made her skin glow more porcelain than ghostly pale. Between her vomit-fest in the restaurant bathroom and sleeping in a drugged-out stupor on the floor of the bookshop, all her efforts had made it look like she'd painted her face with cheap drugstore makeup and then slept on the streets.

Emmy started to walk out of the bathroom and then realized that the two (or was it three) cups of tea had left her with a very full bladder.

Pierce hadn't said anything about peeing, so she called out, "I need to use the restroom," and then taking it for granted that he would say yes, she started to pull the door shut.

"Wait." He put his foot in front of the door before she could shut it all the way.

"What?" she asked. Was he really going to refuse to let her relieve herself?

"Hold on a second." He ran back to the office and in a few minutes came back with a Styrofoam coffee cup. "I know pathology is going to want a sample."

She stared down at the cup in his hand. "A sample?"

He turned red. "A urine sample, so he can see what was in the tea you drank. So he knows what they put in it to drug you."

Emmy took the cup awkwardly. "Right, thank you." She closed the door, her face burning. She wasn't sure why she'd said "thank you" except that in some small way, that embarrassing exchange had made her think that maybe Pierce believed her crazy story.

Chapter 7

Suspect

"I don't know what I'm going to do without him." Emmy stopped to take in the scene before her in the half-opened doorway. Madelyn Sharp was draped against Pierce's chest. "He's the only family I have left since my husband died."

"What about your mom and sisters back in Colorado?" Pierce said. It appeared he knew a lot about the woman he was holding.

She leaned her head against his chest. "I barely speak to them. They never understood me the way Papa Sharp did. He always wanted a daughter, so he *doted* on me. He insisted I stay here with him after Westy was killed in that plane crash."

"I'm sure you'll be"—Pierce stopped as he saw Emmy standing in the doorway—"fine." He pushed Madelyn back toward the chair.

"I left the...er... sample on the sink," Emmy said. She sat back down on the chair. "I didn't know what else to do with it. Also"—she looked at the older woman who was glaring at her from behind Pierce's shoulder—"I threw up in the jade-colored garbage can. Maybe they can analyze that too."

"Right." Pierce swallowed heavily. "I'll let them know."

Madelyn made a face. "Disgusting." She flopped back into the other chair.

Emmy sat for a few minutes, wondering if she dared to make another request. "Am I allowed to make a phone call?" She gestured to the phone on the desk. "My roommate will be worried because I didn't come home last night. I'd like to let her know I'm all right."

Pierce looked at the phone and then back at her. "I guess so."

Emmy picked up the phone from the desk. It was ancient. She could count on one hand the number of times she'd used a corded phone. She was grateful that Ginny's number had a pattern, that it was the same backward and forward. It was one of the few phone numbers she could remember.

The phone rang twice before Ginny answered, "Hello?"

She nearly cried to hear the familiar voice. "Ginny, it's Em."

"Emmy! Where have you been? I called and texted and even did the 'find your phone' thing but you didn't pick up. What happened to you? Where are you? Wait..." She paused for a long moment. "Did the date go *that* well?"

"No!" Emmy yelled into the phone as soon as she realized what Ginny was implying.

"So it was that bad, then?"

Emmy was conscious of Pierce listening in. "I mean it was...well, it wasn't terri—" But it had been, in fact, terrible. "Never mind the date. Look, things are complicated right now. I lost my purse and—"

"Again?" Ginny said.

"Yeah, but that's not the most important thing, I—"

"How long ago did you lose it? Did you retrace your steps? Have you canceled your credit cards? Do I need to come get you? Girl, you have got to stop being so—"

"Stop! Listen to me, Ginny. I'm okay for now, but I think I was drugged and there's this man—"

"Drugged? Was it your date? I knew I shouldn't have let you go alone. Have you called the police? Hold on, I'm calling 9-1-1 right—"

"I'm with the police. The man I was with was murdered." Ginny gasped and then started to say something, but Emmy cut her off. "Not my date." She sighed. "It's a long story. I just wanted to let you know I'm okay."

"Okay? That does *not* sound okay. Do you need me to come down there? I'm grabbing my keys right now." Ginny's mama bear was coming out in a big way. As much as Emmy wanted to have someone there who was on her side, she couldn't drag Ginny into this.

"No, I'll call you when I need you, just...everything's okay. Okay?" But even as she said it, a hot tear rolled down her cheek.

"Do you need a lawyer? I could call Collin or..."

"Absolutely do not call Collin!" Emmy yelled back.

"I'm sorry, Em, I didn't mean to bring him up. Not Collin, but I could find someone, or I could Google it."

"I don't know if I need a lawyer yet." Emmy leaned against the phone. She was tired, and wired, and frazzled. Her stomach was empty and sick and she felt like she was in a bad dream. "Try not to worry. I'll call you back when I can."

"Hang in there, girl. Love you." Ginny didn't hang up immediately, and Emmy didn't want to sever the connection either. Finally she hung up the phone.

As soon as she sank back into her chair, Madelyn sprang up. "I get to make a phone call too," she said as if she were a child trying to make sure everything was even.

"Be my guest." Pierce made a grand gesture toward the phone.

"In private," Madelyn said. "I'm not the one who is under arrest."

"Whatever." Pierce stood up. "Come with me," he said to Emmy. He didn't clarify to either of them whether Emmy was under arrest or not.

Once they were in the hall, Madelyn put her cell phone to her ear and pushed the door shut.

Devoid of even a chair for support, Emmy slid to the floor. Pierce stood over her. "Are you sure you're okay?"

She gave him a look that she hoped conveyed her utter lack of okayness.

"Sorry, dumb question." He leaned against the wall, fingering the radio at his belt. "Who is Collin?"

Emmy looked up at him, dumbfounded that out of everything she'd said on the phone, this was the detail he picked up on. After a second she decided there was no harm in answering that question. "The newest member of the big-shot law firm, Jackson, Jackson, and Hart. Maybe you've heard of them?"

Pierce shook his head. "No, should I have?"

"Probably not." She let out a long breath. Collin's mother had always made it sound like everyone in the state had heard of their famous law firm, but as time had passed, Emmy had decided that none of them were as important as they thought they were. "Collin Jackson is my ex-fiancé."

"Oh." Pierce sounded sorry he'd asked.

The silence between them grew long and awkward. Through the door, Madelyn's voice was alternately weepy and whiny, but Emmy couldn't make out anything she was saying. Her butt cheeks fell asleep, her back hurt, she wondered how long it would be before they hauled her down to the station or wherever they'd take her to begin her interrogation. Maybe she should have had Ginny call a lawyer. Not that she could afford one. She could barely afford the ferry ride back to the mainland.

Pierce's radio crackled to life. The chief's voice came through. "Hamilton, you still got the suspect with you?"

"Of course," he answered.

Suspect. Emmy never thought it was a word that would be associated with her.

"Bring her down, there's someone here who'd like to talk to her. Says they're her lawyer."

Chapter 8

Represented

"Lawyer?" Pierce looked at the radio and then at Emmy in disbelief. "Already?"

"Yes." The chief's voice was clipped with annoyance.

"Looks like your ex came through. Although how he did it that fast..." Pierce looked at her and she could almost hear his thoughts before he voiced them. "Unless you called him before you called 9-1-1."

Emmy's heart had been pounding ever since Ginny had mentioned Collin's name. "I wasn't the one who called 9-1-1," she reminded him.

"Right." The word was weighted with suspicion.

"And I absolutely didn't call my ex. I was passed out on the floor until I heard that woman screaming."

"Right." The suspicion came even heavier.

Emmy had the sudden urge to punch him, or to scream that she was innocent, that this was all some horrible nightmare. She turned away from him and headed down the stairs before she did something that made her look even more guilty. She braced herself for the sight of the man she'd basically left at the altar and for the lecture she was about to receive, something along the lines of, "I told you you'd never be able to take care of yourself without me." She had no idea how Collin knew what had happened or how he was close enough to rescue her. But it seemed like something he would do, if only to prove that she'd made a mess of her life without him.

She descended the stairs slowly and stopped as soon as she could see the room below. The body was gone, but the buzz of activity in the bookshop had increased. The police appeared to have multiplied—taking pictures, making notes, dusting for fingerprints. She scanned the room for Collin, but couldn't see his shock of pale blond hair atop a disapproving expression. Across the room the police chief was talking to an older woman, short, full-figured, in a tailored skirt and jacket with prominent shoulder pads. Her hair was dyed a burgundy-reddish color—nearly the same color as her suit.

Pierce stood a couple of steps above Emmy, waiting for her to continue down the stairs. She looked around the room again to be sure Collin wasn't there. The chief looked up and gestured for her to come down. She stumbled on the bottom stair and Pierce steadied her with a hand on her shoulder. She resisted the urge to shake it off.

"If you're sure about this?" the chief was saying to the woman in the suit.

"As I said, Edward requested I help the girl in any way I can."

"I'm not sure he meant defending her against charges of murdering him," the chief replied.

"If that's what she's facing, she'll need all the help she can get." The woman finished her thought to the chief and then extended her hand to Emmy.

"Ramona Beesley." The woman's handshake was exceptionally firm. "Your lawyer, if you'll have me. I'd like to take you away from this insanity so we can have a few minutes to talk."

"We need to get a statement from her," the chief said.

"You'll get it, as soon as I get the chance to advise my client." Ramona's friendly tone was gone and she was all business with Chief Howe. She turned back to Emmy. "I don't imagine you've had anything to eat or drink this morning." She shot a glare in Pierce's direction. "People get in their minds that you're a murderer and all sense of civility goes out the window. It was the same when I represented the Sheraton Stalker, guilty as sin, a real snake in the grass. Still, even he had the right to some humanity. My office is just down the block." She turned toward the officers to add, "You can meet us there in say, half an hour when Ms. Fox is in the right mind to make a formal statement. Follow me, dear." Ramona put one hand on Emmy's arm and directed her toward the door.

Emmy hadn't been given the chance to accept or reject the older woman's representation, but she went with her anyway. They walked out of the bookshop and through the large crowd that was gathered on the other side of the police line.

"Is that the girl who stabbed the professor?" a man in a white apron called to Ramona.

"Now Stan, you know I can't discuss an open case," Ramona answered. "Tell Stella I'll have to cancel our outing this afternoon, as I'm otherwise engaged."

"Will do, do you want me to tell her when you can reschedule?" the man called back.

"Just tell her I'll call her later today." She nudged Emmy toward a glass door with a little bell on top. Arched gold letters spelled out "Anjuli's Patisserie" in a fancy script. Next to the door was a glass display case of elegant little cakes and pastries, including the infamous petit fours from the night before. "Well, open the door," Ramona directed when Emmy hesitated.

"Your office is in a bakery?" Emmy asked.

"Patisserie," Ramona corrected, "and no, although my waistline might say otherwise, my office is upstairs. All the shops and touristy stuff on Sharp's island are on the bottom floor. Business takes place upstairs and out of sight of the tourists. George Sharp designed the island to be a bit like Disneyland in that regard."

"George Sharp designed the island?" Emmy said as Ramona huffed herself up two flights of stairs.

"In a manner...of...speaking." She stopped and then blew out a breath. "Whew! Remind me to lay off the morning croissants. They make the best crème pat–filled ones first thing in the morning. The smell hits me as soon as I open the door. Hard to resist." She stopped at a wooden door with the words "Ramona Beesley, Attorney at Law" printed in stiff black lettering. "Here we are." She directed Emmy inside.

Ramona's office reminded Emmy more of a grandmother's house than a law office. There was a huge desk in the middle with a tall office chair behind it, only instead of a stately black it was a bright purple. The wall behind it was decorated with the usual diplomas and commendations, but a large macramé planter containing a draping green plant hung in the corner. There was an overstuffed blue couch covered with a multicolored afghan, an assortment of poofs, crocheted doilies and potted plants covered almost every surface, a jar of candy stood half-full on a table next to the couch, and a red basset hound

napped on an orange pillow in the corner. She lifted her eyes and gave
Emmy a sleepy look.

Ramona nodded her approval. "Belle likes you. That's a good sign."

"She barely acknowledged me," Emmy pointed out.

"If she disapproved, you'd know." Ramona took her place on the
other side of the desk and gestured toward the couch for Emmy to sit
down. "I'm sure you have a lot of questions. It would have been nice if
we could have discussed the terms of your uncle's will before the nasty
business downstairs, but what's done is done. We'll have to save the
question of your inheritance until we clear you of this murder rap."
She gave a slight laugh. "Unless you actually killed him."

"Excuse me." Emmy's head was spinning. She wasn't sure she'd
heard correctly. Maybe the drugs hadn't quite worn off. "Did you say
inheritance?"

"Of course, dear. It was all in the letter your uncle sent. He intended
for you to inherit all this." She waved her arm in front of her.

Emmy was too stunned to comprehend what was going on. What
letter? What inheritance? "You mean the man that was murdered last
night left me his bookshop?"

"Don't be silly," Ramona said. "He left you everything: the island,
the town." She chuckled. "For all I know, you own me."

Chapter 9

The Heir Apparent

"**Y**ou don't look very well." Ramona moved to a little counter next to her desk. "Maybe you'd like some tea?"

Clearly this was a huge misunderstanding, or an elaborate and malicious prank. That was it. This was a prank.

There was only one person who was rich, smart, and vindictive enough to pull this off. It took a few deep breaths before Emmy found her voice. "How much is he paying you to do this to me?"

Ramona had poured two cups of tea. She slid one across the desk to Emmy and took a sip for herself. "I'm being paid out of the estate, so technically, I guess you're paying me now. You're perfectly welcome to hire another attorney. I could give you the names of some very good ones, but for now I wish you'd—"

"Collin. How much is Collin Jackson paying you, paying all of you to make my life a living hell?"

Ramona took another sip and gazed at Emmy over her teacup. "You didn't receive the letter, did you?"

"What letter?"

Ramona put her tea down and started rifling through a drawer under her desk. "I told him it should have been an email. No one your age reads letters. You probably don't even get your mail."

"I do." For some reason Emmy felt the need to defend herself on this point, although to be honest, she'd been avoiding the mail, as well as her email and even her cell phone. Her student loans had gone into repayment, and she didn't have enough to cover even the minimum payment. "Are you sure you sent it to the right address? I moved in with a friend recently."

"I honestly have no idea. But considering the money Edward shelled out to that private investigator to find you, I hope he got the address right. It doesn't matter. I have a copy right here." She passed a stiff white piece of paper across the desk.

Emmy took it with both hands. Across the top was written Benson and Associates. Below it read:

Dear Ms. Fox,

After an exhaustive search, I have determined that you are the daughter of my only sister, Margaret Sharp, who passed away some years ago. As I am advancing in years and as I have no blood relations of my own, I would like to meet with you to discuss an inheritance I wish to bestow on you, subsequent to a determination of your worthiness to receive said inheritance.

The name and address of my lawyer is at the top of this document. Please contact them at your earliest convenience so they can arrange a meeting.

Sincerely, Edward L. Sharp

Emmy read the letter three times before she looked up. "This is a joke, right?"

"No joke. Feel free to contact the law office at the top of the page to verify it," Ramona said.

Emmy looked back at the letterhead at the top of the page. "This isn't..."

"Me? No. Edward didn't trust the idea of a woman lawyer handling the riches his family had accumulated over the last three generations. Particularly not a woman he was once married to."

"But you said—"

"I said he asked me to help you." She tapped her finger on the letterhead at the top of the letter. This firm exclusively represents multimillion-dollar estates."

Emmy stared at her in disbelief. "Million. Dollar. Estates?"

"No. Multimillion-dollar estates. A million won't buy what it once did." Ramona shook her head and took another sip of tea like she was talking about the rising cost of a gallon of milk.

Emmy sat back, trying to take it all in. There was no possible way this was happening. "And you're a—"

"Criminal defense attorney," Ramona said firmly. "And a damn good one."

"Why would Professor Sharp think I'd need a defense attorney?"

"If I were to guess, I'd say because someone is trying to frame you for his murder."

Chapter 10
Family History

Emmy leaned forward, for a second she thought she was going to pass out, or throw up, but she'd done enough of both in the last twenty-four hours. "I don't believe you," she finally said. "This is something Collin came up with. He wants to make me crazy. He wants to get back at me for breaking our engagement. He wants to—"

Ramona held up her hand. "Three months ago you received a DNA test as a gift from your step-grandmother, correct?"

"Ye-es," Emmy said.

"Even though they had broken off all contact with you? Didn't you find that odd?"

"Maybe a bit, but—"

"And you took the test, but you never got the results back? Am I right?"

Emmy sat back, trying to collect her thoughts, but they refused to focus. She hadn't eaten anything. She hadn't taken her meds. Everything that was happening reminded her of a trip down a particularly insane rabbit hole. Maybe the drugs hadn't worn off yet.

"I forgot to mail it. Just like I forgot to mail the thank you card to my grandma. I found it when I was cleaning out my apartment, just before I moved in with Ginny. Life's been crazy. First I was finishing my degree, and then planning a wedding, and then I wasn't getting married, and then I had to find a cheaper place to live and I've been trying to find a job—"

"If you had mailed the thank you card, you might have found out your grandmother wasn't the one who sent it. That was just a ruse to get you to take the DNA test. I have the results right here." Ramona went back to the drawer and retrieved another envelope. She set it on the table between them.

Emmy stared at the envelope. She felt violated. Like part of her had been taken without her permission, even if it was a few strands of DNA. "Isn't that illegal, like stealing my DNA or something?"

Ramona pursed her lips. "Do you want to see the results or not?"

Emmy reached for the envelope. The mixed feelings she'd had when she took the test and then mailed it out came back to her. She had mailed it. She remembered that now. It was on the way to sign the prenuptial agreement. It was the first time she'd had serious doubts about marrying Collin.

She held the paper between her fingers for a long moment, wondering what it said about her past, and possibly her future. Emmy's mom had died when she was six. Any memories of her felt like hazy dreams—holding onto her leg on the first day of kindergarten, wearing matching swimsuits to the pool in the summer. Her parents had been Dad and her stepmother Donna. Until recently she'd lived a perfectly normal life with them. Somehow though, she'd always felt like something was missing.

Dad wasn't tight-lipped or mysterious about her mom. He had good memories of his first wife, and answered her questions as they came up. He didn't have many answers about her mom's family, just that she hadn't had much to do with them.

Finally, as if ripping the Band-Aid off a wound that had festered too long, Emmy tore into the envelope. She scanned the results for answers. On her dad's side the list was long and familiar. On her mother's side there was only one name, Edward L. Sharp.

"This could all be faked," Emmy said.

"You're right, and these could be photoshopped." Ramona handed her a file folder of pictures. "But they aren't."

Emmy emptied the pictures on the table. She recognized her mom, standing in front of the building they now sat in, her arm around a much younger, much happier-looking Edward Sharp. There were other, younger pictures of her mother, most of them in places that Emmy could walk to from here.

"He was a lot older than she was," Emmy remarked as she sorted through the pictures with both Edward and her mother.

"Franklin Sharp, your grandfather, was married twice. He had one child from each wife. Edward never quite got over his parent's divorce, or forgave his dad for remarrying. I assume that's why he and your mother didn't get along." She sighed and picked up a family picture. "Not that many people got along with Edward."

"Why me?" Emmy asked, realizing that she was starting to believe this crazy story.

"You're all that's left. If our son and that disaster of a wife of his had given us any grandchildren before he died, I doubt Edward would have taken the trouble to track you down. As it is, you're the last of the Sharp line. Blood was everything to them."

Emmy sat back. She rubbed her hands across her eyes. "I need a minute to process all this."

"Of course you do," Ramona said. "Unfortunately there aren't many minutes left before Chief Howe comes in and starts demanding answers. The way I see it, the only way for you to beat this murder rap and get your inheritance is to figure out who's framing you. To do that, we'll have to find out who killed your uncle."

Chapter 11

Bugged

"You're sure that's all you remember?" Chief Howe sat on the couch next to Emmy while Ramona monitored every word that came out of either of their mouths. Emmy was beginning to see the "damn good" defense attorney behind the grandmotherly Ramona.

Pierce was there as well, perched uncomfortably on a tufted yellow poof. The basset hound Ramona had called Belle bayed once when they arrived, sniffed Pierce's shoes, and then made herself comfortable with her head on Emmy's lap. Emmy kept her hand on the warm, soft head of the dog. She appreciated the comfort of the hound's velvety ears.

"Clearly someone knew about the impending change in the will and is trying to frame my client for the murder of Professor Sharp." Ramona leaned forward like a chess player about to make a critical move.

Chief Howe matched her stance. "Not to be morbid, but if the killer really wanted Ms. Fox out of the way, wouldn't it have been easier to just kill her too? Especially if she were as incapacitated as she claims she was."

"You make a good point, Chief. One that opens up a whole other realm of possibilities. If the killer wasn't interested in the inheritance, maybe they drugged Ms. Fox because they didn't want to have to kill her as well as the professor."

"Or the drugging part is a convenient lie," Chief Howe said.

"I guess we'll have to wait for the lab results on that one," Ramona said it cheerfully, like she already knew what the results would be.

"In the meantime, I'll be taking your client into custody while we await those results." Chief Howe rose, already reaching for the handcuffs Pierce wore on his belt.

Emmy shrank back, but Ramona didn't even blink. She took another sip of tea. "In the meantime, you don't have an arrest warrant or enough evidence to acquire one." She set her cup down. "And if you do arrest Emmy, I can have her out on bail within an hour."

"She can't touch the money in Professor Sharp's will until that will is found, substantiated, and she's been proven innocent so we know she's not benefiting from a crime," Chief Howe said.

Ramona smiled. "And here I thought you had to prove her guilty and she was already considered innocent."

"You know what I mean," the chief shot back.

"Do I?" Ramona stood. "Let's cut to the chase. Emmy will not be going to jail. She will stay here in the vacant apartment above the bookshop. I will ensure she doesn't leave the island. You can do your investigation and let us know when you find the person who killed Edward so Emmy can collect her inheritance and go about the business of managing Sharp Island." She nodded toward Pierce. "You can even leave your guard dog here to watch over her and make sure she doesn't leave the island." Ramona turned her gaze toward him. "I believe your grandmother always keeps your room ready for you."

Emmy looked at Pierce. His face was red. She wasn't sure if he was mad or embarrassed or both. He hadn't told her his grandmother lived on Sharp Island. When he made the date, he'd only said he knew of a little island where they could go for a good dinner and if things went well, a beautiful sunset.

"It's actually not a terrible idea," Chief Howe said begrudgingly.

Pierce opened his mouth to protest. "I don't think—"

"I'd like a chance to consult with my officer," Chief Howe said. "In private."

"Be my guest," Ramona said. "There's an empty office next door."

"Thank you." The chief and Pierce left the room. In a few minutes another door down the hall opened and shut.

Emmy moved closer to Ramona. "Does that mean I'm not allowed to—"

"Shh." Ramona reached under her desk and flipped a switch. A hidden speaker crackled to life.

The chief's voice came through. "You keep saying you'd like to get a spot in a bigger city with a bigger department. This might be your chance. Helping solve a murder looks pretty good on a résumé."

"Isn't this illegal? Listening in on the cops?" Emmy hissed. She wondered if it even mattered to Ramona.

"My place, my rules. They didn't ask me if it was bugged," Ramona said. "Now hush."

"Sharp Island is the smallest beat in the department. It's not even a beat, just an every-other-day check-in, a couple of parking tickets, a noise complaint here and there," Pierce said.

"And now a murder. You know this island better than anyone I've got. Babysitting our prime suspect aside, you're the closest thing we have to an expert on the families and politics that make up Sharp Island. Considering the status of the victim, I'm sure the DA is going to want to send in his own experts. I want you to be here to represent the interests of our department. Keep our hand in the pie so to speak." She lowered her voice. "Not to mention this will give you a chance to protect your personal interests."

There was a long moment of silence before Pierce finally spoke. "I don't—"

"The less I know the better. I won't ask again, but if you refuse this assignment I won't be able to continue to look the other way when…" The chief's voice became garbled. Emmy and Ramona leaned over the desk to try to catch the last few words, but nothing more came out.

Ramona banged on the speaker. "This whole damn system is getting old."

"It's settled, then." The chief standing at the door sent Emmy scrambling back to her chair and Ramona back to a more upright position after she clicked the switch under the desk. Emmy wasn't sure how the chief gotten out of the other room so quickly. "You're not to leave the island, and Officer Hamilton here"—Pierce appeared behind her—"is your new best friend."

Pierce's lips stayed in a straight line.

Emmy forced a smile back at him. "Maybe we'll get to see that sunset after all."

Chapter 12

Room Service

E mmy rolled over on the unfamiliar bed and opened her eyes to the unfamiliar surroundings. It took her a second to remember where she was. When she did, the full force of everything that had happened in the last two days hit her. She had no idea what time it was. Her phone was still gone and the heavy drapes on the windows hid any hint of whether it was light or dark outside.

A knock sounded at the door. Emmy hesitated. There were only two people on the island who knew where she was—her attorney and the police officer who was playing her babysitter. She wasn't sure if she wanted to face either of them.

She got up and slipped on the oversized robe that Ramona had loaned her, trying to decide whether to answer the door or pretend she was still sleeping. She drew back one of the thick gold curtains in the bedroom. It looked out away from the town and toward the far side of the island. The view was breathtaking. A clear blue sky met a clear blue ocean, hedged in on either side by towering evergreens and rocky cliffs, a nostalgic lighthouse perched at the highest point.

Emmy stretched in the sun coming in through the window. Despite an anxious night in a strange room, she felt rested. The king-sized bed was definitely more comfortable than the pull-out couch she'd been sleeping on in Ginny's apartment. In the light of day, she surveyed her prison. Despite the insanity of her circumstances, she had to admit the apartment was nice. Nice in a vintage 1960s English flat kind of way. Her uncle must have liked things with a British flair. Maybe that's why he insisted on calling the store the bookshop.

This hadn't been his apartment. Ramona had explained it was a guest residence, but it still had touches that reminded her of the shop downstairs. There was even an assortment of old books in the book-case and some on her bedside table. The bedroom was huge, bigger than her entire college apartment. It had an attached sitting area and a luxurious private master bath. The rest of the apartment consisted of a large living room, a guest suite, a cozy study, and a beautiful kitchen.

And it was hers.

Or at least it could be. Ramona had explained that with few exceptions, the entirety of the shops and buildings on the island were still owned by the Sharp family—by her. If the DNA test was right, she was the only Sharp left.

There was a part of her that was waiting for the moment when someone told her this whole thing was a big mistake. Most of her hoped it was. But other pieces of this situation felt more like a dream, even like a fairytale. Except in this story, she had to prove she hadn't slain the dragon to inherit the kingdom.

The knocking grew more insistent.

"I'm coming," Emmy padded across a soft shag carpet to the front door. She pulled it open, fully expecting to see Ramona or even Officer Hamilton.

"Oh, excuse me." The red-headed waiter from the restaurant stood at the door. He was wearing a tight white polo shirt with White Sails—the name of the restaurant—over his well-defined left pec. "I assumed you'd be dressed by now."

Emmy looked down. Her robe had come open so she was showing him the oversized T-shirt and a too-big pair of shorts printed with dogs that she had borrowed from Ramona to sleep in. She wasn't exactly undressed.

"I woke you up. Sorry." But his grin showed that he really wasn't. "Ms. Beesley asked me to bring you something to eat. She said you didn't have a chance to buy any food yet."

Emmy studied him skeptically. "And you brought it all the way up here?"

His eyes crinkled. "We provide room service for our most important customers."

"I didn't realize I was an important customer," Emmy said.

"But you are. It's been a long time since Sharp Island had such a celebrity. Or such a scandal."

Emmy stared at him for a long moment. She wasn't sure how to take this man at her door. He was unabashedly brash and it felt like he was flirting with her. She remembered her first assessment of him at the restaurant—the rogue with a checkered past and a heart of gold. "I'm sorry, I'm not used to being a celebrity, or a scandal."

"That's not what I heard."

"Oh really. What have you heard about me?"

He tried to look mysterious. "Let's just say it's a small island and you are the most interesting thing to come along in a while." He lifted the bags of food. "Can I come in before all this gets cold?"

"I can't let you in. I don't even know your name." It surprised Emmy that after everything, she was still capable of some bantering.

"Jonathon. Jonathon Moore." The waiter shifted the bags so he could shake her hand. "Nice to meet you." He held her hand for a long moment. "Now can I come in?"

Emmy dropped his hand and then stepped back to let him in. The bags of food he was carrying smelled delicious, like strawberries and eggs and bacon. Her stomach rumbled. "Put those in the kitchen, I'll go grab my—" Then she remembered she didn't have her purse, or any way to pay for the breakfast. Even if she had her purse...she mentally calculated how much the food he was carrying must cost. "I'm sorry. I lost my purse when I was at the restaurant, so I can't pay you now but..."

"Oh, you don't need to pay me." He set the bags on the cabinet. "Ms. Beesley told the manager to let you order whatever you wanted and to put it all on the Sharp account."

His mention of the restaurant manager made Emmy remember how horrible that man had been to her. She was glad Ramona had ordered the food up to her apartment so she didn't have to face him again, especially since she still didn't have money to pay for anything.

The waiter looked around the kitchen. "This is a nice place."

"Thank you. It's not exactly mine," Emmy admitted. "It's just an empty apartment Ramona is letting me use."

"I guess you can choose whatever apartment on the island you want, unless..."

"Unless I'm convicted of murder?" Emmy asked.

For the first time the man seemed to consider some tact. "I didn't mean—"

"Actually, I think you did. Half the town saw me in the bookshop, next to Professor Sharp's body. I know what it looked like. If I wasn't me, I'd probably think I was guilty." Emmy perched herself on one of the kitchen chairs. She was curious. "Besides the obvious, what are people saying about me?"

The man hesitated. "That you're the long-lost niece of Professor Sharp. That he left everything he had to you and that—"

"That I killed him?"

He shrugged. "Yeah, some people are saying that. But since you aren't locked up yet, I assume they're wrong."

"But I am locked up." Emmy spread her arms. "This is my cage until they figure out who actually killed him."

"You can't leave the apartment?" Jonathon asked.

"I can't leave the island," Emmy admitted.

"I don't think that's such a horrible thing." Jonathon moved to start opening the bags. "The island is a decent place, pretty, if a little touristy. Maybe a little boring. I'd be happy to give you the grand tour."

"Have you lived here long?" Emmy asked.

"Only about four months. I came for the tourist season, but now that it's winding down. I think I might stay longer. Especially now that we have a celebrity murderer to make things interesting."

"Glad I could provide entertainment for the masses." Emmy slumped in the chair, all banter gone out of her.

"I'm sorry. I should have been more sensitive to how you're feeling. I can't imagine what it would be like to be in your place." Jonathon opened a few cupboards until he found the plates. Emmy noticed that he had two as he set them on the counter. He rummaged through the food containers. "But I wouldn't worry. Ms. Beesley is a great attorney. She'll take care of you."

He laid thick slices of French toast stuffed with strawberries and cream cheese out on the plates and covered them with strawberry scented syrup. "And I'm happy to show you around, or give you someone to talk to, or—"

"Share my breakfast?" Emmy said.

Jonathon looked down at the second plate he'd dished up. "Sorry, I didn't mean to presume—"

"Again, I think you did." Emmy found two forks and laid them next to the plates. "But it's okay. It's a ton of food and I could use someone to eat with. As long as your manager isn't going to be mad if you take too long with this delivery. He didn't seem to be the most understanding guy when I met him."

"Artie's not a bad guy. He's just been under a lot of stress lately. Most of the shopkeepers around here are."

"Why is that? This seems like such a quiet, laid-back little place, and you said the tourist season was winding down."

Jonathon hesitated with a bite of French toast poised on his fork. "Your uncle just increased everyone's rent, and he's written a whole bunch of statutes for the town about everything from the color of paint in the restrooms to what color and how many flowers should be planted out front."

"He seemed pretty nice to me, and isn't it in everyone's interest to keep things nice?" Emmy wasn't sure why she felt like she should defend the uncle she hadn't known more than a few hours.

"You're right, but Professor Sharp had a bit of a god complex when it came to the town."

Emmy leaned closer. It was in her best interest to find out what she could about the people in this town. "I bet that frustrated a lot of people."

"It definitely did. I hate to say this, since he's dead and all, but I don't think there was a single person in town who liked your uncle. Of course, everyone pretended to like him, especially that terrible daughter-in-law of his." He sat back, like he was thinking. "I wonder what's going to happen to Madelyn. She's been completely dependent on Professor Sharp for everything. I'm sure she assumed she'd be the one to get everything he owned. I can't imagine she's very happy with him right now, or with you."

Jonathon finished his last bite and took his plate to the sink, then he came back for hers. She was surprised when she realized her plate was empty too.

"Thank you. It was very good," Emmy said.

"Glad you liked it." He reached across the table to gather the rest of the food.

Emmy stood. "You don't need to clean up. This isn't the restaurant and you should probably be—"

Another knock startled her. She turned at the same time as Jonathon and her hand knocked the little bottle of syrup he was holding. It splattered across his white shirt.

"Oh, I'm so sorry!"

"Don't worry about it." But he was already pulling off the polo shirt. He moved to the sink. "I need to rinse this out right now though. I have a sweatshirt in my car and another shirt at the restaurant."

A long jagged scar on Jonathon's left pec caught her attention. She stood up.

"How did you..." She wasn't sure if it was polite to ask about scars.

The knocking morphed into a full-fledged pounding.

Flustered by the mess in the kitchen and the bare-chested man at her sink, Emmy turned toward the door. "I'd better get that."

This time she was sure it was Ramona. Instead, Pierce was standing at the door.

"Good morning," she said, attempting to use her body as a shield between the police officer and the half-dressed man in the kitchen, but it was no use. Jonathon had come over to see who was at the door.

"I found your purse," Officer Hamilton said. He looked Jonathon over. "And you have a bit more explaining to do."

Chapter 13

Stolen Property

E mmy blushed and started talking fast. "Jonathon brought me breakfast and he spilled some strawberry syrup on his uniform. He was just washing it out."

Pierce remained stone-faced. "I meant about the contents of your purse and where it was found."

"Oh, of course, I just—" Emmy was sure her face rivaled the strawberry stain that had caused Jonathon to remove his shirt.

"Can I come in?" Pierce said.

"Of course I—" Emmy stuttered, moving out of the way.

Jonathon stood in the doorway, bare-chested and blocking Pierce's path inside. "I don't think you should talk to him without your lawyer present."

Pierce and Jonathon glared at each other through the doorway, like they were waiting to see who would be the first to back down.

"He's right," Emmy said, although it came out like an apology. "I'd better call Ramona before I let you in. You didn't happen to find my phone along with my purse, did you?"

"Unfortunately, no." He turned to Jonathon. "I did find the note I asked you to give Ms. Fox, stuffed in the same dumpster as her purse. You wouldn't happen to know how either of those things ended up in a dumpster outside the restaurant?"

Jonathon made an exaggerated sniff. "Ah, you've been dumpster diving. I thought I smelled something."

Pierce's jaw tightened. "Answer the question. Unless you feel it necessary to consult *your* lawyer."

Jonathon leveled his gaze at the officer. "I left your poor excuse for an excuse on the table when I finished my shift. I would have stayed to make sure Ms. Fox got your note and made it home okay, but I had to catch the ferry off island. My niece's birthday party was that evening and I didn't want to miss it. I don't remember seeing Ms. Fox's purse at the table or anywhere around it."

"And I'm sure someone can vouch that you were on the ferry and at the party?"

"I have pictures," Jonathon pulled his phone from his pocket, scrolled back and presented a picture of himself and a little red-haired girl in a party hat. After showing Pierce the picture he turned it around to show Emmy. "Adorable isn't she? Her name is Taylor."

Emmy studied the picture for a second before she handed the phone back to Jonathon. "Cute. How old is she?"

"She just turned six." Jonathon took his phone. "Do you want me to call Ramona for you or—"

"No need." The older woman huffed toward the door. She was wearing the same suit coat she had on yesterday, except in yellow. The blouse underneath was black with white zebra stripes. "I hope you saved some breakfast for...Heaven's sake, Jonathon, where are your clothes?"

Jonathon shook his head. "I spilled the strawberry syrup and I was trying to keep it from staining."

"White vinegar and rubbing alcohol on a clean white cloth, keep blotting it until the stain comes out, although you may be past that point with as much water as you poured on it. I hope it wasn't hot water."

"No ma'am and thanks, I'll try that." He picked up the sopping shirt and made a little bow to Emmy. "I'd better get out of here, but if you'd like to take me up on that offer to tour the island, I'm off by four."

"Thanks," was all Emmy could get out with the dark look from Pierce and the subtle shake of Ramona's head. Despite their unspoken warning, Emmy's mind was already racing for a way to see Jonathon again. She needed to find out what he knew and why he'd lied about going to his niece's birthday party.

Chapter 14

Message in a Bottle

"What is this I hear about Emmy's purse being found, and there being drugs inside?" Ramona pushed her way past Pierce and into the kitchen.

"Drugs?" Emmy asked, her blood going cold. How much worse could things get for her?

"Don't tell me you and Jonathon ate all the French toast," Ramona said instead of answering her.

"No, but the syrup's gone."

"Now that your lawyer is here, can I come in?" Pierce asked.

"Whatever you'd like." Ramona waved him inside. "Emmy, why don't you pull on some clothes and the good officer and I will finish off breakfast and talk about what he thinks he found. When you're ready, you can join us."

Emmy hesitated for a minute as Ramona pulled out another plate from the cupboard.

"I don't think this can wait," Pierce said.

"Where do you have to go?" Ramona said, opening up the cardboard containers and loading up her plate. "Sit and have a civilized breakfast. You're not going to get any more out of her if you interrogate her in her pajamas than if you let her get dressed."

"I don't really have anything to change into." Emmy was suddenly feeling self-conscious. "The clothes I brought I've worn for two days and—"

"Thanks for reminding me." Ramona picked up a bag she had dropped beside the table. "I guessed at the size, but I'm usually pretty close. You can wear these today."

"Thank you." Emmy picked up the bag. She was sure it contained more of Ramona's colorful castoffs. She headed back to the bedroom as Ramona dished up the remaining French toast.

Emmy set the bag on the unmade bed and sighed. She wished she could climb back in the bed, pull the covers over her head and wake up...where? On the pull-out couch in Ginny's living room? In the Seattle apartment she had picked out with Collin? In the house she'd grown up in, long sold to pay off her dad's debts? There was no place left anywhere that qualified as home for her. She didn't have anywhere to go even if she could leave.

She opened the bag and discovered a pair of jeans and a frilly blouse in the exact shade of apricot she'd picked out for her wedding—what used to be her favorite color. Ramona was good at guessing sizes. The jeans hugged her hips and tapered just above her ankles. The shirt was soft cotton, stretchy, but not too tight. The tags on both items showed she couldn't have afforded either. The shop name on the tags was "Look Sharp." She recognized it as a clothing store she'd passed on her way to the bookshop.

Emmy glanced at the mirror and wished for the little makeup case and hairbrush that she kept in her purse. It was pointless to ask for them now. Even if it had been found with her purse, she was sure both items were tagged in some evidence room along with...drugs? What kind of drugs could Pierce have possibly found in her purse?

Leaving her feet bare, Emmy went back into the kitchen.

"Oh, you look lovely, dear," Ramona said. "You'll have to wear that around town. Madelyn will be furious when she realizes I bought it for you."

"Madelyn?" Emmy asked.

"She owns Look Sharp. It's a business venture Edward let her have to give her something to do. I had one of the girls who works there pick this out for you. Doesn't she look lovely, Pierce?"

Pierce looked up, coughed, and then swallowed a piece of French toast that seemed to be stuck in his throat. It took him a few minutes to find his voice. "About what we found in your purse." He set a prescription bottle on the table. It was tucked into an evidence bag. "Do you know where this bottle came from?"

Emmy picked it up with relief. "These are my ADHD meds. I have a hard time focusing or concentrating without them." She looked up at Pierce. "I haven't taken any for a couple of days. Can I keep them?"

"Not just yet."

"If this is an essential medication, I don't see how you can keep them from her," Ramona said.

"This wasn't the only bottle we found in your purse." He handed her a second bottle, also in an evidence bag.

This one didn't look familiar to Emmy. She read the name on the bottle: Bethany Gregory. "These aren't mine." She studied the label. "Ketamine?"

"Do you know what ketamine is?" Pierce asked.

"Yeah. It's used to treat severe depression and suicidal tendencies. It was also an anesthetic for animals, and it was used as a date rape drug in the '90s at raves and stuff."

Pierce stared at her. "How do you know all that?"

"I was a pharmaceutical major for"—she did some mental calculations—"about three semesters, but it wasn't for me. Too many details to try to keep straight."

She handed the bottle back to him. "This was in my purse?"

He took the bottle and set it back on the table. "Yes, and more than that, the toxicology report came back in from your body fluids sample." Emmy wanted to crawl under the table, thinking about what body fluids he was talking about. "They found ketamine in your system."

Emmy nodded slowly, but her mind was racing. She'd been drugged with ketamine. Her vague memories of the night before matched what she knew about its effects.

"Do you want to explain how a controlled substance like this, prescribed for someone else, got in your purse?" Pierce asked.

Emmy's mouth was suddenly dry. "I don't—"

"It looks to me like you were taking a known recreational drug that didn't belong to you. I think you used these pills as a cover for murder. You threw your purse in the dumpster by the restaurant, killed Professor Sharp, and then took the medications so you could claim you were drugged."

"How could she have taken the drugs if they were in her purse in a dumpster behind the restaurant?" Ramona asked. "Why get rid of the whole purse? Why not just the medicine bottle? Why..."

The argument between Ramona and Pierce faded into white noise as something on the side of the bottle caught Emmy's attention.

"This prescription is a fake," she said suddenly.

"What?" Pierce asked.

"Fake?" Ramona asked.

"Yeah." Emmy picked up the bottle and turned it around. "The date on this bottle is May 10, 1998. Ketamine wasn't prescribed in pill form like this until about ten years later."

"Let me see that bottle." Ramona reached for the prescription and studied it for a second. "You didn't do a lot of research on this prescription before you came to accuse my client, did you, Officer?" Ramona said.

"I didn't...I don—" It was Pierce's turn to sound flustered

"Because if you had, you might have figured out the significance of the name and the date on the prescription."

Pierce blanched and took the bottle from Emmy.

Ramona poked her finger at the date. "That bottle of pills may have been prescribed ten years too late for Ms. Gregory." She looked up at Emmy. "But maybe just in time to send a message to you."

Now both Pierce and Emmy stared back at her.

Ramona sighed and took the bottle from him. "Bethany Gregory killed herself on May 10, 1998, by jumping from Professor Sharp's office window. I represented your uncle in a wrongful death suit after she died."

Chapter 15

Attention to Detail

"**C**ome back when you're more committed to doing your job," Ramona said as she closed the apartment door behind Pierce. She waited a few beats and then turned to Emmy. "You don't think I was too harsh on him, do you?" She had morphed from the hard-core attorney back into a benevolent grandmotherly figure. "Pierce is actually a fairly decent cop. Too stiff most of the time. He needs to learn to loosen up. He's been like that since he was a little boy—Boy Scout, straight A student, the whole thing. Smart kid. Although his grandmother thinks he's way smarter than he really is."

Emmy sunk into a bright green settee. There were so many thoughts spinning in her mind that she couldn't focus on any one of them, much less the endless stream of words Ramona was spewing out.

"Sorry. I keep going on. I know this is a lot for you to take in." Ramona sat in the chair next to her. "I'm impressed that you figured out the prescription was faked. You pay attention to details. That's a great quality. That will help out a lot as we try to make heads or tails of what's happening here."

"Random details I can handle. It's the big picture stuff that I have a hard time with, especially now, when I've been without my medicine for a couple of days."

Ramona patted her hand. "I can get on the phone with the judge right now and make Pierce return the pills to you."

"That would help. I have a few stashed for emergencies, left from when I was too distracted to remember to take my pills. I need to call Ginny and have her bring me some things." Emmy stared out the window for a minute, thinking about everything that had happened this morning. Finally she turned back to Ramona. "Who was Bethany Gregory? The girl whose name was on the prescription bottle."

"A talented young journalism student who had the misfortune to end up in Professor Sharp's class," Ramona said.

"He was a teacher?" Emmy said. Of course he was; where else would the title "professor" have come from?

"He taught journalism at the University of Washington for a few years. I'm not sure how he got the job. His only credentials were a purchased degree from Harvard and a family newspaper empire."

"So what happened to Bethany?"

"She killed herself after he wrote a letter to the editor at the *Seattle Times* stating that she wasn't a good candidate for an internship she'd worked all year to earn."

Emmy winced. "Ouch. And her family filed a wrongful death suit against Professor Sharp for it?"

"Yes. As terrible as it all was, they really didn't have a leg to stand on. Bethany was a talented writer—Edward was completely wrong there. I think he was actually jealous of her in that aspect. But she was also emotionally and mentally unstable before Ed destroyed her chances with the internship and her self-esteem. We dug up all sorts of evidence to that effect before the trial. I'm not saying he didn't make things worse. He was the kind of man who should have never been let loose among impressionable young minds. Still, she was likely to have self-destructed without his help. At least the judge thought so. The whole thing was thrown out before it went to trial." Ramona sighed, and Emmy got the idea she regretted her part in the case. "Her family thought otherwise. It's possible they're still holding a grudge and that's what the pill bottle was about."

"Wow. Sounds like I have quite a legacy to live up to," Emmy said.

"Live down is more like it. But I think you're up to the task, or you will be once we clear your name." Ramona stood and retrieved her large yellow handbag from beside the counter. She dug through it until she found a notebook computer with a leopard print case. She sat back down and perched the computer on her lap. "I think we should start a list of suspects."

"You're serious about this?" Emmy said.

"Of course I am. Didn't you say you loved a good mystery?"

Emmy stared at her for a second. She had said that to the professor, not to Ramona. She thought back to the semiconscious, drugged state she was in just before Professor Sharp was killed. She'd had the impression that someone else was there and she was sure the professor had been talking to someone. Could it have been Ramona? And if she had been there, why hadn't Ramona said anything to her or the police about it?

Ramona continued to look at her, a silver stylus poised over the notebook. She looked expectant, maybe like she was waiting for Emmy to call her bluff. Emmy decided not to, not yet anyway. "I love reading a good mystery, not one where I'm at the center of it."

"Fair enough. But as you're stuck on the island until this thing is solved, and you have a vested interest in finding an alternate suspect, I think we should get to work, don't you?"

"Fair enough," Emmy added, but for the first time since she'd met Ramona Beesley, she wasn't sure if the woman was really on her side.

"We'll start with Bethany Gregory's family." Ramona wrote on her tablet as she spoke. "How are you feeling?"

"A little shaky and out of sorts, but other than that, fine. Why?"

"We might have to come up with a sudden injury or illness, maybe something that happens in the middle of the night. Something that would get you into the clinic."

"The clinic?" Emmy asked.

"Dr. Gregory is mostly retired, but he runs a little clinic on the island. It's the only place for medical care after hours. Maybe you can have a possible case of strep throat one of these nights?"

Emmy didn't like the idea of confronting someone with that kind of a grudge against her family. "Is it something you could do? I'm not a very good actress."

Ramona patted her hand. "It doesn't have to be tonight. It's something we can figure out as we go along." She looked over at her notebook again.

"So Professor Sharp knew Bethany before she went to college?" Emmy asked.

"Knew her and the whole family. Most of the people who live here have been here their whole lives."

Emmy shook her head; it made what her uncle had done even more despicable. "The pill bottle is a pretty obvious clue. Too obvious maybe."

"Maybe. But we'll need to check out his alibi anyway."

"Alibi." Emmy remembered the alibi Jonathon had given Pierce and the picture he showed her. "What do you know about the waiter from the restaurant downstairs? The one who brought me breakfast?"

"Jonathon? Not a lot. He came here at the beginning of the season. He's nice to look at and a decent worker from what I've heard, but I don't know much of the backstory on him. Why do you ask?"

Emmy took a breath. She wasn't sure whether she should tell Ramona about the picture and the fake alibi, but she needed to tell someone. "He said he left the island last night on the ferry, and that he went to his niece's party. He had a picture, but the picture wasn't taken yesterday. It had to be at least fourteen months old."

Ramona sat up, suddenly interested. "Why would you say that?"

"It was taken at Happy Hippos, that chain pizza place where they do kid's parties. Jonathon was with some little girl in a party hat, he said it was his niece, but Lottie Llama was in the background and she wasn't dressed right."

"Lottie Llama?" Ramona looked at her like she was speaking another language.

"Lottie Llama is one of the characters from Happy Hippo. I worked at Happy Hippos for about a month in college. I wore the Lottie costume a few times."

"Okay, but what does a llama costume have to do with a fake alibi?" Ramona still looked confused.

"They changed the Lottie Llama costume in all Happy Hippos restaurants over a year ago. The one in the picture was the old costume."

"Are you sure some restaurants didn't keep the old costumes?"

"Positive. Corporate banned the old costumes after they received complaints that the outfit wasn't culturally sensitive."

"Interesting." Ramona tented her fingers under her chin. "I guess the question is, did Jonathon show you that picture to establish his alibi, or was he just trying to earn points with a pretty girl by showing a picture of him and his niece?"

"I don't know," Emmy said.

"We can check the ferry records to see if he was on the ferry that left the island."

"I suppose I could poke around his social media sites to see if he really has a niece or if she really had a birthday party," Emmy said. She didn't want to admit that there might be other reasons for her to be interested in Jonathon's social media sites.

"We definitely need to add him to our suspect list. He had the most direct access to your purse and the opportunity to plant the prescription bottle and discard your purse in the dumpster. Besides the restaurant, he does deliveries for both the tea shop and the patisserie, so he may have had access to the food the professor served you." Ramona ticked off the points on her fingers. "And now you've caught him in a lie about his alibi for the time of the murder."

"You said he was an outsider. What motive would he have for killing my uncle?"

Ramona smiled at Emmy like she was a child who didn't understand how the world worked. "That I'm not sure of, but give it time.

Soon enough you'll understand that nearly everyone who came into contact with your uncle had a motive for killing him."

Chapter 16

Lies and Alibis

E mmy stared at her for a long moment. "What about you?" she finally asked.

"Me?" Ramona opened her eyes wide with innocence.

"Did you have a motive for murdering Professor Sharp?"

Ramona leaned back. "I *was* married to him, wasn't I? And the spouse or ex-spouse is *always* the first person everyone suspects. Well, except in this case it's the person found with blood on her hands next to the body." She gestured to Emmy.

Emmy shook off the flippant reference to her own guilt. "Do you have a motive for murdering Professor Sharp?"

"Yes actually." Ramona almost seemed pleased that Emmy suspected her. "The stingy old bastard tricked me—yes, me, up-and-coming, brilliant lawyer that I was—into signing a prenup that left me with virtually nothing after our divorce. The Sharp men have used the same boilerplate prenup for generations." She ticked the points off on her fingers. "You get nothing in the case of divorce, you lose everything if you remarry, even if your husband is dead, and they get full custody of whatever offspring you produce. So yes, I had as much motive to kill him as anyone else."

"Did you kill him?" Emmy asked.

"Would I be helping you if I did?" Ramona laughed.

"I'm not sure. Actually, I'm still not sure why you're helping me."

"A couple of reasons. One, I think you're innocent, and two, Edward prepaid my legal fees, so I'm obligated to help you. It might be the only bit of my ex-husband's fortune I ever see. It was very important to Edward that his estate go to a blood relative."

Emmy met the older woman's eyes. "You didn't give me a direct answer to my first question."

"No. I did not kill Edward Sharp. There have been times over the years that I've definitely considered it, but it wasn't economically feasible and besides, I dislike killing anything, even bugs. I don't have the stomach for murder." She held up the tablet again. "But if it will make you feel better, I can add my name to the list."

Emmy shook her head. "No. I believe you." But she wasn't sure she did.

"Okay, so we have the Gregory family, Jonathon, and Madelyn. Anyone else?"

"Jonathon said Professor Sharp had just increased the rent on the restaurant. Maybe the owner was angry about it. He didn't seem like a very pleasant person."

"If we start adding disgruntled shopkeepers, the list will get long pretty fast," Ramona said. "But it might not be a bad idea. I could go back to my office and we could go through some of the files on whose lease was increased, and by how much. There's also a town council meeting tonight that you could attend that might give us an idea—"

Emmy was looking out the window again, her mind wandering. She'd never been good at research that involved sitting still and sifting through facts. "Maybe I should talk to some of the people on the island, then I'd get a better idea who might have had a grudge against the professor."

Ramona folded the tablet back up in the case. "You're right. It's time for a field trip. We can start with Ms. Lee's Teas and the patisserie. We can find out what they know about the treats that were delivered to the bookshop yesterday."

"Good plan." Emmy stood up. Breakfast had been loaded with sugar, but her mouth still watered as she thought about the little cakes she'd had in the bookshop, even if they had turned out to be drugged.

Ramona seemed to be thinking the same thing. "I could go for a midmorning pick-me-up." Her phone rang as she tucked the notebook back in her bag. She said a cheerful "hello," but then her face got serious. "Already?" She shook her head. "Of course she's challenging the will… Not in your office." She stood, pacing away from Emmy to the far side of the room. "He should have signed that months ago, after he got the file from the p—" She turned her face away from Emmy's and whispered something into the phone. "I know he was eccentric, but really? All right, yes. She's right here. We can be there by one." Ramona hung up the phone and let out a loud breath. "If I could divorce him all over again …"

"What was that all about?" Emmy asked.

"That was your uncle's lawyer," Ramona answered. "I called him this morning, first thing mind you, before his office was even open, to tell him that Edward was dead and request a copy of Edward's will. He was waiting to sign it until he met you in person. Which apparently he did last night."

"After he met me?" Emmy said.

"Yes."

"And after I was drugged."

"I'm not exactly sure..." Ramona was starting to squirm.

"But you're sure it was signed?"

"Yes. Definitely."

"How can you be sure?"

Ramona suddenly looked guilty.

"You can be sure, because you were there." Emmy crossed her arms over her chest. "I knew your voice was familiar."

Ramona put her hands up in surrender. "I didn't see you. Edward met me at the counter in the front of the store. He explained that he had met you in person and had decided that you should inherit everything. He had the will already drawn up. He asked me to witness it and he signed it in my presence. He said he would get it to his lawyer first thing in the morning."

"Who else was there?" Emmy asked suddenly. "If you didn't see me, someone else did. I heard Professor Sharp talking to someone."

"No one else was—"

Emmy narrowed her eyes. "A will isn't valid without at least two witnesses. Who else was there when my uncle signed the will?"

Ramona twisted the strap to the yellow bag. "See this is where things get complicated. I don't know who the other man was. I didn't recognize him. He was already at the bookshop when I got there. Edward called him Dr. Green. We both witnessed him sign the will, and then he sent it with Dr. Green to be delivered to his lawyer."

"Why didn't you tell the police any of this?" Emmy asked.

"To be honest, I panicked when I found out Edward was dead. There was no time written on the signature on the will. I didn't want the police to know that I was in the shop just before Edward was murdered."

"But Dr. Green, whoever he is, will tell the police that you were there and what time it was."

"He probably will." Ramona looked thoughtful. "Like I said, I panicked. Well, I guess I'll face whatever consequences come up soon enough. Your uncle's attorney is meeting us at my office at one to read your uncle's will."

"So soon?" Emmy said.

"That was one of the stipulations in the will, that it be read within twenty-four hours of his death."

"Why so quickly?" Emmy asked.

Ramona sighed. "I don't have all the details, but let's just say your uncle's murder was expected, and he made provisions in his will to that end."

Chapter 17

Where There's a Will

Hammond Benson, in Emmy's opinion, looked exactly the way a man with two last names should look. He was old and distinguished, clean-shaven, tall with broad shoulders, and half a head of silver hair. He wore a full suit that appeared to be part of him. He was every bit the proper attorney, especially when contrasted with the colorful image of Ramona Beesley, who let him have her desk while she perched on a purple stool next to him.

Madelyn and Pierce were both there. Pierce was standing respectfully near the door in his police uniform. Madelyn, dressed in black, was taking up the entire couch. Another distinguished gentleman, the mysterious Dr. Green, sat on one chair. Emmy sat across from him. Victoria, the bookshop assistant, had taken the smallest chair pushed into the farthest corner of the office.

"Thank you all for coming on such short notice," Hammond Benson said. He made a show of straightening a pile of paperwork. "Professor Sharp made it clear that he wanted his will read as soon after his death as possible. Once you've seen the contents, I think you'll understand."

Emmy looked at the circle of people around her. Everyone looked uneasy about the way this was being presented. Only Ramona nodded her head.

"I apologize, as the contents of the will are rather odd. But as you all know, Professor Sharp was a highly opinionated man, with a fondness for puzzles, and...er..."

"Making things difficult on everyone around him?" Ramona supplied.

The attorney cleared his throat, but made no comment.

"Can we get on with it?" Madelyn dabbed at the corner of her eye, as if a tear would have the audacity to threaten the sheen of her flawless eyelashes. "I have arrangements to make. As the only living relative, the funeral responsibilities fall to me."

"You'll be happy to know that all the arrangements have already been made," the attorney said. "Professor Sharp made sure everything was in place before he passed."

"And less happy to realize you are not Professor Sharp's only living relative," Ramona added.

Madelyn looked incensed. "But I've been here for him. For the last ten years since Westy died. I've stood by his side and—"

"Squandered the money you inherited from my son," Ramona appeared to be making an aside to Emmy, but everyone heard.

"You're just bitter that nothing was left to you. You didn't even get alimony payments thanks to your prenup," Madelyn shot back.

"I've done just fine for myself without help from my ex," Ramona said. "Some of us don't need to be supported by—"

"Ladies," Dr. Green said. "We're only going to drag things out more."

"Of course." Madelyn dabbed at her dry eyes once more. "The whole thing is just so emotionally draining."

"Yes, well." Hammond Benson reshuffled the paperwork on the desk. "We'll proceed with the will as it appears in the deceased's own words. Ms. Beesley, if you'd be so kind as to get everything set."

Ramona stood and opened a cabinet in the back of her desk to reveal a large screen. She cycled through inputs with a remote and finally settled on a frame of video. Professor Sharp's face was frozen on the screen in what appeared to be something between a smile and a sneeze. "Pierce, could you hit the lights?"

The lights dimmed and Ramona un-paused the video.

"I suppose you're all wondering why I called you here." Professor Sharp's voice was somber, and then he laughed. "I've always started my meetings that way, even when everyone knows damn well why we're here." He coughed, cleared his throat and went on. "If you're all watching this, then I guess I'm on some slab in the mortuary, awaiting my autopsy. Or perhaps I've already been sliced open with my cold naked guts splayed for the world to see. At any rate, once the details have all been hashed out, I'm sure the verdict will be that I was murdered."

A collective gasp went through the room.

"He knew he was going to be—" Madelyn covered her mouth in a kind of shock. It was the first emotion from her that Emmy thought was remotely genuine.

"Yes. I knew what my end would be," Professor Sharp appeared to answer her. "And though I hope the method was neither too painful nor too gruesome, I knew that this was the end that I would ultimately come to. I have no shortage of enemies or money, both qualities that lend themselves to a good old-fashioned murder mystery." His face broke into a mischievous grin. "With this in mind and knowing I had no living relatives or friends who deserved my fortune, I came up with a delicious plan to make my heir work for their inheritance. But first I had to find someone who would be worthy of the task. It took a good deal of my time and my own investigative prowess to find my sister's only child."

"Or, you know, he hired a PI," Ramona whispered to Emmy.

"Once I ascertained that she was, in fact, a blood relative, I decided to test her further. First with an in-person meeting and now with this challenge." Professor Sharp's video-enlarged eyes seemed to find Emmy in the corner of the room. "Emerson dear, I know you better than you think I do. I know you like mysteries, I know you like reading. I know you are in a precarious financial position. I know that you recently walked away from an engagement to a man who would have solved all your financial problems. I applaud that choice. Far too many women and even men marry for money, thinking it will solve all their problems, only to find that their problems have been multiplied rather than subtracted." Now the video gaze seemed to fall on Madelyn.

"This act shows that you have gumption and the tenacity to solve your own problems—something that has been a hallmark of the Sharp family for generations. But the question is, how much gumption and tenacity do you have? How much of you is Sharp? To find that out, I devised a sort of game, or more appropriately, a challenge to see if you're a worthy heir to the Sharp name." The professor paused for a long moment, long enough that everyone in the room leaned forward, waiting.

"I know you like a good book. By virtue of your blood alone, the bookshop is yours, along with the apartments and offices above. You can live here on this island, with all property taxes paid for the duration of your life. You can rent out the offices and sell books for a bit of income. Your living as a bookshop owner may not be opulent, but it will likely be quiet and comfortable. Your mother chose quiet comfort over opulence. I, on the other hand, never had the luxury of quiet." He paused and something like regret passed over his face. "I was meant for greater things, as I believe you are."

"If you have the ambition, the whole of the Sharp fortune can be yours—the island, the town, the contents of my varied investments and bank accounts. You only have to complete one simple task." He leaned forward, his eyes gleaming. Everyone in the room leaned closer to the TV. He waited; even in death he was aware of the spectacle he had created.

"You must find my murderer."

Chapter 18

Impossible Puzzle

The professor's expression froze on the screen in a twisted smile that was almost menacing. For a few heartbeats, everything was silent.

"That's it?" Madelyn shrieked. "No mention of me at all?"

"I believe you were the aim of the 'too many people marry for money, thinking that will solve all their problems' comment," Ramona said.

"You horrible old witch!" Madelyn came out of her chair toward Ramona. "You did everything you could to drive me and Westy apart for our entire marriage, and now that he's gone, you have the nerve to tell me that I only married him for his money."

Ramona met the hysterical Madelyn with measured boredom. "If the gold-digging pick-ax fits—"

"Ladies, ladies." Hammond Benson's tone suggested he didn't think of either of them as ladies, but had too much decorum to use names he thought might fit better. He waited until they both looked at him. He sighed deeply. "As it turns out, there is more."

"More?" Madelyn's voice was small, with a faint glimmer of hope.

"Yes. If you can resume your seat."

Madelyn sat.

"Besides bales of legal jargon associated with Professor Sharp's bequest, there are a few provisions. As was said, Emerson can choose to accept the challenge or not. If she would rather just take the bookshop, then the remainder of the estate, including Sharp Island and the town that inhabits it, will be divided up and sold to benefit various charities."

There was silence for a long moment. Finally Emmy found the courage to speak up. "What if I can't figure out who killed the professor?"

The lawyer reshuffled the paperwork. "If you choose to take this ridiculous challenge and you fail, then the bequests outlined in Professor Sharp's original will, will stand."

"What exactly was in the original will?" Madelyn did her best to keep her voice even.

"Certain bequests will go to the university. A smaller bequest will go to a shelter for stray cats and a few other assorted charities." He paged through his notes. "The bookshop goes to Victoria."

"Me?" The little woman squeaked out the first word she'd said since everything began.

"Yes," the lawyer acknowledged her. "The remainder of the estate will go to"—Madelyn drew in a breath as the lawyer made his own dramatic pause—"you, Madelyn Sharp, widow of the professor's only son, Weston Sharp..."

Madelyn let out a held breath in an unearthly squeal. It cut off as soon as he finished with, "to be shared with Edward Sharp's ex-wife, Ramona Beesley..."

"Me?" Ramona said.

"Her?" Madelyn said in the same instant.

"Equally," the lawyer finished. His expression was stoic, but behind it, Emmy sensed he didn't think either of them should inherit anything.

It felt as if the air had been sucked out of the room. Emmy looked at Ramona and then at Madelyn. Ramona shook her head, still in disbelief as she met Emmy's eyes.

Madelyn glared at Ramona and then Emmy. "What if something happens to her?" Pierce, who had silently guarded the corners of the room suddenly took a step forward, stopping just short of standing between Madelyn and Emmy. Madelyn looked up at him, her face transforming into a picture of innocence. "Chasing down a murderer is dangerous work. Something could happen to her. Unless, of course, she is the murderer."

Madelyn turned back to the lawyer. "What if Emerson is the murderer and she just admits she did it?" Her eyes widened in a kind of realization. "Does that mean she gets everything? Is that why you killed him?"

The lawyer rolled his eyes toward the ceiling. "If Ms. Fox murdered Professor Sharp, then the law will prevent her from benefiting from her crime. As to your first question, if something happens to Ms. Fox before the terms of the will are fulfilled, then the former will stand."

Ramona moved to the front of the room and snapped off the screen. Professor Sharp's last expression faded to black as she turned to face them. "To summarize this in lay-person terms, Emmy can solve the mystery of her uncle's death and inherit everything, or she can choose to take a quiet life in the bookshop while the rest of the town is divided up and sold to the highest bidder."

"What if I say no? What if I don't want any of it?" Emmy said.

Hammond Benson looked tired. The crisp collar on his suit appeared to have melted since the meeting began. "I suppose you could do that. In that case, the original will stands."

"And the town becomes a bone where every little piece is fought over by these two..." Pierce paused, as if the word he was planning to use wasn't quite appropriate, "...mortal enemies."

Dr. Green spoke up for the first time, addressing Emmy. "And if you choose to take only the bookshop, we all know who the highest bidder will be for the rest of the island."

Emmy looked back at him, confused. "I don't."

He nodded. "I guess you haven't been here long enough to be confronted by Khonico."

"What is Khonico?" Emmy asked.

"A big hotel corporation that's been after Edward to sell Sharp Island for decades. They want to turn the entire town into a resort," Ramona explained.

"If that happened, all the shops would be closed or placed under Khonico's control. Any private citizens who live on the island would be evicted." Pierce's eyes shone with indignation. Emmy remembered that his grandmother was one of those private citizens. Even Madelyn appeared incensed by the idea.

Emmy nodded; the full weight of what was happening draped over her shoulders like a lead blanket. She turned back to the lawyer. "How long do I have?"

"How long?" Pierce's question came out like she had just said she was dying.

"There's no way Professor Sharp gave me an open-ended amount of time for this. How long do I have to solve his murder?" Emmy asked.

"One month," the lawyer said.

"One month?" Pierce repeated, his voice full of shock. "Murder cases take years to solve."

The lawyer nodded. "As I said, this challenge is ridiculous. If you were my daughter or granddaughter or even just my client, I would advise you to choose a peaceful life and take the bookshop." He held up his hand against the protests that came from every side. "Perhaps this town has been stuck in a time warp for too long." He straightened the papers one more time, put them in four large envelopes. He delivered one to Madelyn, one to Ramona, and another to a red-faced Victoria before he stood in front of Emmy. He held the last envelope out.

"Take some time to think about your decision. And by time I mean the next forty-eight hours. That was also a stipulation in the will; forty-eight hours to decide your course of action, one month to solve the murder." He nodded toward Ramona. "I know Ms. Beesley here has been advising you, but as you are now on opposite sides of this travesty of an inheritance, I suggest you seek counsel elsewhere. Say the word and I can have a troop of lawyers here to advise you by tomorrow afternoon." He handed Emmy the envelope and nodded his goodbye. "Best of luck to you."

Chapter 19
Advice

Emmy stared at the envelope in her hands. She was aware of the weight of all the eyes in the room on her. Combined with the weight on her shoulders, she wasn't sure how she was still upright. Her thoughts raced and she wished again for her medicine and some time alone to make her decision. Hammond Benson's card was stapled to the top of the envelope. Maybe she should take him up on the offer of a dozen lawyers to give her advice. That would only make things worse. She never did well when she was presented with too many choices to make. That was one of many reasons wedding planning had been a disaster.

"If you want my opinion—" Madelyn began.

"She doesn't," Ramona cut her off sharply. "And you shouldn't take mine either." She exhaled. "That man. He managed to trap us all in a no-win situation, most of all you, Emmy. I'm sorry for this. He was always conniving and manipulative. All this is just his way to get the last word on everything."

"She could just back out." Madelyn spoke as if Emmy wasn't part of this decision. "Mommy Dearest and I will just divide everything down the middle. She controls one side of the island and I control the other."

"Which side would you take?" Ramona said.

"The business side, of course," Madelyn said.

"You mean the side that makes money."

"You're old, close to retirement. You don't want to have to manage a town. Besides, you're always bragging about how you don't need the money. It makes the most logical sense."

"To you," Ramona said. "But where does that leave Emmy?"

"Exactly where she was before. She won't have lost anything that she has any right to in the first place. She never even *knew* Eddy. I was the one who's taken care of him all these years."

"You mean he's taken care of you. Given you the boutique to run into the ground. Given you a free place to stay and a generous allowance," Ramona said.

Emmy found her voice again. "What if I don't want to go back to where I was?"

Everyone turned to face her.

"Basically, I'm homeless, drowning in debt with a do-nothing degree."

"And you're still a murder suspect," Pierce pointed out. "You couldn't leave right now if you wanted to."

"Thank you for that reminder," Emmy shot back at him. She passed her hand over her face. "I need some time to think about all this. I need my meds."

She had said it almost to herself, but Dr. Green answered. "I might be able to help you there. If you give me the name of your doctor, I can get in touch with them and write you a temporary prescription."

Emmy looked at the mostly silent man with gratitude. "That would be great, I—"

"Who are you?" Pierce's question was abrupt and full of suspicion. "I haven't seen you around the island and you weren't mentioned in the will. Why are you even here?"

"Sorry, there wasn't really time for introductions before. I'm Carson Green. I've been Edward Sharp's private physician for the last three years, since his diagnosis."

"Diagnosis?" Ramona appeared shocked and so did Madelyn. The only one in the room who didn't look surprised was Victoria, still sitting in the corner, clutching her envelope. She nodded sadly.

"Excuse me, I assumed he would have told you all," Dr. Green said.

"Told us all what?" Madelyn asked.

"I can't exactly... doctor-patient confidentiality." He cleared his throat.

"Professor Sharp is dead," Emmy said. "Everything will come out in the autopsy in a day or two."

"I guess that's true." Dr. Green still sounded reluctant, but he went on anyway. "Edward was dying. He didn't like going to the doctor, so the cancer was caught too late. I assume that's why he didn't go to the police when he started receiving threats."

"He received threats? From who?" Pierce said.

"He didn't know," Victoria said softly. "They were just book pages. Torn from books in the shop with the words blacked out so that all that was left were threats."

"Where are those pages now?" Pierce asked.

"In the files he set aside for me to give to the police and to Emerson after he was gone. He also stipulated that all police reports, medical examinations, and anything else the police take into evidence be shared with her," Dr. Green said.

"Why didn't you give those to the police before all this happened? Maybe we could have protected him," Pierce said.

"And ruined his little game?" Ramona snorted. "Edward wouldn't have allowed it."

"Withholding evidence like that could make you an accessory to his murder," Pierce said.

Dr. Green looked more thoughtful than concerned. "I suppose you could make that case, although doctor-assisted suicide is legal in this state. Still, suicide by murder might make for an interesting court case."

"Where are the files?" Emmy asked.

"Files?" Dr. Green said.

"You said Professor Sharp had files to give me. I'd like to see what evidence there is before I make my decision."

"Good girl," Ramona said. "I, for one, think you have the brains to solve this case. I'd offer my assistance, but as Hammond said, we're on opposite sides of this now." She shook her head. "Just like Edward to make us allies and then find a way to drive a wedge between us. Not that I care about the money."

"Then just give it all to me." Madelyn spoke up again. "If you don't care about the money, let me have it. I can pay off Emerson's student loans, get her a nice apartment, and a new wardrobe." She turned to

Emmy for the first time. "We can make a deal. You don't have to go through all this."

"I don't care about the money, but I do care about the town," Ramona said. "And if you think for one minute I'm going to leave Sharp Island in your incompetent, conniving, money-grubbing hands, then you really are as stupid as everyone thinks you are."

"I'm not stupid!" Madelyn shouted. "I have an advanced degree in marketing and I was running a successful business before I met your son. You just couldn't stand that Westy chose me over you."

"Successful? Hah! You went after Weston so he could save your sinking ship, and then it sank anyway after he tried to bail you out." Ramona turned to Emmy. "Whatever you do, don't make a deal with her. You can't trust that one. She'll—"

"Stop. All of you!" Emmy's voice came out more forceful than she had intended. "I'll make up my own mind about all this. Dr. Green, I need my medicine and those files as soon as possible." She turned to face Pierce. "And I'll need whatever the police have collected and the autopsy report as soon as it's available."

Pierce looked unsure of himself for the first time. "I'm not sure how that—"

"Make it happen." Again, the voice was Emmy's but she barely recognized herself. "Ramona, you said there was a town council meeting tonight. I'd like to attend it. I need to get more information about this place before I make my decision."

"Yes ma'am." Ramona shot her a salute. She smiled and patted Emmy on the shoulder. "For what it's worth, I believe Edward thought you could do this. As despicable as he sometimes was, he was a pretty fair judge of character. He wouldn't have put you up to this challenge if he didn't think you could do it."

"Thanks," Emmy said, but despite her sudden influx of bravery, all she could feel were doubts about her chances of solving anything.

Chapter 20

Suspects

"This is a great place."

Emmy looked up from the pile of torn book pages in front of her, startled by the sudden appearance of Ginny. She blinked a few times before she stood up and threw her arms around her best friend. "I'm so happy to see you!"

Emmy had called Ginny on the landline in the apartment and explained everything and then asked her to bring her clothes and everything she'd need to stay on the island.

Ginny hugged her back. "Good to see you too. I was so worried when you didn't come home. I was sure I'd convinced you to go out with a serial killer. Which reminds me"—Ginny put her hands on her hips and assumed her motherly pose—"the door was unlocked.

Do you really think that's a good idea? Wasn't someone murdered downstairs yesterday?"

"Was that only yesterday?" Emmy sighed and slumped back down in the chair.

"You're in one of your hyperfocus modes, aren't you? I knocked for a long time before I tried the door." Ginny looked at the papers spread around the table. "What is all this?"

"Evidence," Emmy said.

"So you're going to go through with this? You know this is actual murder and not one of your puzzle games?" Ginny sat at the table next to her.

"I know," Emmy said. "Thanks for bringing my stuff." She indicated the suitcase Ginny had brought with her.

"No problem. I found an old phone I thought you could use. I tried to activate it on your account. I even pretended to be you but the jerk on the other end said your bill was a couple of months overdue."

"I'll order a new one and pay off the bill. My old one hasn't turned up yet," Emmy said.

"No offense, but with what money?" Ginny asked. "I thought you didn't get anything until you solved the case."

"I have an 'investigation fund' that was provided for in the will, so I have money to live on for the next month."

"So you've already made up your mind?" Ginny asked.

"No." Emmy moved the pieces of paper around in front of her. "I don't know."

"But this could all be yours? For real?" Ginny spread her arms. "This apartment, the island, everything? It's like some sort of fairytale."

"Deranged fairytale," Emmy said.

"The island is a lot like this apartment: beautiful, if a bit dated. The people are nice though. The Uber driver who brought me here was hot. He told me to ask you if you wanted him to bring up something for us for dinner."

"Jonathon? He was your Uber? Apparently he does everything around here." Emmy pointed to a paper menu on the counter. "Get some food if you're hungry. I don't have time. I'm heading to a town meeting in an hour."

Ginny walked over and picked up the menu. "Have you figured anything out yet?"

"Professor Sharp had a lot of enemies. The family of a girl who killed herself because he said her writing was no good. A disgruntled ex-wife who likes to pretend the money means nothing to her, but I think it does. A gold-digging daughter-in-law who thought she was getting everything until this morning, and a town full of angry renters who thought he was overcharging and cheating them. Those are just the suspects I've unearthed in the last twenty-four hours."

"Wow, your uncle sounds like a real peach," Ginny sat back down at the table.

"He was." Emmy twirled her pen between her fingers. She was thinking about the night the professor died. "Two voices."

"What?" Ginny looked up from the menu she was studying.

"There were two voices in the library when I was drugged. Two people came in and talked to the professor. One was Ramona, his ex-wife. I think the second voice belonged to the killer. Only my memory is so muddy I can't remember even if it was a man's or a woman's voice." She stared into space for a few minutes. "There was a knife, and a pile of books. And I cut my hand." Emmy shook her head. "I can't think."

"You need food. How does pasta sound? Or…seafood? How much did you say you have to spend?"

Emmy pushed back her chair. "We'll have to get something on the way to the meeting. We're out of time. Besides, it will give me a chance to talk to the restaurant manager. I hope he's nicer today."

Chapter 21

Dumpster Pancakes

"Hey ladies." Jonathon stood at the counter of the White Sails restaurant. "I'm glad you decided to come down to eat. Sit anywhere." He made a swoop with one arm that took in the entirety of the empty dining room. "As you can see, as of this morning the tourist season is over."

"Is that why you're driving Uber and delivering food?" Emmy said.

"Yeah. If I'm going to stick around I have to get a couple of side hustles." He followed them to a table by the window and put a couple of menus in front of them. "What would you like?"

"Something quick. I'm going to the town council meeting," Emmy said.

Jonathon whistled as he filled their water glasses. "You're brave."

"Why is attending a city council meeting brave?" Ginny asked.

Jonathon looked for a minute like he shouldn't have said anything, then he relented. "It may be called Sharp Island, but most of the people here would prefer it if they had nothing to do with the Sharp family. Indentured servitude, I think that's what Artie calls it."

"Is he here?" Emmy was almost afraid to ask.

"No, he left already. I think some of the shopkeepers are having a kind of pre-meeting to discuss what the professor's death means for them."

"If everyone is so unhappy with the way things are run, why do they stay here?" Ginny asked.

"From what I can tell, most of them have some kind of family tie to the land or the store, so this is home. But I think the biggest reason is debt. The way the leases have been run by the Sharp family make it incredibly hard for anyone to get out from under the lease or whatever they owe for their shop."

"But I'm not like the rest of the Sharps. I don't know anything about the island or the family ties here, and I know almost nothing about business, aside from my one semester stint as a business major, back when I thought I would make millions as an entrepreneur."

Jonathon leaned across the counter. "Better to make it the old-fashioned way, by inheriting a fortune from an obscure relative you didn't know existed."

"Especially since marrying for money didn't work out." Ginny picked up the menu. "What do you recommend?" She was full-on flirting with Jonathon, but Emmy had lost her appetite for both food and guys.

She walked over to the booth across from the counter where she had sat with Pierce the night of the murder. She thought about everything that had happened in the restaurant, trying to picture everyone who was there.

She and Pierce were here. Jonathon was back and forth between the tables. The professor was at the corner table, eating... She closed her eyes. "There was no food on his table," she said out loud.

"What?" Jonathon and Ginny turned toward her like they just remembered she was there.

"Did Professor Sharp come here often?" Emmy asked.

"Almost every night. He always ordered the most expensive things on the menu, although he ate next to nothing and stayed long after his plate was cleared. I think he came more to people watch or to see how things were run at the restaurant. He snooped around all the shops in town like that, ordering this or that, always comped. He was like Sharp Island's personal food critic, or quality control expert. He always had some complaints, and everything went on his 'tab,'" Jonathon said. "Artie's blood pressure always went up when he saw Sharp coming in."

"Artie didn't seem very happy when I talked to him that night," Emmy said.

"To be fair, Artie's not much of a people person himself."

"My drink," Emmy said suddenly. "Who ordered my drink for me? It was here when I sat down. I didn't realize it had watermelon in it until I drank it."

"You drank something with watermelon?" Ginny looked horrified.

"Is there something wrong with watermelon?" Jonathon asked.

"She's allergic to it. It makes her puke," Ginny said.

"Yeah, we got that." Jonathon made a face. "Actually, Pierce ordered the drink. I remember how embarrassed he was when I got him to admit he was on a date with a girl he'd met online." He chuckled. "Not that there's anything wrong with that, but he was super-nervous. He tried to play it off cool, but he said something like, 'I need a lemonade with just a hint of watermelon. I did some snooping and found out that was her favorite drink.'"

"I wonder where he got that idea," Emmy said. "I haven't exactly broadcast that I'm allergic to watermelon. But I definitely wouldn't have said it's my favorite drink."

"I don't think it was an accident that the watermelon ended up in your drink," Ginny said. "Someone clearly wanted you to leave the room. Maybe long enough for them to steal your purse and plant that medication in it."

"She was sitting with a cop," Jonathon pointed out.

"A cop who was called away," Ginny replied. "As if that wasn't convenient. Do you know what the call was about?"

Jonathon visibly squirmed for a minute before he answered, "I probably shouldn't mention this, but since it might be important, I'll tell you that the whole 'police call' was a lie."

"It was a lie?" Emmy asked.

"Yeah. I have a police scanner app on my phone, so I know there wasn't any kind of call or police activity anywhere on the island," Jonathon said. "I don't know why he left."

"Maybe he just wasn't into her, or he was expecting something else," Ginny said. "What profile pic did you use?"

"I'm sure he didn't leave because he wasn't attracted to her," Jonathon said.

Emmy's heart fell and her face went red. It was humiliating to listen to Jonathon and Ginny discussing why a guy would have walked out on a date with her.

"Who's to say the cop didn't take Emmy's purse and cell phone," Ginny said. "Maybe he needs this case for his career and so he decided to frame Emmy for the professor's murder."

Emmy thought about the discussion she'd heard between the Chief and Pierce. It sounded like she had been hinting at exactly that. She also hinted at Pierce having something to hide.

"Your phone wasn't with your purse," Ginny said suddenly. "Have you tried tracking it?"

"Tracking it?" Emmy thought. "Oh right, you set that up on your phone after the last time I lost mine."

"I wish I'd thought about it last night," Ginny said. "It's probably dead now, since you never remember to charge it, but just in case." She pulled out her own phone and activated the "find my friends" app. After a few minutes she said, excitedly, "It's somewhere close." She zoomed in on the image. "Like behind the restaurant."

"We can cut through the kitchen," Jonathon said. "The only person back there is Birdy, the cook. It's been slow so she's probably reading with her headphones on. She won't mind as long as I go in with you." The three of them walked into the kitchen, past the cook who was sitting on a stool with her back to them, and to the open back door.

"Can you tell where now?" Emmy asked.

Ginny stared at the map. "It's not that accurate, but maybe I can get it to make a sound."

After a few seconds they heard a faint chirping sound. It grew louder the closer Emmy moved toward the dumpster. "No," she said. "I think it's in the dumpster. I wonder why they didn't find it with my purse?"

"Because it wasn't in there then," Jonathon said. "It couldn't have been. Pierce went through the whole thing himself, almost lost his lunch a couple of times, but he was thorough. Besides, the dumpster was emptied this morning. Somebody had to ditch the phone after that."

"We need to get it," Emmy said.

"Ew," Ginny replied. "I'm not going dumpster diving."

"I'd offer," Jonathon said, "but I'm still working. I can't exactly smell like garbage for the rest of my shift."

"I guess it's up to me," Emmy said.

"The good news is there's only about half a day's worth of yuck in there. The bad news is, it sounds like it's down at the very bottom," Jonathon said. "We could just call Pierce to come sift through it again. He's going to want to take the phone into evidence anyway." He chuckled again. "That might be fun to watch."

"I want to see what's on my phone before I hand it over to the police." Emmy turned to Jonathon. "Can you help me get in?"

"Of course ma'am," he said gallantly. "Hold on a second, you're going to need to get out too." He went back into the kitchen, yelled for Birdy to watch the front, and came back with a step stool and a pair of rubber gloves which Emmy gratefully put on. He lowered the step stool into the dumpster first and then boosted Emmy up to the top.

She sucked in a breath and descended on the stool. She could hear her phone chirping for help from the bottom of the pile. Luckily most of the garbage was sacked up and easy to move. Emmy was thinking she might be able to do this without getting her hands dirty, when she realized the sound was coming from the very bottom bag.

Taking another breath, she ripped the bag open. Crumbled bits of pastry and frilly pink napkins poured out. She dug through the mess until she found her own rose gold phone. She wiped a bit of frosting off the screen with her gloved hand; the phone screen glowed 6:55 and then went dark. She held it up triumphantly. Then it hit her. The city council meeting was in five minutes. She was grateful she'd avoided the smelliest of the garbage. She might even be able to...

Something about the garbage she'd just dug through was off. She didn't know what kind of desserts the restaurant served, but she was sure the frilly pink napkins were out of place. She pulled one out, smoothed out the wrinkles and read the gold writing on it. It said Anjuli's. Digging a bit more, she realized that this wasn't garbage from the restaurant. It was garbage from the patisserie.

The garbage bags were even different, white instead of black. She stepped back to see if there were any other bags from the patisserie and tripped. She fell backward onto a big black garbage bag. It burst. She screamed and she found herself sitting in a pile of leftover pancakes sticky with syrup, slimy egg bits, and biscuits soggy with coffee and gravy.

"Emmy, are you okay?" Ginny yelled.

Jonathon vaulted himself to the edge of the dumpster and peered down at her.

"I'm fine." She stood. "Disgusting, but fine."

Somewhere the church bells began to chime. It was seven o'clock and she was supposed to be at a town council meeting so she could get to know the town she might possibly own, and she was covered in this morning's breakfast leftovers.

Chapter 22

Town Meeting

All eyes turned toward Emmy as she stepped into the town hall at 7:23. A quick wash-off in the restaurant sink and a change into semi-wrinkled clothes from the suitcase Ginny had brought did little to take away the lingering smell of eggs and bacon with a side whiff of rotting garbage. The meeting had come to a screeching halt when she walked in, so Emmy could only assume she had been the topic of discussion.

"You're late," Ramona pointed out when Emmy and Ginny slid into the empty seats next to her. She sniffed. "Did you stop somewhere for pancakes?"

Emmy didn't bother to respond to either whispered comment. She sat in beet-red silence as the councilwoman at the front of the room resumed the meeting. "As I was saying, the future of Sharp Island for the time being is up in the air. Until the contents of Professor Sharp's will is made pub—"

"We all know what's in the will." Artie, manager of the White Sails restaurant, spoke up. A murmur washed over the room.

"At this point everything is speculation and rumors." The councilwoman tried to regain control. "So until we get the official word—"

"I, for one, feel like we should stand together to contest the will." From the center of the room, Madelyn Sharp stood up. She was dressed in a black suit that was at once conservative and racy—tight black slacks, and a fitted black jacket over a lacy red camisole. It looked like it was designed for a black widow to wear to her husband's funeral. Three-inch black heels clicked all the way from her seat to the front of the room. "I was present at the reading of the will. I can only describe the recent alterations my dear father made to his will as the wanderings of an afflicted mind."

"Father-in-law," Ramona corrected, not quite under her breath.

Madelyn sniffed loudly. "Edward Sharp was suffering the effects of the last stages of cancer. He wasn't in his right mind, and the provisions of the will are ludicrous."

"She probably had to look that word up," Ramona said to Emmy.

Madelyn shot a dark look in the general direction of Emmy and Ramona's row. "As the only surviving member of the Sharp family, a business owner, and longtime resident of this island, I think we should fight back."

"So you're one of us now?" Emmy couldn't tell where the man's voice had come from, but it was dripping with sarcasm.

Despite the remark, Madelyn soldiered on. "The idea that a town as beautiful and cultured as ours should be handed over to a stranger, a young woman who took seven and a half years to barely graduate from college with a degree in University Studies, is the definition of lunacy."

Emmy wished she had stayed in the garbage bin. Madelyn had obviously done her homework. Murmurs, turning and whispering, and outright angry stares all flooded in Emmy's direction. Ramona started to stand, but another voice from the corner of the room spoke up first.

Emmy didn't know who the hunched woman was, but she knew this could only be another voice against her.

"And who should be put in charge?" The woman's voice crackled with age tempered by a soft British accent. She reminded Emmy of one of the witches from Macbeth. "The too-good-for-all-of-us gold-digging daughter-in-law of the crazy man who made all our lives hell for the last ten years? In my line of work, that's out of the teapot and into the fire for all of us."

"Ms. Lee of Ms. Lee's Teas," Ramona whispered. "She's a spitfire."

Emmy could only nod as the woman continued. "Nearly all the businesses on this island have survived and flourished in spite of the unreasonable demands put on us by our taskmaster—and yet yours, with a constant influx of cash from that same source, has floundered. And you want us to trust you?"

"You know nothing about business and even less about fashion," someone from the crowd yelled.

"Anjuli from the patisserie," Ramona said.

"Ms. Lee makes a good point." A slender young woman with long dark hair stood while balancing a baby on her hip. "But so does Madelyn. Neither option seems like a good one."

There were voices of assent and growing indignation floating through the crowd. Emmy wished she'd stayed in the apartment. Better yet, she wished she'd never set foot on Sharp Island.

A broad-shouldered man stood head and shoulders above the crowd. "Any option that has us under the thumb of any member of that family..."

"Brighton Redding," Ramona said. Emmy searched her scattered brain for where she'd heard that name before. It seemed familiar somehow. Ramona continued, "...boat rental place."

Emmy didn't know yet what Mr. Redding's beef with the Sharp family was, but she was sure he had one.

"Would you rather the island be sold?" Ramona spoke up. "If Emmy doesn't want it, the whole thing goes to some greedy corporation and we all lose our homes and our livelihoods. I would suggest that you treat the rightful heir to the Sharp fortune with some common courtesy, so she doesn't decide to take what's hers and make a run for it."

More voices—anger, fear, and tension flooded the room.

"You're conveniently leaving out your part in all this," Madelyn said. "If Emerson steps away from the inheritance, it goes to Ramona and me to manage jointly. As much as I dislike the idea of managing the town with my dear monster-in-law, we all know that is the least of the three evils that are left to us."

"Especially if one of those evils is a murderer," Artie roared. "We all saw the professor's supposed niece at his shop, with his blood on her hands." Madelyn opened her mouth, but before anything came out Artie continued, "and we all know Madelyn has been waiting for the old skinflint to kick the bucket. Maybe she got antsy and hurried the process up."

"I would nev—" Madelyn said.

"And what about the ex-wife? Don't tell me that's not an obvious—" Artie's words were drowned out in shouts of agreement and dissent. At the front of the room, the chair pounded on the podium for order, but no individual voice could be heard over the arguments. Emmy saw Pierce lift the radio from his belt and speak into it. She was positive he was calling in backup for what was shortly to become an angry mob. She had visions of her, Madelyn, and Ramona all being carried out of the building to be thrown into the ocean or burned at the stake.

A long screech from the back brought the room to dead silence. An elderly woman had dragged a pointed cane across a forgotten chalkboard in the back of the room. "Good to know that trick still works." The woman slowly made her way to the front of the room. Pierce took a couple of steps to intercept her, but she stopped him with a glance.

"You should all be ashamed of yourselves," the woman said. "I taught most of you better manners than this in this very room. That was years ago, and yet here you all are, acting like spoiled children." She shook her head. Her effect on the crowd was like some sort of spell. The chair stepped aside to give the woman the microphone. The silence lingered and many in the crowd were actually hanging their heads in shame.

"Emerson Fox, could you come to the front of the room?" The woman had obviously been a teacher, and a good one. Although she wasn't sure she had the strength to move, Emmy discovered that she also lacked the strength to resist the woman's command. She stood.

"Confidence," Ramona whispered. "Or they'll eat you alive."

Emmy squared her shoulders and worked to keep her legs from shaking as she met the woman in the front of the room.

The woman's stern face split into a smile as Emmy got closer. "You remind me of your mother, dear. She was one of my favorites." She extended her hand. "I'd like to be the first to welcome you to our little island. I know your first couple of days here have been anything but warm, but I predict that will change, right now." She looked around the room with the same stern expression. "The way I understand it, Emmy is the best shot we have at maintaining our way of life on Sharp Island. She has a daunting task ahead of her. I know she's up to it, but she'll need our help. Whatever we thought of Edward Sharp, there is a murderer on the island. My guess is he or she is here in this very room. Only when we find out who that is will we have peace. I'm asking you to pull together to help her as only this island can."

As the woman's voice faded, Emmy waited. For what, she wasn't sure. Maybe for applause, maybe for the arguments to start up again, maybe for someone to object to the old woman's intervention.

After a few awkward moments of silence the chair resumed her place. "Next item of business are the new streetlamps on Port Avenue."

The old woman walked with Emmy back to her chair. She patted her arm as she sat. "After the meeting, come to my house. I have something for you that you're going to want. Pierce will walk you back."

Emmy looked up to find Pierce standing behind her. "Gran, I was going to—"

"I can get myself back fine enough. You stay here and do your job. Emerson will need far more protection than I do. Besides, you could use another intelligent woman in your life." The woman winked at Emmy, and Pierce turned bright red. "I'll see you both in about an hour. If this drags on longer than that, just duck out the back. That's what I always did, even when I was mayor."

Chapter 23

The Whole Picture

Ginny was yawning before the meeting was over. She leaned over to Emmy. "I'm heading back to the apartment."

"Me too," Emmy said, standing.

Ginny gently pushed her back toward her chair. "You have to stay. This is your town now, and besides, I think you have a date." She nodded toward Pierce, who was still standing guard against the back wall. His eyes swept the crowd and found Emmy's. They both looked away at the same moment.

"A date with the police officer who thinks I'm a murderer, or a date with his grandma?" Emmy whispered back.

"Having an in with the grandma is not a terrible thing," Ginny observed.

"Even if he wasn't sure that I'm guilty, and he didn't already express his disinterest by stepping out on our date, I don't have time or energy for anything remotely like a romance right now." Emmy waved her hand at the crowd around her. "Town to run, murder to solve. You know, the usual."

"Give him another chance. Whatever happens you need to live your life. Besides, you look good together." Ginny stood. "See you back at the apartment." She slipped out the back of the room.

As soon as the meeting ended, Emmy wished she'd gone with Ginny. She decided to get away quickly and meet Pierce at the edge of town before the flood of curious and hostile questions began.

Unfortunately, as soon as she stood, her path was blocked by a woman about her own age. She was wearing nice tan slacks, a cream-colored blouse, and a pink blazer. "So you're the famous Emerson Fox." She stuck out her hand. "Nice to meet you. My name is Kirsten Loche."

"She doesn't want to meet you." Ramona, who had been dozing in the corner of the room, suddenly stood up and moved between the two before Emmy could reciprocate the handshake.

The other woman smoothed a few strands of her light brown hair back into place. "Maybe you should let Ms. Fox make that determination."

"And maybe you should introduce yourself honestly," Ramona said. "Emmy, this woman is a spineless lackey who works for the Khonico corporation. She's here to get the dirt on the will and to find out if she can weasel you into selling our island."

Kirsten laughed. "Ms. Beesley is correct in my intentions." She drew a card out of her pocket and handed it to Emmy. "Except that I'd say I'm here to relieve you of the incomprehensible burden of running an entire island."

"It's all about how you sell it," Ramona said.

Kirsten ignored her. "We're prepared to offer you a generous deal that's in your best interest, and honestly the best interest of Sharp Island and the people who live here." She'd slipped easily into a sales pitch. Before Emmy could answer, Kirsten had opened her briefcase and was pulling out what Emmy was sure were artist's renderings of what the Khonico corporation had in mind for the island.

"I'm not sure I want to—"

Kirsten didn't miss a beat. "We only want to build on the natural beauty of this place and the quaint closeness of this town to make it accessible to more people. It's not fair that so few people get to enjoy a place as lovely as this. Our resorts cater to families to help them build memories together. Wouldn't you like all children to have the experiences you had as a child when you visited Sharp Island?"

Emmy bristled. This woman was trying to play on her emotions. "Unfortunately I didn't have the experience of visiting Sharp Island as a child. Up until forty-eight hours ago, I'd never set foot on this island."

The woman looked perplexed. Emmy noticed she'd stopped mid-pitch, in the act of offering some sort of brochure. Emmy took the paper, but it wasn't a brochure. It was a glossy photo taken on the island. The image was idyllic—a beach scene with a little girl digging in the sand as her two adoring parents held hands in the background. A glorious sunset painted the sky crimson behind them.

There was something familiar about the couple, something familiar even about the little girl who couldn't be more than five years old. It took a couple of seconds for Emmy to place where she'd seen both the family and the beach before. The beach was the one she'd walked past between the ferry dock and the restaurant when she first came to the island. The family, she'd seen in a picture she'd found buried in a box in the back of her father's closet when she was fifteen.

The little girl was her.

She put her hand over her mouth. "I've been here before, but I didn't remember." She leaned closer to the picture. This must have been just before my mom died." She looked up at Ramona for an answer. "Professor Sharp said my mom didn't want anything to do with the island."

"Maybe you'd better save the rest of your pitch for another time, Kirsten," Ramona said almost gently.

The other woman blinked and then nodded before she put the briefcase away. She turned to Emmy. "Call me when you've had time to process all this. Khonico will make you the best offer when you decide to sell." The enthusiasm had been swept out of her voice and she walked away without saying anything else.

Emmy stared at the picture in front of her. The sea of people leaving parted around her like she was a rock in the middle of a stream. She'd been sure everyone who'd spoken up at the meeting would want to say something to her, but the room emptied without any more interruptions. Emmy had the feeling that everyone around her knew some terrible secret about her past that she didn't.

Pierce was suddenly beside her. "Are you ready to—"

"Give us a minute, okay?" Ramona said to him. She took Emmy by the elbow and steered her toward a side door. It led to the courtyard at the center of the town.

She sat on a bench and directed Emmy to sit next to her. She took a deep breath. "What do you know about how your mother died?"

Emmy looked up at her, not quite registering the question. "She died in a car accident when I was six. I was at a family friend's house."

Ramona shook her head. "I'd guessed your dad never told you the truth. I probably would have lied too if I were in his place."

A rock of fear and confusion wedged itself in Emmy's chest. "What are you talking about? What happened to my mom?"

"He was honest about one thing: she did die in an accident, only it wasn't a car accident. It was a boat, just off the coast there." Ramona pointed through the buildings and to the ocean beyond. "And you were at our house—Edward's and mine. Your parents had come for your grandpa's funeral. We agreed to watch you so they could have some time together to process everything. Your mother had just inherited Sharp Island."

Chapter 24
Family Secrets

"What?" Emmy's heart was racing. "That can't be right. You're..." But Ramona didn't look like she was lying. "You must have me confused with—"

"Edward got the bookshop and enough money to live comfortably, a similar deal to what he's offered you. Our son, Weston, got a trust and some fairly lucrative properties on the mainland, all of which Madelyn squandered soon after he died. The island he left to your mother. She was able to enjoy her inheritance for just over forty-eight hours before she died."

Emmy was afraid to hear more, but she couldn't stop herself from asking, "What happened on the boat?"

"No one knows for sure. Your father said the boat was sinking when he woke up. He found a rubber life raft, but not her. It was three days before they found her body, washed up on the far side of the island. She'd drowned. Some people speculated that the pressure got to her and she..." Ramona stopped, looking at Emmy with pity. "...sabotaged the boat. It was officially ruled an accident." She hesitated again, her hand on Emmy's shoulder. "But a lot of people believe it wasn't an accident at all."

Emmy sat for a minute as the words sank in. "They think she was murdered?"

Ramona nodded. "When they found the wreckage, there was some evidence that the boat had been tampered with, that it was sunk on purpose. Your father said that someone drugged both of them and then slipped onto the boat while they were sleeping and caused it to sink."

Something in her tone made Emmy think Ramona didn't believe that version. "What do you think happened?"

Ramona shook her head, "I don't know. Edward believed...well...he thought your father had killed her for the money she'd just inherited. That he didn't realize everything would revert back to Edward after she died."

"I don't...he wouldn't..." But her father had been convicted of doing a lot of things she hadn't thought he was capable of. And if he thought her mother had been murdered, why hadn't he looked for a killer? Why had he lied? A memory pushed its way into her mind, something the judge had thrown out at her dad's trial. The prosecuting attorney wasn't allowed to bring up any past investigations that had involved her father. It hadn't sunk in at the time. She didn't know there *had* been any past investigations involving her father.

"I don't know what the truth is," Ramona admitted. "Edward accused your dad, your dad accused Edward. There was no proof either way. They never spoke to each other again."

Emmy sat reeling as the sun set and the shadows moved in around them. Like everything else that had happened the last two days, this was too much to take in. An uncomfortable thought settled in her mind. "What did I inherit from my grandpa?"

Ramona sighed. "A very large trust fund, which I assume your dad used to raise you."

More thoughts swirled in her brain, things she didn't want to think about but that somehow pushed their way past her lips. "So he probably never really made money from his investments. He was using my money. Then when it ran out..." She looked up at Ramona as the full force of everything hit her. "Do you think my dad murdered my mom?"

"I don't know," Ramona said. "I never believed your mom's death was an accident, but I know the Sharp family had its share of enemies, then and now." She gripped Emmy's shoulder. "You need to be careful."

Chapter 25

The Bookstore Dragon

"Nice night out." The rhythmic but empty sound of her and Pierce's footsteps and their breathing must have finally driven him to say something.

"Yes, it is," she answered numbly. After everything she'd learned, Emmy should have said no to going to visit his grandmother when Pierce came to find her, but she was suddenly desperate to learn anything she could about the mother she'd never known.

"Fall is one of the prettiest seasons on Sharp Island. I always look forward to it. It's like the island is putting on its best show for the locals. Almost all the tourists are gone by the time the leaves change, so it kind of feels like our little secret," Pierce said.

It was so out of character from what she had seen of Pierce over the last two days that Emmy was shocked out of her trance. He sounded much more like the man she had been chatting with over the dating app than the stiff and disgruntled police officer she'd seen over the past couple of days. "That was almost poetic," she said.

"Was it?" Pierce awkwardly rested his hand on his gun. "I probably picked it up from a book somewhere."

"Do you like to read?" Emmy asked.

"I used to," Pierce said.

"Why did you stop?"

"There's too much going on. I've been putting in a lot of hours trying to get promoted to detective," he said. "I don't have much time or patience for fiction anymore."

"That's sad," Emmy said. "There's so much about life you can learn in stories."

They left the lights of the town and started down a semi-dirt path that led toward the water. "Now that sounds like something out of a book."

"Actually it came from my uncle, from the one conversation I had with him. He said, 'the answer to everything can be found in a book.' Only I got the idea that he'd lived too much of his life in his books."

"What exactly did you discuss in your one conversation?" Emmy could tell that Pierce had discreetly slipped into interrogation mode.

"Books," Emmy said simply. "He asked me if I liked mysteries and which ones I'd read."

"Did he give you any indication that he knew he was going to be murdered, or if he knew who that person was?" Pierce asked.

"No. He didn't really talk about himself, only about the bookshop and the shops around town. He gave me tea from the tea shop and cakes from the patisserie." She thought back to that night. "He wanted me to try all of it, but he didn't eat anything himself. He only drank the tea. Oh!" Emmy slid on a piece of loose gravel.

Pierce caught her arm to steady her. "Be careful, it gets steep here."

"Thanks." Whatever important thought she'd tried to grasp had fled her mind.

"Why was he so insistent that you try the food?"

Emmy shrugged. "Maybe he was trying to impress me. He said Sharp Island had the best of everything."

"Interesting," Pierce said. "I don't think I ever heard him say anything good about our town."

Emmy walked in silence for a few minutes. "Maybe he's like my dad. I didn't feel like I measured up to his expectations most of my life. But when his friends came around they'd say things like, 'Is this the daughter you brag about so much?'"

Pierce kicked a rock ahead of him. "My mom is kind of like that. She pushed me hard to make something of myself. I always felt inadequate around her, but I'd like to think she said nicer things about me when I wasn't around." He kicked the rock again. "What kind of work does your dad do?"

Emmy suddenly wished she hadn't brought up her father at all. "He used to work for a big investment firm. We had a lot of money when I was growing up."

"That must be nice."

He said it in the way her friends had said it to her in high school. *Must be nice to have Daddy pay for everything. Must be nice to get a new car for your sixteenth birthday. Must be nice to go to Cabo for Spring Break.*

"It was nice, I guess." Emmy thought about how it was all a lie, that the money he'd used on her was her money. Money that could have been saved for college.

"Let me guess. Your dad is a workaholic who made tons of money but was never around," Pierce said. "At least he cared enough to send you a check once in a while."

Something about his "poor little rich girl" attitude got to her. "He cared enough to write checks on someone else's account until he got caught."

Pierce stopped. "Oh."

Emmy wished she could take the words back, but Pierce would probably find out anyway in the course of his investigation. He might as well hear it from her.

"My dad's in jail and the stepmom who raised me wants nothing to do with me. I think she blames me for my dad messing up so badly. Just before she cut ties she said, 'He was trying to give you everything. He wanted to make up for you losing your mom, so the princess got whatever she wanted, but it wasn't ever enough for you.'" The words stung just as bad coming from her own mouth as they had from the woman who had been her mom for almost her whole life. She hadn't known another mother. She was a little kid when they got married. Emmy tried to remember her parents' anniversary. How long had he waited after her mother had died to get remarried?

Pierce was talking to her. It took a second for her to focus back on what he was asking, "Is that why you have so much money in student debt?" Emmy stared at him for a long moment and he started talking quickly. "Ordinarily I'd say that's not any of my business, but your financial situation was the first thing that came up in our investigation. We had to look into your motive."

"I got into a college I couldn't afford because Dad said he would pay for it. Like an idiot, I stayed after he went to jail because it was prestigious and my friends were all there. It was my only stability. I wasn't smart enough for a scholarship, but I could pay for it all with loans. Then I couldn't come up with a major, and then I think I was afraid that if I did graduate, people would expect me to be an adult, and I didn't feel ready for that." Emmy shivered with a sudden vulnerability.

"I thought you said you'd gotten your PhD?"

Emmy blushed, but there was no reason to lie about that. "I said PhD as a question, because I'd missed what you just said, not because I'd gotten one, and then I didn't know how to backtrack."

"I guess my conversation at the restaurant was pretty boring," Pierce said.

"Not as boring as I was, apparently," Emmy said.

"What makes you say that?"

Emmy looked down at her feet. She wasn't sure how to admit that she knew he'd ditched her.

"Looks like the meeting went longer than usual."

Emmy looked up. She'd been so focused on her conversation that she hadn't realized they were at the house. The elderly woman from the meeting was sitting on the dark front porch, pushing with her feet to make the wooden swing she sat on creak and sway. The house was a small, gray clapboard with red geraniums in window boxes, set on a bluff overlooking the ocean. A simple house with a million-dollar view.

"Stop with the interrogation, officer. Emmy is our guest for tonight, not our prisoner." The woman stood and Emmy met her at the top of the porch stairs. "I don't think I ever introduced myself. I'm

Clara Hamilton, Pierce's grandmother. Come inside. I have a pot of coffee on the stove and some homemade cookies on the table."

"They smell wonderful," Emmy said, following her through the door.

"They're a bit rough and ready, as they say," the woman said. "Not like those cookies Anjuli keeps in her shop, but Pierce seems to like mine anyway. You might want to get one or two before they're gone." Pierce looked up, guilty, half a cookie already in his mouth.

"Thank you." Emmy took one. Mrs. Hamilton sat at the table and patted the seat next to her. Emmy sat.

"Pierce, why don't you make sure the doors are shut tight on the barn and the greenhouse. There's supposed to be a storm later tonight."

Emmy suspected that Mrs. Hamilton just wanted to get him out of the house. The air around the house felt heavy, but the sky was clear. Pierce grabbed a handful of cookies and headed back out the door.

"You said you knew my mom," Emmy said after he'd walked out.

"I did," Mrs. Hamilton said. "I knew most of the children on the island. I taught school in the building before it was converted into the town hall. We were there for over forty years until the district decided it was more equitable to ferry the students across to the mainland and shut down our little school. Not quite a one-room schoolhouse, but still a small bunch. We had three classrooms and four teachers for thirty to forty students from K–8, and everyone pitched in." Mrs. Hamilton's face shone with nostalgia. "It was a simpler time. I think having the kids on the island for school made everyone closer." She leaned forward and blew on her coffee. "The few kids who are left get up before dawn to catch a ferry. Everyone is tired and grouchy and in such a rush these days."

Emmy waited for a few minutes, nibbling at a cookie. She didn't want to appear as one of the people in such a rush, but she wanted to know what Mrs. Hamilton had wanted to show her. She was sure it had something to do with her mother.

Finally Mrs. Hamilton stood and stretched her arthritic legs. "But you didn't come here to listen to me pine away for the old days. I told you I have something for you. We might as well go get it."

They moved at a snail's pace to the next room. On the floor was a pile of boxes. Mrs. Hamilton opened the top one and started to dig through it. Emmy could see that it was full of children's drawings, probably collected over years of teaching. "Pierce is after me to get rid of some of this stuff. He says I'm a hoarder of other people's childhoods."

"That's a good way to put it," Emmy said. For the second time she was struck by how poetic Pierce's words were.

"Not this one," Mrs. Hamilton pushed the first box aside and moved to another. She mumbled to herself, "The class with the twins. Third grade? Fourth?" She dug into a third box.

Emmy leaned to help. "If I knew what you were looking for, maybe I could—"

"Aha!" Mrs. Hamilton pulled out a stapled-together construction paper book. She handed it to Emmy. The words "The Island Princess and the Bookstore Dragon" were written in red crayon in a neat but childish scrawl. Below that it said *by Maggie Sharp.*

"Maggie?" Something in Emmy's memory stirred when she read the name. Her dad had always called her mother Margaret when he referred to her. It hadn't occurred to Emmy that her mom might have been Maggie as a child.

She looks like Maggie. The mystery person at the bookshop had known her mother.

Emmy flipped through the pages. It was the story about a little princess on an island who had to defeat a dragon who lived in a bookstore to become queen. "I take it Edward and my mother weren't very close."

"Keep reading," Mrs. Hamilton encouraged.

Emmy flipped to the next page. The story continued with a sea witch attacking the island. The princess and the bookstore dragon had to work together to defeat the sea witch using a spell they found in an old book in the bookshop. It ended with the two ruling the island together. The last words on the page came from the dragon saying to the princess, "The answer to everything can be found in a book."

Emmy looked up at Mrs. Hamilton. "My uncle said the same thing to me just before he died."

Mrs. Hamilton's eyes twinkled. "I suspect your mother had some collaboration on that story. Some of it seems a bit above a third grade level."

"Were they close, my mom and Edward?"

"They were very far apart in age and Edward resented his father getting married again, but I think your mother eventually won him over. Edward was always a bit aloof, but he didn't truly turn into the bookshop dragon until after she died. He had the weight of responsibility put on his shoulders. Add to that the tragedy of her death, and the knowledge that his father hadn't trusted the island to him. It was a heavy burden for him to carry. Losing his son just over eleven years later nearly broke him."

"How do you think my mother died?" Emmy asked.

Mrs. Hamilton shook her head. "I can't answer that one for you, dear. I'm just a retired teacher. I'll leave the sleuthing to you and my grandson."

"So you think I should do it? You think I should try to solve my uncle's murder and inherit the island?"

"That's not my call to make."

Emmy looked out the window at the waves crashing against the shore. "What would my mother have done?"

"The brave little girl I knew never backed down from a challenge. The young woman she grew into didn't either. I believe that's why your grandfather meant for the island to go to her."

Emmy shook her head. "I'm not my mom. I never even knew her."

"True. And I don't pretend to know you. But I see some of the dragon charmer and sea witch slayer in you." She nodded at the book. "You can keep that. I think there are a lot of clues to who your mother and your uncle were within its pages. Who knows? That book might end up being the answer to everything."

Chapter 26
The Phone Call

The phone ringing made Emmy jump even though she'd been waiting for it. Maybe because she was waiting for it. She let it ring three times before she found the courage to move toward it. On the fourth ring she picked up the piece of paper where she had written down her list of questions. She didn't want to forget anything. On the fifth ring, the one she knew would be the last, she finally answered the phone.

"You have a call from the Yakima Penitentiary. Will you accept the charges?"

"Yes," her voice squeaked. She listened to the message that always played at the beginning, reminding her that the call would be recorded.

There was a click and then a familiar voice got on the line. "Em? Is that you?"

She breathed out, forgetting her resolve with the sound of his voice. "Daddy."

"Baby, I'm so glad you called. It's been ages."

Six months. They hadn't talked in six months. The last time she'd called, the conversation had been brief. She'd finally worked up the courage to tell him she'd broken off her engagement and that she was trying to make things work on her own. There was a long silence before he said, "Are you sure about this, baby? Collin will take good care of you. I only want you to be taken care of."

Behind his words she'd heard disappointment and desperation. Having a daughter marry into a family of prestigious lawyers was obviously important to a man in prison. It had hit her wrong and they'd argued. Then they got cut off.

She hadn't called back.

The silence had stretched out enough that he must have felt like he had to fill it. "It's so good to hear your voice. How have you been? Did you work things out with Col—"

"What really happened to my mom?" She'd rehearsed how she was going to lead into this discussion a hundred times. None of those imaginary conversation starters began with her blurting out that question.

He breathed on the other end for a long moment before finally saying, "You're on the island, aren't you?" When she didn't answer, he pushed forward. "What poison has my dragon of a brother-in-law been feeding you?"

"Funny that you should mention poison." Emmy went for the punch. "Professor Sharp is dead."

"Dead? Edward is dead? Really." The disbelief in his voice was convincing. If Emmy had harbored a passing thought of adding her father to her list of suspects, it was gone. Not that he could have afforded a hit man even if he could have hired one from the confines of his cell. When she didn't answer immediately, he continued his speculations out loud. "So the old dragon finally kicked the bucket. I thought he was too stubborn to die."

"Dad, he was stabbed."

"Stabbed?" he asked, like he was unfamiliar with the term.

"He was murdered," Emmy finished.

"Murdered? Are you sure?" Again, his shock seemed genuine.

"I was there when it happened. I...found the body. They read the will this morning."

"Will? Does that mean...Emmy, are you telling me you inherited Sharp Island?" There was a thinly-veiled eagerness in his voice.

It bothered Emmy that he'd skipped right over the part where she witnessed her uncle's murder and gone right to the possibility of her as the heir to the Sharp fortune. Actually he'd skipped over a lot of things, about twenty-two years worth. "Why didn't you tell me what really happened to my mom, or about Sharp Island, or that she had a brother, or any of this?"

There was a long silence on the other end. When he spoke, her dad's voice was tender almost to the point of tears. "I didn't want to lose you, Em. I didn't want to lose you like I lost your mom."

"What does any of this have to do with you losing me?" Emmy asked.

"That world, your uncle, all of it. They would have sucked you in and taken you away from me. He said as much after she died. He was going to sue for custody. He wanted you to grow up there. Your mother never wanted any part of it. She wanted you to grow up normal, far away from her belligerent older brother, the island, and her insane family."

"That doesn't explain anything, Dad. My mom went down on a sinking ship in the middle of the night and drowned. You told me she died in a car accident. Ramona said—"

"Ramona? That old bat is still around? What did she tell you about me?" Before Emmy could answer he plunged forward. "They both thought I'd killed Margaret, but why would I have done that? I loved your mother. She was my world. It destroyed me when she died." He said the words like they were rehearsed, like he'd said all this before. "More likely they killed her so Edward could have the island and all the money to himself. They accused me when they were the ones with the motive."

"But you had the opportunity," Emmy said quietly. "You were the only other person on the boat."

He let out an angry breath, "Emmy, don't tell me they've turned you against me. This is exactly what I was afraid of all those years ago. Why I cut ties and moved you across the country as soon as your mother's death was ruled an accident."

"Was it an accident, Daddy?" Emmy asked.

His breath caught like she'd stabbed him through the heart. It took a second before he spoke again. "Whatever terrible things I've done, I didn't kill my wife. I'm not capable of something like that."

Emmy tried to forget that he'd used those exact words when he was first accused of embezzling money from his company. She was no longer sure if she knew what her father was and wasn't capable of.

"What happened the night my mom died?" Emmy asked, hoping he was at least capable of relating the story.

"We took off on the boat so we could get away from Edward and Ramona. We needed time to think about what our next step was.

We talked into the night and we both drank too much champagne. I passed out in the cabin below deck. When I woke up, the boat was going down and your mother was gone."

"Champagne? What were you celebrating? Her dad had just died and you said she didn't want anything to do with the island. That doesn't sound like something to celebrate."

"It's complicated, baby. We were nearly broke. My business ventures weren't panning out. Your mom had been overly generous to a couple of old friends who couldn't pay her back. We were heavily in debt and the inheritance would have set us for life. Surely you understand what that's like."

Emmy winced internally at her father's jab at her financial situation. Then she remembered it didn't need to be that way. "What happened to my trust fund? Ramona said—"

"I used it to take care of you." Her father's voice had gone from tender to defensive in a breath. "You had the best of everything, private school, a nice car, expensive vacations, all the things I only dreamed about when I was a kid."

"But you didn't ever tell me that it was my money we were using. You pretended it was the money you were making. You didn't give me the choice of what I wanted to do with *my* money. If you had, maybe I wouldn't be so—"

Her father snorted. "You in control of your own trust fund? You would have spent it by the time you were ten. At least I made it last for eighteen years and gave you a pretty damn good life in the process. If you'd had control of it—"

"You have used up your allotted phone time. You will have the opportunity to call again in—"

Emmy hung up on the robo-voice before it could hang up on her. She felt like she'd gotten more questions than answers. Her dad's last words stung nearly as much as him lying to her. She held the phone to her chest and answered his last accusation to herself. "I would like to have been given the chance to try."

Chapter 27

The Skeleton Key

A crack of thunder pulled Emmy from a fitful sleep. She'd been dreaming about dragons and bookshops and a little princess lost on a sailboat in the middle of the ocean. Far away she could hear the sound of the storm-tossed ocean through an open window. Ginny was snoring away in the spare bedroom.

She went into the kitchen to get some water. The clock on the wall was ticking through the hours she had left to make her decision.

Spread out on the table was the picture of her family at the beach, her mother's book, and the list of suspects that Ramona had printed out for her. Emmy shook her head when she saw Ramona's own name third down from the list. "At least she's thorough," she said to herself.

She turned the paper over and wrote her own list of suspects, but these were people who might have killed her mother, not people who might have killed her uncle. She started with her uncle's name and then added her father. In the spirit of equality she added Ramona to that list too. She put the pen down and thought long and hard. Despite everything he'd done, she'd always stood by her dad. Up until six months ago she'd called him every week while he was in jail. He'd confessed to writing bad checks and embezzling money from his company. She'd actually felt guilty about it, because she believed what her stepmother had said, that everything he'd done had been for her.

She thought about everything he'd done for her—the car for her birthday, the vacations, her prom dress custom-made after a fitting in New York. But he'd bought things for himself too. They had a beautiful house in an upscale neighborhood. He'd always driven a luxury car and had an expensive country club membership. He and her stepmother, Donna, had traveled a lot without her.

What had her uncle said about her mom? "Your mother opted for quiet comfort over opulence. I never had the luxury of quiet." What if her mom had lived to inherit Sharp Island? Would they have lived in luxury on the island? Would she have sold it? Did she really not want any of it, or was that just what her brother decided?

Lightning flashed outside her window and a few seconds later thunder crashed again. The storm was right on top of her as much as it was brewing inside of her. She had to do something.

She picked up the book her mom had made and studied the cover. She recognized the bookshop in the rudimentary drawing of a princess holding a sword, while a dragon lay behind her, curled around the bookshelves. Emmy smiled at the third-grade interpretations of the genres her mother had added above the shelves—*miss torri, si fy,* and *kids* because apparently the word "children's" was too hard to spell.

The bookshop was drawn again on the third page. This one was a closer look at the *miss-torri* section. There was something off about the shelf of mystery novels. It was at an odd angle, like it had been pulled forward. There was some kind of light shining from behind it.

Emmy thought back to when she'd been lying incapacitated on the floor of the bookshop. There was a light that seemed to come from within the walls, or maybe from a little room behind the bookshelves.

What if the drawing from her mother's book was accurate and there really was a room behind the mystery bookshelf?

Emmy wrapped up in her favorite sweater and crept out the door of the apartment. She didn't have to go outside to get to the bookshop. It was right below her. She just had to go out into the hall and then down the stairs to the door Pierce had taken her to, the one beside the fireplace.

She padded down the wooden staircase and reached the door below. It was locked. She stood in front of it in quiet frustration. She stared at the lock that kept her out. Like the front door to the bookshop, the lock was wide and old-fashioned. Somewhere in the makeup case Ginny had brought, there was a bobby pin. Maybe she could pick the lock.

She walked back into the bedroom and considered her options. Was it considered breaking and entering if the bookshop had the potential to be hers? Would she get into more trouble? She knew she should just let it go. She might be able to get her uncle's assistant to let her in tomorrow, but the question of what was behind the shelves had caught hold, and she couldn't let it go. She was heading to the bathroom to look for the bobby pin when a book on the nightstand caught her eye. It was an old 1930s' mystery. The title was *The Skeleton Key*.

It seemed too obvious, too unbelievable, but she opened it anyway. There was a hollowed out space in the book. A long narrow key was tucked inside. Emmy pulled it out and held it in her palm. She wondered if it was really what the book advertised it to be, a skeleton key that would open any lock. At least any of the old-fashioned locks she'd seen around town.

There was only one way to find out.

Chapter 28

Behind the Shelves

The long key clicked and the door at the bottom of the stairs swung open with a creak. Emmy couldn't believe the key had worked. She turned it over in her hand and wondered what else it might open.

The empty bookshop was dark and creepy. She knew exactly where her uncle's body had lain and kept her eyes anywhere else in the room. She didn't want to turn on the overhead lights and broadcast to the world—or at least the empty streets outside—that someone was inside. She turned on one of the lamps. Its shade cast a dim golden light across the room that didn't quite chase away the shadows. She headed for the mystery bookshelf.

In cheesy mystery shows, a hidden doorway in a bookcase was activated by the right book or a statue. Emmy thought about the books she'd discussed with Professor Sharp, but then decided to try a more practical way to find the door. She got down on the floor in front of the bookcase and looked for evidence that the shelf moved. A long braided runner was pushed against the shelves. Emmy pulled it back and found a place where the floor had been scratched in a semicircle.

She ran her fingers along the edge of the shelf above the scrape marks, but she couldn't find anything. She moved some of the books, feeling along the back of the shelf until she found a handhold and pulled against it. The shelf wouldn't budge. Some kind of latch held it in place.

Back to the cheesy mystery idea, she tugged at the books the professor had mentioned, but none of them worked. She scanned the titles again and then laughed to herself as she reached for a book with the title *Imposter*. It wasn't a real book. It was attached to some kind of lever and when she pulled it forward, the latch gave way. This time when she reached into the handle inside the bookshelf, the shelf slid forward.

Behind the shelf was a little room. It held a lamp, a comfortable chair, and a little desk. On the other side was another shelf of older books. She was disappointed in the room's lack of mystery. It was just a private office. She turned on the lamp and pulled the shelf closed behind her. When she did that she could see cut-out areas on all sides of the shelves that made up the walls of the secret room. Each one looked out on a different side of the bookshop. The hidden room seemed to have been built as a place to sit and spy on anyone who might be in the shop.

She stopped. She had been in this little room before, but it had seemed so much bigger then. She got down on her knees, remembering when she'd looked through the bottommost opening from her tippy-toes, spying on the people in the shop.

Shh, be quiet. They don't know we're here. It's our secret.

Someone had brought her into this little room a long time ago.

She stood up. Someone had been in this little room the night the professor was killed. She didn't know if they had been the killer or a witness.

There was a smudge of brown on the spine of one of the books. Leaning closer, she realized it wasn't just a smudge, it was a fingerprint. A fingerprint preserved because it was made with blood.

She noted the title of the book and almost laughed. The title of the book was *Red-Handed*. She should leave the fingerprint for the police, and she would show it to Pierce, eventually. Right now it felt too much like a planted clue. As little as she knew about him, it felt like her uncle's humor.

There was a box of tissues on the desk. Emmy used one to take the book off the shelf without getting her own fingerprints on it. She set it on the desk and it fell open to a bookmarked page. She scanned the page, but couldn't find anything that could be significant. She was about to put the book away, when she looked closer at the bookmark. It was a printed jade dragon covered in green scales. It took a second before she realized the dragon's scales were tiny words. Forgetting about fingerprints she opened the drawer and found a magnifying glass. She held it above the bookmark.

It was a letter from her uncle.

Dearest Emerson,

I don't know where you are in solving the mystery of my death or if you've even decided to take up my challenge. If not, maybe a complete stranger is reading this and the bookshop has long been sold. But if you are Maggie's daughter, I don't believe you'll let this go.

It's taken me this many years to understand why my father wanted to give Sharp Island to her and not to me. He saw the Sharp tenacity and drive in her that he didn't see in me. In many ways she was just like him—never backed down, never gave up. In other ways, she was nothing like the rest of us. While the rest of the family looked at the island and saw dollar signs, she only saw people. She was the perfect mix of stubbornness, strength, and compassion. I'm convinced she wouldn't have made the mess of the island that I have.

I admit, I left you with no good choice and my game isn't fair, but I need you to understand, this isn't about me, or about you, or even about the island. It's about my sister, your mother—a woman who didn't get the chance to make a mess of this island or even raise her only child. A woman whose murder has never been solved.

That's where you come in. I was never one for math, but in this case I believe you need to look for the common denominator. Whoever murdered my sister will eventually take my life as well. Although I couldn't be sure where or when, or even who, I knew this was coming.

That is why I want you to solve this. If no one cared enough to solve my sister's murder, then people will likely care even less to solve mine. I may have deserved my fate, but she did not.

She loved this island with all her heart, but she loved you more. Use that love to find out who killed her, but be careful. I believe our killer won't rest until they have relieved the world of the last of the Sharps.

Sincerely yours,

The Bookshop Dragon

 Emmy held the bookmark between her fingers. Her uncle's words found a place inside her that she didn't know existed. Of all the things she'd given up on in life, she couldn't give up on this one. Whatever happened, inheritance or no inheritance, she needed to find out who killed her mother.

She needed to solve this mystery.

Chapter 29
The Decision

"Jonathon." Emmy was flustered and confused when she opened the door after the bell rang. She'd made four calls and three people were gathering at the apartment. One would be joining them via a video conference call. None of them were the red-headed waiter/Uber driver/delivery guy.

"I called him," Ginny said. "I thought you might need some food to keep up your strength."

Jonathon held up a bag from the restaurant.

"Thanks, but now is not—"

Two of the three other guests stood at her doorway—Ramona and Pierce. Pierce glared at Jonathon, who said something about putting the food away before he disappeared into the kitchen.

Ramona looked curious. She glanced at the cat-shaped clock twitching its tail and rolling its eyes back and forth above the sink, counting down the last of the forty-eight-hour deadline. "I assume this means you've made your decision."

Pierce looked more wary than curious. "Your time is almost up. What did you decide to do?"

"I don't want to say anything until everyone is here. Ramona, did you bring your laptop?"

"Of course." Ramona hoisted an obviously very heavy, flowered combination briefcase/purse onto the dining room table. "I'll get it set up for you."

"Thanks," Emmy said.

"Are you sure about this?" Ginny squeezed her hand. She was the only one in the room who knew what decision Emmy had made. She's spent the last hour trying to talk her out of it.

"It's what I have to do," Emmy said.

"Emmy," Pierce's voice had a warning note to it. "If you decide to do this, I can't legally help you with any of it. I can't let family in on the details of my investigation."

"Last I checked, your investigation centered only on Emmy, and since you're wrong about her, who's to say you aren't wrong about everything? In other words, she's probably better off without your help," Jonathon said, coming into the dining room.

"Last I checked, none of this was any of your business," Pierce said. "Why are you here, anyway?"

"Don't mind me, I'm just the delivery guy," Jonathon said, but he didn't act like he was in a hurry to leave.

The doorbell buzzed at the same time Ramona said, "Do you have the link?"

Jonathon went to the door as Emmy turned her attention to the computer. When he opened it, Madelyn stood there in all her glory. She looked surprised, almost shocked, to see Jonathon. "What are you doing here?"

"Food delivery." Jonathon tapped the White Sails restaurant logo on his pec.

"I didn't know this was a party." She swept by him. "Why are we all here?" She turned to Pierce. "And why haven't you arrested that woman yet?"

"You didn't have to come," Ramona pointed out.

"Yes I did," Madelyn said. "I assume this is about the ludicrous stipulations my father—"

"In-law," Ramona finished. "You have no blood relation to the man, stop acting like—"

"Can you hear me?" The lawyer from the reading of the will came on the little screen and Ramona and Madelyn forgot their fight as they crowded around the laptop.

"We can hear you," Emmy said.

"Good, although I believe the person we all want to hear is not me, but Emerson. I assume you called this meeting together so you could let us know what you've decided."

All eyes turned on Emmy. She was suddenly positive she'd made the wrong choice. She rethought everything she'd learned in the last twenty-four hours. Her life wasn't what she thought it was. It hadn't been her own for a long time, maybe never. She'd relied on first her dad and then Collin, and they'd both let her down. It was time she learned to rely on herself.

"Well?" Madelyn asked.

Emmy's eyes fell on the stapled together book she'd left on the coffee table in the living room. She owed her mother some justice. No. She owed it to herself to find the truth.

"I've decided to take the case."

Chapter 30

Private Investigator

"This is a terrible idea." Pierce's hands were balled into fists of frustration. "Why would you do something as stupid as trying to solve this mystery on your own? This isn't one of your mystery novels, this is real life. With real danger and real bad guys."

"You don't need to lecture me about what is real." Emmy matched his tone. "I was there, remember? Less than three feet away when Professor Sharp was murdered, but I couldn't stop it. I had his blood on my hands, literally." Hot, frustrated, angry tears gathered in the corners of her eyes.

Ginny put a hand on her shoulder. Emmy moved back, working to wipe the tears away before anyone saw. She hated how weak they made her look. She couldn't tell anyone that she wasn't crying because she was scared or worried, or even because of her uncle's death. She was crying because until last night, she hadn't known that her mother's death might not have been an accident. More than that. She hadn't known that her father had lied to her all these years and that there was a possibility he had been the one who killed her mom.

Madelyn, queen of drama, picked up on the tears immediately. "Now you're crying? You barely knew Edward and now you shed crocodile tears, to make us think you care about anything but his money?"

"Hello pot, this is the kettle..." Ramona said.

"What does pot have to do with any of this?" Madelyn asked.

Ramona looked heavenward and shook her head. "I, for one, am impressed that Emmy has the gumption to try to tackle this on her own. More power to her."

Pierce huffed, "If you think I'm going to turn over any of our police files, you're crazy. I don't care how rich your uncle was, he doesn't get to dictate who has access to our investigation."

Ramona looked thoughtful. "There might be some legal precedent that could—"

"For once shut up with the legal jargon," Madelyn said. "I'm going to go call my lawyer and see if any of this is—"

"Legal?" Ramona finished for her.

Madelyn turned her back and stomped out. Pierce followed her. "You're making a big mistake, Emmy. I only hope it isn't a fatal one." He shut the door behind him.

"Was that a threat? That felt like a threat to me." Ramona stood up, and the stack of bracelets that encircled her wrists jangled. "I'm off to look for legal precedent. If there's a way to get the police files on this case, I'll find it. That was one of my specialties when I was a defense lawyer, I could always find a loophole. I hope for your sake I can find one this time. You need all the help you can get, and Pierce is not going to offer it willingly."

Ginny stood at the door for a long moment after Ramona left. "I hate to desert you especially now, but I have to catch the ferry if I'm going to make it back to work tomorrow. I have a rent payment coming up and I don't have a rich uncle to take care of me." She walked over and gave Emmy a quick hug.

Emmy considered asking her to stay. With the stipend she was getting, Ginny could quit her job, at least for the month. Emmy had gotten used to her being around to help her remember things, like taking her meds and charging her phone. Pierce was right; she wasn't going to solve this on her own. But if Emmy failed, then Ginny would have lost her job, maybe even her apartment, and it would all be for nothing. She couldn't ask her to take that risk. And having Ginny babysit her wasn't exactly doing it all on her own.

"Call me, okay?" Ginny finished. "And if none of this works out, my couch is still available."

Emmy nodded and hugged her back. She was too overwhelmed to answer. After the door closed for the last time, she sank back in a chair. She felt utterly alone. What had she done? She couldn't solve a murder. She couldn't run an island. She could barely run her own life.

"You look like you could use this." Jonathon came out of the kitchen carrying a plate of food. Emmy was surprised to see him; she thought he'd left before the lawyer came on.

"Thanks, but I'm not sure I have the stomach to eat anything."

"You need to keep your strength up. You have a mystery to solve." He set the food in front of her.

In spite of herself, she picked up a fork. The food looked delicious. "I think it's going to take more than a shrimp and spinach salad to get us out of this one, Scoob."

He laughed and then sat down across from her. "You're probably right." He hesitated for a long moment, looking around the room like he expected someone to be listening. "I might be able to help you."

Emmy took a bite of the salad. "Help me with what?"

"With solving this case."

Emmy looked at him, waiting for the punchline, but for once, Jonathon appeared sincere. "You're serious? How could you…"

Jonathon bent his head toward her. "No one else on the island knows this, but I'm actually a PI."

"A PI?" Emmy asked.

"A private investigator. I did some intelligence work in the Army, until I was wounded. Once I recovered, I decided to go into the private sector."

Emmy looked at him skeptically. It sounded like a far-fetched story. "Are you kidding? You did intelligence work for the Army? And you were wounded?"

He lifted up his shirt and made an x across the scar she'd seen before. "Cross my heart and hope not to die."

"That's from—"

He lowered his shirt. "A sniper bullet, yeah. I was lucky. I've been lucky a few times."

"Then why are you a waiter/Uber driver/delivery guy on a tiny little island?"

"I was working for a client. A rich guy wanted me to spy on his wife who was vacationing here, turns out with another guy."

"Ouch," Emmy said.

"Yeah."

"But the tourists are all gone, and I assume so is the rich guy's cheating wife. Why are you still here?"

"I'd sent my report to my client, deposited his check, and was about to leave. Then something came along that intrigued me, or maybe I should say, someone." He reached across the table and put his hand on top of Emmy's.

Her stomach fluttered. She let his touch linger for a minute and then pulled her hand away. "I don't know…"

"The point is, I can help you. I guarantee I'll be more help than that stiff overgrown Boy Scout who obviously doesn't even want to be on this island. At least give me a chance to try." He leaned closer. "I already have some information that might help you."

Emmy's interest was piqued. "What?"

"Our friend Officer Hamilton has a dark secret."

For some reason, the accusation made Emmy bristle. "What kind of a secret?"

"A secret that nearly cost him his badge, a secret that has kept him from advancing in the police force, like he'd like to. A secret that I believe has relevance to this case."

Emmy sat back, annoyed with his dramatic build up. "Okay…"

"His mom is in prison," Jonathon said.

Emmy swallowed hard. Pierce had the same secret that she had. She knew better than anyone that it didn't mean he was a bad person, but it did mean he had a lot to overcome, especially as a police officer. She almost didn't blame him for not mentioning when she'd told him about her dad being in prison. "What is she in prison for?"

"Insurance fraud," Jonathon finished dramatically.

"What does that have to do with anything?" Emmy could see where that might keep Pierce from advancing in the police force, but she didn't know what the connection was to her or her uncle.

His ego seemed deflated by her lack of enthusiasm. "I'm not sure. Yet. But I have a feeling it has some kind of connection to this case. At the very least, it's something Pierce has to live down to advance in the police force. Maybe it's like your friend said, maybe Pierce needed a big case to overcome the fact that his mom is in prison."

"So he killed my uncle so he'd have something to investigate?" Emmy asked.

"It's just a theory. I think it would pay to have a lot of them as we go about this," Jonathon said.

"We?" Emmy asked.

"If you'll have me." Jonathon slipped into a sales pitch. "You can't do this alone, not in the time you have. You can't ask Ramona for help or really anyone on the island—too many conflicts of interest. Pierce has to do his duty. I'm an outsider, with no vested interest in the case. I'm your best bet at making this happen."

Emmy looked at his earnest green eyes. "What's in it for you?"

He smiled. "I'd like to say I'm doing this out of the goodness of my heart, but a man needs to eat."

"I won't be able to pay you until I get my inheritance. *If* I get my inheritance."

"We can discuss payment when we get this in the bag. In the meantime, I'll settle for a good excuse to spend extra time with a beautiful woman." He extended a hand. "What do you say?"

Emmy hesitated. She felt like she was handing over control to someone else, just like she always had, but he was right. Where else was she going to find someone to help? She took his hand, the picture of the impish rogue with a heart of gold still firmly in her mind.

"Okay."

Chapter 31

Bookstore Mouse

The scream and clatter of metal and glass woke Emmy with a start. She looked around her. Even though she was sitting in the green wingback chair instead of passed out on the floor, waking up in the bookshop gave her a sick feeling of déjà vu.

The smell of mint/lavender tea and sweet cinnamon wafted around the broken things as tea seeped into the rug in front of the unlit fireplace.

"Stay back!" Victoria, her uncle's assistant, was standing next to the shattered teapot, one of the pokers from the fireplace raised above her head.

"It's me," Emmy said, realizing that maybe the fact that it was her could be the exact reason the woman screamed.

"Right." The woman reluctantly started to lower the poker. She peered at Emmy over thin gold-rimmed glasses. "You're Edward's niece. The one who— Who—" The woman's hand trembled. Emmy wanted to take away the poker before it clattered to the ground next to the tea set, but she was afraid the woman would see that as a threat.

"I'm so sorry I startled you," Emmy said. "I couldn't sleep, so I came down to read. I must have fallen asleep in the chair." She'd started poring over the books she and her uncle had talked about the night he was murdered. She assumed there would be an answer in one of them. She'd fallen asleep in the middle of *Rebecca*, by Daphne Du Maurier, a book that talked about a woman who had drowned in a boating accident. It seemed like the most likely place to start.

"It's okay." Victoria twisted her lips into something that was probably supposed to be a smile, but didn't quite make the bend. "Edward used to do that all the time." The smile came then, sad and wistful.

Emmy knelt to help pick up the things that had spilled from the tray. "I didn't expect anyone to be in the bookshop this morning."

"I didn't either." Victoria dropped to her knees, picking up pieces of the blue teapot so quickly that Emmy was sure she was going to cut herself. "Sorry I screamed. After what I came upon here the other morning, I'm a bit shaky."

"That's completely understandable," Emmy helped stack the broken glass on the tray. "Do you have a vacuum or..."

"I've got this, don't worry," Victoria said, but her hands trembled as she watched Emmy place a particularly sharp bit of pottery on the tray.

"Of course you do." Emmy backed off. "I'm sorry I ruined your breakfast."

"It wasn't my breakfast, it was for..." Victoria's voice trailed off. "I mean, I'm in the habit of picking up tea and something from the patisserie every morning on my way in. It was only natural to stop this morning. I'd set up the tea things before I remembered." Victoria's eyes grew wide and moist and she reached for a tissue box strategically placed near the romance section.

Emmy studied the older woman, wondering if she was someone she should add to the suspect list. As his assistant, Victoria was one of the closest people to the professor. She had easy access to the bookshop and she was the one who had brought the tainted cakes that Emmy had been drugged with. She had plenty of opportunity, but did this soft-spoken, gray-haired bookworm have a motive?

"How long have you worked here?" Emmy asked.

"I've been Professor Sharp's assistant for nearly thirty years. But I've lived on the island my whole life. I'm a good worker and I love books, I wouldn't want to be anywhere else even if..."

"Even if someone hadn't been murdered here recently," Emmy supplied, but the expression on Victoria's face told her that wasn't what she'd been about to say.

"Even if I had to take a cut in pay," Victoria finished for her. Emmy realized the woman was worried about losing her job. That was confirmed when Victoria started talking quickly. "I don't know what your uncle told you about my financial situation, but Dr. Gregory has agreed to take me on as a part-time receptionist, so as far as the money I owed him, I ca—"

"Wait, you worked for him, but you owed him money?" Emmy asked. "How does that happen?"

Victoria blushed. "Oh, I assumed you already had all of Edward's financial information. It was just a small loan Edward gave me when I was in trouble. I told him I'd work it off. I could have too, in just a few short years, but Edward refused to take the money out of my paycheck. He said he was afraid if the debt was paid, I'd leave him." Victoria opened her eyes innocently. "He didn't need to do that. I would have stayed whether the debt was paid off or not. And I'll still stay. If you'll have me."

Emmy wasn't sure what to say. Victoria must have taken her hesitation as proof that she wasn't planning on keeping her. "I'm only at the clinic a couple of days a week. I can work nights or weekends, whatever you need. Just let me—"

Emmy chose her next words carefully. "I'm not sure what's going to happen to the bookshop or anything else on the island right now."

"So you've decided to sell it?" Victoria's horrified expression caught Emmy off guard.

"No. At least not yet. I need to—"

"I thought you were trying to find Edward's murderer. You haven't given up already, have you?" Victoria looked equally horrified by this idea. "You can't give up on him. I know a lot of people hated him, but he was always nice to me. He wasn't the man everyone says he was." A little blush colored the woman's cheeks and her eyes shone with unshed tears.

Emmy started to wonder exactly what this woman's relationship had been with the professor. Other than Madelyn's dramatic show, these were the first tears anyone had produced over his death.

"Could you tell me a little about my uncle?" Emmy said. "I barely got to know him."

There was a strange awe in Victoria's voice as she spoke of the professor. "Oh, he was a great man. An important man, but he always took time for our books." She'd said the phrase with the same pride that one might say *our children*. "He was always looking for old books, rare books, or just interesting stories. He restored the very old ones. He kept all the book restoration supplies in the office. I could show you."

"Another time, maybe," Emmy said.

"He taught me how to do most of it." Victoria looked hopeful. "That's another useful skill that you might want to consider if you keep me on."

"Yes, book repair is a great skill to have," Emmy said, although she was wondering if anyone really repaired books anymore.

Victoria finished picking up the last of the pieces and stood. As she did, a jade green necklace in the shape of a curled dragon at her throat caught Emmy's eye. It seemed familiar. "That's a beautiful necklace," she said. "Did you get it from one of the shops in town?"

"Oh." Victoria grasped the necklace like she wanted to hide it. "Um, I don't know where it came from. It was a gift."

Emmy pressed her. "I'd love to get something like it. Who gave it to you?"

"It was a gift, from...um...a gift from Edward...for..." She hesitated for a long moment. "For being a loyal employee and putting up with the bookshop dragon." She chuckled nervously. "He meant himself. He always referred to himself as the bookshop dragon."

Emmy nodded. "That's an interesting nickname."

"I don't know where he got it." Victoria moved toward the door. "I could get more tea and pastries if you want."

"No, I'm okay," Emmy said. She couldn't shake the feeling that she'd seen that jade dragon before, maybe not in a necklace, but something important.

"Okay." The woman acted like she was still afraid of Emmy or just nervous. She fluttered around the shop like a trapped bird.

"Could you tell me about the tea and cakes that were left at the bookshop the night before Professor Sharp died? Did you get those at the local shop?"

"Yes." Victoria nodded. "Edward left me a note saying he was meeting someone special for tea after dinner. He asked me to get the best cakes I could find and leave everything on the table. He told me to leave work early." Victoria hesitated and Emmy could sense something behind it.

"But you didn't leave work early, did you?"

Victoria twisted her hands. "I only wanted to see who Edward was so excited to see."

Emmy remembered the bump from behind the bookshelves and what her uncle had said about a bookshop mouse that lived behind the shelves. If he was the dragon, then the woman in front of her was definitely the bookshop mouse. "You were spying on us."

The woman turned bright red and became flustered. "I didn't...I wouldn't...I...I ..."

Emmy moved closer to the stammering woman. "Are you the one who put ketamine in the cakes? Who told you to do that?"

"I...I didn't do anything to the food, besides bring it from the shop. I didn't stay very long after you got here. I was afraid you might be..."

"Might be who?" Emmy probed.

The bell at the front of the shop rang before she could answer. Pierce strode in.

"I have a few questions for you."

Chapter 32

Options

"Questions?" Victoria turned ashen and slumped into a heap on the floor.

Pierce had come in looking gruff and official and now he looked as helpless as any man when confronted with a fainting woman. "What did I say?"

Emmy moved to the woman on the floor. "I don't think it was you. She seems to be terrified of everything."

"I guess so," Pierce said. "Help me get her to the couch."

The two of them lifted the woman to the aptly named fainting couch. "Should we call the doctor or something?" Emmy asked.

"No doctor." Victoria was coming around. "I don't have health insurance. I can't afford to go to the hospital."

"You worked for this place for thirty years and you have no insurance?" She was incensed that her uncle wouldn't have provided this poor woman who was loyal to a fault, in his debt, and most likely in love with him, some kind of health insurance.

Victoria tried to sit up, but she was still very pale. "I'm sorry, Officer. I can answer your questions now. It's just been a trying few days."

"Oh, I don't need to ask you any questions now." Pierce stepped back like Victoria was going to explode. "You look pale. You don't feel, um...sick at all, do you?"

"I'm okay, really. I overreacted. I'm happy to talk to you, if you don't mind my answering questions while I stay on the couch."

"I didn't come to question you." He turned his gaze toward Emmy, who was in the tiny bathroom wetting a paper towel to put on the back of Victoria's neck. "I came to ask *you* a few questions, starting with when did you get your phone back?"

Emmy covered her mouth with her hand, realizing the huge mistake she'd made. She was in such a hurry to get changed and make it back to the meeting that she hadn't told Pierce about finding her cell phone. "I found it in the dumpster behind the restaurant, just before the town meeting."

"You should have left it where you found it. That phone is an important piece of evidence and you what, just stuffed it in your pocket and held onto it?" Pierce had obviously recovered from his fit of compassion. "Doing stupid, mindless things like that make you look guilty."

His words stung, but Emmy knew she deserved it. "It was dead and then I was in such a hurry to get to the meeting that I didn't even look at it."

"Have you used the phone since you got it back?" Pierce asked.

Emmy remembered the one call she'd made on her phone, to her dad in prison, something that would definitely look suspicious. "Only once. I'm used to just having it, I...didn't think."

"No, you didn't." Pierce shook his head. "You need to bring me the phone, and you need to show me exactly where you found it. If Jonathon hadn't mentioned it today I wouldn't have known it had been recovered until I tracked it back to your apartment."

"When did you talk to Jonathon?" Emmy asked. In a weird way it felt like a betrayal for Jonathon to tell Pierce about the phone, but he probably thought she'd turned it over to Pierce after the meeting.

"When I went in for breakfast this morning, he asked when I wanted to search the dumpster. He said he'd been holding all the trash back, but that he couldn't hold it much longer."

"My phone's upstairs in the apartment," Emmy said.

"Under the circumstances, I can't let you go get it alone," Pierce said. "Not that you haven't had ample time to delete whatever might have been on in or wipe away any evidence that might be on it."

"You can subpoena the phone records, and I doubt the person who took it left any fingerprints." Emmy tried to keep the irritation out of her voice. Mostly she was irritated with herself, not Pierce.

"Will you be okay alone for a while?" Pierce asked Victoria.

"I'm alone most of the time," Victoria said with a little sniff. "I always manage."

"Okay, well, Ms. Fox, I'll follow you," Pierce said.

Emmy led him up the back stairs that led to the apartment. He was all business, but something was on her mind. Something she needed an answer for. "I've been thinking about this. I think someone who knew I was allergic to watermelon put it in my drink, so I would have to leave the table to um...because I was sick."

Pierce turned a shade of pale green. "I'd rather not—"

"Maybe they needed my phone or my purse for something, or—"

Pierce stopped at the door, waiting for her to open it. "Or maybe they knew they had to do something to get me away from you, so you would go with the professor. But that presupposes that someone knew enough to put watermelon in your drink, except the only ones with access to your drink were Jonathon and me."

"So it had to be one of you," Emmy said.

"It seems pretty convenient that twice in one night something slipped into your drink," Pierce said.

"Actually I think the ketamine was in the cakes." Emmy turned to face him.

Pierce raised his eyebrows. "You seem pretty sure of that. Is it because you took it yourself?"

"No. Because Professor Sharp didn't eat any of the cakes, but he did drink the tea, and he wasn't drugged. Besides, why would I take enough ketamine to pass out?"

"Maybe you hired someone to kill your uncle, but took a drug known to induce amnesia so you could say you didn't remember anything."

Emmy was getting flustered and frustrated with his questioning. "But I do remember things. For example, I remembered last night that someone was in the secret room behind the bookshelf. I went back to check to see if I imagined it, and there really is a room behind the bookcase."

"There is?" Pierce sounded skeptical.

"I can show you after I get my phone. Victoria knows it's there, she—" Emmy stopped herself, remembering that Victoria had been the person hiding in the little room. But Emmy was sure she was there because she wanted to see who Professor Sharp was meeting with, because she was jealous, not because she was a killer. But if she was there, had she seen the killer? She hadn't gotten the chance to tell Emmy whether she saw who was with the professor.

"Are you going to let me in?"

"Right, sorry." Emmy had been stuck in her own head. She fit the key into the lock, but the door swung open before she could turn it.

"You left your door open?" Pierce said. "Considering everything, I don't think that's a—"

"Sorry, we let ourselves in." Jonathon was standing in the apartment.

"We?" Pierce asked.

"I'm here too." Ramona stood up from the living room couch. "Jonathon told me Pierce was looking for you and your phone. I wanted to make sure you had an attorney present if your apartment was searched."

"But you said you couldn't be my attorney any more." Emmy was thoroughly confused, especially when a third person stepped into the room. This one was a young, dark-haired man.

"That's why I brought my associate," Ramona said. "You didn't think I'd leave you high and dry, did you?"

The man extended his hand, "Hi, Kenneth St. Williams here. Of course you don't have to hire me, but—"

"How many people are in my apartment?" Emmy said. It felt like she didn't have anything like privacy on this tiny island, and she was tired of people making decisions for her.

"By my count five, but I was just leaving." Jonathon stood by the door. "If you're still up for that island tour, I can meet you at the bakery in about an hour."

"Patisserie," Ramona corrected.

"Right," Jonathon said. "I'll pick up a picnic lunch. Anjuli's sausage rolls are to die for."

"I really don't think she has time right now for a—"

"Ms. Fox, I really need to see—"

"My client is not required to turn over her perso—"

"She's not your client yet."

"Emmy don't tell him anything until—"

Ramona and the lawyer crowded toward her, giving out bits of advice. Jonathon waited expectantly for her answer while Pierce looked ready to haul her off to jail. Emmy felt claustrophobic. She hadn't asked for Ramona to find her another lawyer. She hadn't invited any of them into the apartment that wasn't technically hers, but was still the only place she had to herself on Sharp Island, and she hadn't agreed to go anywhere with Jonathon. She felt completely out of control. Worse, she felt like everyone was trying to control her life in the name of taking care of her, just like her father. Just like Collin.

"Enough!" Emmy said. The room grew silent as all eyes fell on her.

She turned to Ramona. "Thank you for trying to help, but I'm not going to be able to navigate any of this with a lawyer breathing down my neck, advising me what I can and can't say and do." She turned to the lawyer. "I respectfully decline your offer of representation. I need to do this my way."

Ramona and the lawyer both opened their mouths in protest, but she turned to Jonathon. "I'll meet you Thursday morning, at 10:00 a.m. at the patisserie. I'll put together a lunch. Then we can go on that island tour. I can figure out my own meals between now and then. Thank you."

Jonathon bowed; he looked impressed and maybe a little amused at her taking charge. "I'm at your service, milady."

"And you." Emmy turned to Pierce. He was the only one she couldn't exactly send away. "Give me a second. I left my phone on the charger."

"I can wait," Pierce said as everyone else filed out of the room.

Emmy went into her room. She had automatically plugged the phone in without thinking, and then because she was thinking too much, she hadn't picked it up again.

As she turned it back on, she realized there were ten new messages she hadn't checked before she called her dad. Seven of them were frantic texts from Ginny leftover from two nights ago. Two were from an overpriced bridal shop where she'd gone dress shopping. She couldn't make up her mind, so luckily she hadn't purchased anything. The tenth message was from Professor Sharp.

Chapter 33

Messages from the Dead

BY THE TIME YOU READ THIS, I'LL BE DEAD...THAT'S ANOTHER THING I'VE ALWAYS WANTED TO SAY AND NOW I'VE FINALLY HAD THE CHANCE. TOO BAD I'M TOO DEAD TO APPRECIATE IT. BUT I'VE ALSO ALWAYS WANTED TO BE THAT VOICE FROM BEYOND THE GRAVE, GIVING ADVICE AND CLUES TO THE LIVING, AND SO IT IS I OFFER YOU THIS BIT OF WISDOM.

TO SOLVE THE MYSTERY, YOU NEED TO EX-
PLORE SOME HISTORY.

The text message from her uncle was attached to a picture of three teenagers dressed for prom—two girls and a boy. Her mother's red curls and impish grin stood out against her royal blue dress. She was dwarfed by a tall girl with bright blue eyes in a red dress on one side, and a muscular dark-haired guy who looked like he'd rather be wearing anything but a tuxedo on the other.

Emmy sat on the bed and stared at the text. According to her phone it was sent from "Dear Old Uncle Ed," even though she obviously didn't have Professor Sharp in her contacts when she'd lost the phone. The text was sent Friday night, just before he died. Was the text really from him? What did he mean, history?

"Emmy, are you okay?" Pierce stood beside her. He seemed to have forgotten both his frustration with her and his vow not to use her first name.

"Fine," Emmy scrubbed at her eyes. She wasn't crying, just tired, just overwhelmed.

"What's on the phone?"

Emmy held it up. "He sent me a text."

"Who sent you a text?" Pierce moved closer.

"My uncle, or someone pretending to be him. Sometime between the time I lost my phone and the time he died."

Pierce took the phone. "Whoever sent it, it wasn't the professor. Besides the fact that he was already dead when this was sent, Professor Sharp didn't have a phone. He hated technology."

"Do you recognize any of the people in the picture?"

Pierce looked uncomfortable. "The one on the end is Brighton Redding, the man who rents boats on the other side of the island. I'm guessing the one in the middle is—"

"My mom, yeah."

Pierce didn't comment on the other girl in the picture. Instead he scrolled back to check the number in the contacts.

Emmy leaned closer. "Do you think you can trace it?"

"There's nothing to trace. It was sent from this phone." He blew out a frustrated breath. "You sent this text to yourself."

"Let me see that," Emmy took the phone back and checked the date and time on the text. "Lucky for me I have an airtight alibi for the time this text was sent." She showed him the phone. "I was with you and the Chief being interrogated in Ramona's office."

Pierce's face wrinkled in concern. "So whoever stole your purse sent the message. Probably the killer."

Emmy turned to him, surprised. "So you're saying I'm not the killer?"

"I haven't officially ruled you out yet," he said.

Emmy sensed that something had changed in him. "But you don't believe I did it anymore."

"Officially, you're still a suspect."

"Unofficially?" Emmy probed.

He took a breath. "Unofficially, if you're not the killer, you're in serious danger."

It wasn't what Emmy expected him to say so she turned to face him. "Beyond the obvious, why would you say that?"

"It's like you said, someone has been setting this whole thing up for a long time and honestly, I don't think it was your uncle. I don't think this is a benevolent little game of finding clues and solving a murder.

This is a game of cat and mouse, and I think your uncle may have been just as trapped as you are now."

Emmy squared her shoulders and faced him. "Then I guess it's time I learned to be a cat."

Chapter 34

The Doctor

"Are you okay?" Jonathon walked in and sat next to Emmy in the waiting room of the tiny clinic that was Sharp Island's only answer to medical attention.

"What are you doing here?" Emmy asked.

"I saw you walk in and I thought I'd see what was wrong."

"Nothing...just some...detective stuff." Despite her resolve to be more aggressive in this investigation, Emmy still felt like she she was an imposter pretending to be Sherlock Holmes or Miss Marple or even Nancy Drew.

"Detective stuff?" Jonathon looked confused for a second, and then realization dawned on him. "Wait, didn't Ramona say the doctor had a grudge against your family?"

"That is exactly why I'm here," Emmy said.

"Are you sure about this? I mean, confronting someone who might be a murderer might not be the best way to start this off. Not to mention it could be dangerous."

"I'm not confronting him, I just want to talk to him, feel things out." Emmy looked over the paperwork she'd been handed, trying to decide how many lies she was willing to tell.

Jonathon read over her shoulder, "Sore throat? You might want to rethink that particular ailment."

Emmy looked back at him. "Why?"

"If you have a sore throat you aren't going to be doing much talking," he observed.

"Good point." Emmy looked back at the part of the form that said *Why are you here today?* "I guess I could fake a headache."

Jonathon walked up to the empty reception desk and retrieved a new form. Emmy reached for it, but he held it back. "Maybe you should leave the faking to me. I'm used to this detective stuff, and you're too sweet and innocent to be a convincing liar. Let me go talk to the doctor, and I'll tell you everything he says."

Emmy took the paperwork from him. "I need to do this myself."

"I appreciate your independence, I just don't want to see you get hurt." Jonathon covered her hand with his and squeezed.

Emmy pulled away. "Ow. If you don't want to see me get hurt, maybe you shouldn't be smashing my cut." She looked down at her hand, still bandaged and sore from whatever she'd cut it on in the bookshop.

Jonathon cradled her hand in his. "That looks like it might be getting infected, maybe you should have it looked at."

Emmy met his eyes and smiled. "Perfect," she said as she continued filling in the form. "I'll have the doctor look at the cut on my hand."

"How are you going to explain how you got it?" Jonathon said. "Aren't you trying to do this incognito?" He gestured to the line that said "name" where Emmy had written *Sarah Barr*.

Before Emmy could answer, the nurse came into the room. "We have a room ready for you. You can finish filling out that paperwork in there."

Jonathon stood with her, but the nurse stopped him. "Our rooms aren't very large, so unless your friend is under eighteen or incapacitated, I'm afraid you'll need to wait out here."

Jonathon sat back down. As she walked away he mouthed the words, *Be careful*. Emmy nodded, but she was sure he was overestimating how dangerous the doctor might be.

"I'm afraid it might be a bit," the nurse said after she took Emmy's vitals. "We only have Dr. Gregory and there are two other patients ahead of you."

"I can wait," Emmy said.

As the nurse walked out of the room, Emmy saw a gray-haired man in a white lab coat leave an office across the hall. Emmy heard him say, "I might need your help with this one," to the nurse. She followed him down the hall. After a few breathless minutes, Emmy decided the doctor's private office was as good a place to begin her sleuthing as anywhere. She slid off the table and went across the hall.

The first thing she noticed was a picture of a pretty young woman on the doctor's desk. She had dark brown hair and haunted gray eyes. Emmy guessed this was a picture of the doctor's daughter who had killed herself. Glancing over her shoulder she opened one cupboard and then a couple of drawers. She wasn't sure what she was looking for until she spotted a row of empty prescription bottles. Another drawer was filled with labels for those bottles. The labels were similar to the one on the bottle Pierce had found in her purse.

Emmy had never heard of a clinic so small that they filled their own medications. It would make it easy for the doctor to create a label and fill a bottle with the ketamine to send her a message. She slipped one of the labels into her pocket and closed the drawer.

She went back to the picture on the desk. The woman was standing in front of a brick building with a sign next to her. Emmy reached to pick the picture up so she could read the writing. A throat cleared behind her. She jerked her hand back and knocked the picture onto the floor.

"Are you lost, miss?"

Emmy turned around to face the white-coated doctor.

Emmy thought fast, her heart pounding in her ears. "I...I saw the picture from across the hall...she looked familiar so I came to see if it was someone I knew."

The doctor bent down and retrieved the photograph. He set it back on the desk with a sad reverence. "I don't think so. She died soon after you were born."

"I'm sorry," Emmy said. "She was beautiful."

"She was. Too beautiful and too good for this world. Her life was cut short because of the greed and selfishness of a horrible man." He stepped back to get a better look at Emmy. She looked down, afraid he might see something of that man in her. "I keep her picture on my desk to remind me that life can change in a heartbeat."

"But that's not why you're here, is it?" He stepped to the door and directed Emmy back into the exam room. Emmy sat on the table and he pulled a little stool up next to her. "I hear you have a cut on your hand?"

"Yes," Emmy said as he unwound the bandage.

He shook his head. "How did you manage this?" He turned her hand back and forth, examining the cut. "It had to be a very thin, very sharp, double-sided blade for it to have cut both your palm and your fingers."

"Extremely sharp kitchen knife." Emmy tried to laugh it off. "I'm not very good with knives."

"The doctor raised his eyebrows. "I don't know of any kitchen knife that is double-edged like this. It almost looks intentional, either by you or by someone else. You don't have a dagger do you? Maybe a set of throwing knives?"

"No." Emmy laughed again, but it came out as more of a strangled cough. "It was just a dumb accident."

The doctor's penetrating gaze seemed to look straight through her. Finally he sat back. "If you're sure there's nothing more you want to tell me about your wound."

"I'm sure," Emmy said.

He sighed. "And as long as you're current on your tetanus shot—"

"I got one just last year." Emmy was happy to talk about anything other than where the cut on her hand had come from. "I sliced my foot on a rusty can at the park. My fiancé told me not to wear sandals, and he was furious that I didn't listen to him. He complained about it the whole time he drove me to the hospital."

The doctor looked concerned. "Your fiancé? The man you came in with? Does he often tell you what to do? Does he often yell at you?"

Emmy backtracked quickly. "Yes, I mean no, this was my ex-fiancé. The man who came with me is just a friend."

"I see," he said, but he hesitated, like he wanted to say more, but then he shook his head. "If you're sure about the tetanus shot, I'll just rewrap your hand and put some good antibiotics on it. It's long but probably not deep, so I won't bother with stitches, maybe a bit of skin glue." He turned and rummaged through the drawers.

"Do you fill prescriptions here?" Emmy asked.

He turned back around, a suspicious look on his face. "Very few and only in emergencies. If you think you're going to get pain meds for this cut—"

"Oh no...I don't need...I mean, that's not what I was asking." Obviously the doctor thought she was some sort of drug addict who cut her own hand in the hopes of getting prescription painkillers. She searched for a legitimate reason for her question. "I need to refill my ADHD meds and I was hoping to do it here."

The doctor went to work cleaning the wound on her hand. "As I said, we fill prescriptions only in emergencies. You're better off going to the mainland for those."

"What if I can't go back to the mainland?" Emmy blurted out.

The doctor stared at her for a long moment as Emmy realized how many mistakes she'd made. "I guess you'll have to have someone else get your medication for you."

He continued to work in silence until her hand was patched up neatly. He took off his rubber gloves and tossed them in the garbage can. "Watch for infection and come back if your hand gets red or hot or you develope a fever."

He stood to leave, pausing at the doorway to catch her in his gaze. "You should be more careful, Ms. Fox. Sharp Island is a dangerous place for people who pretend to be something they're not."

Chapter 35
The Tea Shop

After her visit to the doctor, Emmy should have known there was no hope of anonymity anywhere on the island. Still, she was caught off guard when she walked into the tea shop and Ms. Lee hurried forward to personally greet her. "Only the best for the young heiress," she said as she sat Emmy at a table with a view of the harbor. In less than five minutes, she was back with a little white pot of tea and a plate of strawberry crumpets.

The shop was bustling. Everyone coming in and going out took a second to stare at Emmy. None of them spoke to her, but she felt like she should talk to all of them—find out who they were, what they were like, and where they were the night Professor Sharp died. But she couldn't make herself do it. She felt defeated. She'd gotten more questions than answers from Dr. Gregory's office at the clinic and if he didn't already hate her just based on her family name, he probably hated her now for lying to him.

She'd wanted to do this investigation her way. She wasn't sure what that meant, but right now it felt like her way was just making a mess of everything.

She sipped her tea, and focused her attention on the bent but surprisingly quick and efficient shop owner. She wished Ms. Lee would slow down enough to talk to her. She needed to find out if the woman hated her uncle as much as everyone else or if Ms. Lee had some motive for killing him. After all, the tea at her uncle's house had been from her shop.

Before she could come up with a good reason to flag Ms. Lee down, the older woman took off her apron, called to her assistant in the back that she was going to be taking a break, poured herself some tea and then sat across from Emmy.

Ms. Lee took a sip of her tea. Emmy could feel her appraising her from over the cup. "So you're our only hope." Her tone was conversational, friendly even, but there was an undercurrent of suspicion that Emmy caught there too.

"Only hope?" Emmy asked.

"Our only hope to save the island from being bought out and turned into a resort," Ms. Lee said. "I don't believe for a minute that Madelyn Sharp won't sell us out as soon as she gets the chance and Ramona makes a big show of being on our side, but she's been trying to get her claws into the island since the first time Edward Sharp brought her here."

"Ramona?" Emmy asked. "Ramona said she doesn't want the island. She basically said the same thing you did, that I'm the only hope to keep this place the way it is."

Instead of commenting, Ms. Lee sipped her tea for a few more seconds, regarding Emmy with spectacled dark eyes. Finally she said, "Don't you have any questions for me? If you want to be a detective, you're going to have to ask questions."

"I didn't ask to be a detective," Emmy said defensively, even though that's exactly what she was working up the courage to do.

"No. But you need to be one."

"Right." Emmy thought about all the things she needed to ask Ms. Lee. "Okay, then tell me where you were the night my uncle was murdered," Emmy said.

"You're interested in my alibi?" Ms. Lee looked pleased. "That's a good first step. I was at our weekly outing with the rest of the ladies."

"What exactly did your 'weekly outing' entail?" Emmy asked.

Ms. Lee smiled mischievously. "This week it was ax throwing."

"Ax throwing?" Emmy looked at her in disbelief.

"I keep my own set, if you'd like to see them." Ms. Lee sounded proud enough that she might actually bring her axes to the table.

"And you do this regularly?" Emmy was trying to picture the hunched Ms. Lee hurling an ax.

"Sometimes we do knives instead, other days it's archery or the shooting range, really whatever kind of weapon suits us for that evening. We all have our own specialties. If there's ever a zombie apocalypse, I can tell which of the women in town would most be likely to survive and what her weapon of choice would be."

Emmy was trying to picture the older women in town lining up to practice deadly aim. "I don't think…"

"Aren't you going to ask who was with me, who can verify my alibi?"

"Right, who was there?" Emmy asked.

Ms. Lee seemed to be enjoying herself, "Stella, the owner of the bed and breakfast; Ramona; Anjuli, who owns the patisserie; Gretchen Redding, Brighton's wife; Annabelle, the doctor's wife; and me. We can all vouch for each other's whereabouts from seven o'clock to nearly midnight, although Ramona slipped out for about half an hour."

Ramona had already explained about the signing of the will, so Emmy expected that one.

"Aren't you going to ask me about the tea?" Ms. Lee said. "I heard you were drugged and that's why you don't know who killed the professor three feet away from you."

"I don't think the drugs were in the tea," Emmy said. "Professor Sharp wasn't drugged. He drank the tea, but didn't eat any of the cakes."

Ms. Lee almost looked disappointed. "Well, I guess your next step is the patisserie. That is, if you don't have any further questions for me."

Emmy tried to think of other things she should ask Ms. Lee. She knew there had to be more, but for some reason, only one question came to mind. "What do you know about Pierce Hamilton?"

"Officer Hamilton?" A wide smile spread over the older woman's face. "He is very handsome, isn't he?" Emmy blushed. That wasn't why she wanted information about Pierce.

The older woman continued, "He's quiet. Too serious. He was always serious, even as a child, but even more so now. He's had a hard time with things ever since his mother—" She stopped like she'd said too much.

"His mother?" Emmy prodded, even though she already knew, thanks to Jonathon, what this particular secret was.

"It's not my secret to share." Ms. Lee leaned forward, as if she was prepared to spill the secret anyway. "But between you and me, what

Nancy Hamilton did was out of the goodness of her heart. She helped a few people in this town get out from under your uncle's thumb before she got caught."

"Under my uncle's thumb?" Emmy was surprised that Ms. Lee would be so blunt about it.

Ms. Lee leaned back and shook her head. "Oh, honey, I hope people aren't selling you some romanticized notion of what kind of man your uncle was."

"No," Emmy admitted. "I've heard he was a pretty bad landlord."

"Bad is an understatement." She looked thoughtful for a minute. "He wasn't always that way. In the early days, right after your grandfather died and he inherited the island, he was kind of bumbling and backward in his business dealings, but not vicious. Everything changed after his son died. Edward turned into as much of a tyrant as his father had been. He upped everyone's rent and micromanaged everything on the island. Some even said he was spying on all of us.

"He was quite the loan shark too. He was always happy to loan some poor, struggling businessperson money—for the good of the island. Turned out it was more for Edward Sharp's good." She bit off the last words and shook her head as she took another sip of tea.

Emmy thought for a minute about what that might mean. If Pierce's mom was in jail for insurance fraud... "So Nancy Hamilton sold insurance to businesses on the island and then helped them have an accident so they could get insurance money to pay off loans from my uncle?"

"You didn't hear it from me," Ms. Lee said, taking one of the crumpets she'd set on Emmy's plate. "But some people considered her more of a Robin Hood than a criminal."

"How does Pierce fit into all this?" Emmy asked. "Did he know what she was doing? Were they close?"

"Thick as thieves when he was younger, if you'll pardon the expression. He never knew his father, maybe that's why they were so close. I doubt he knew what his mother's business was really about; he'd just started college when the whole thing came crashing down. I couldn't speculate how he feels about her now, but maybe you could ask him." Ms. Lee nodded in the direction of the door, just as the little silver bell rang. "He comes in like clockwork every evening at six whenever he's in town."

"I don't need to question him," Emmy said, trying to hide the blush that had started again as soon as Pierce walked through the door.

Ms. Lee patted her hand. "Oh darling. You need to question everyone." She stood up and went back behind the counter to greet Pierce like she hadn't just been dishing on his family secrets.

Emmy couldn't bring herself to approach Pierce, so instead she watched him. She was thinking about how they were living strangely parallel lives. His mom was in prison and her dad was in prison. Her mother died when she was a little girl and he never knew his father. These similarities hadn't come up when they chatted online and he definitely hadn't mentioned them on their ill-fated date.

Emmy noted that Pierce didn't go for the tea everyone seemed to love. Instead he ordered a coffee, black. On the way to the door he noticed her, took a detour and came to her table.

"Ms. Fox." He nodded.

Emmy took a breath, Ms. Lee was right, she needed to question everyone. "So we're being formal now?"

"I thought that given the change in our situation, I should probably not call you by your first name anymore," Pierce said.

"You mean the fact that I'm a murder suspect and you're a police officer," Emmy said.

"Something like that," Pierce shuffled his feet, like he wasn't sure whether to sit or take his coffee somewhere else.

Emmy decided two could play at his game. She gestured across the table. "Officer Hamilton, would you like to sit down?"

"I don't think—" he began.

"I don't think it's good police business to miss out on a chance to casually question the prime suspect in a murder investigation," Emmy said.

He sat. "And I don't think it's good amateur detective business to miss out on a chance to question a police officer assigned to the case you're trying to solve. And I didn't say you were the prime suspect."

"Oh, has something changed?" Emmy opened her eyes wide and stared at him over her tea. "Who would you say is the prime suspect?"

"Interesting question. There are a lot of potential suspects in this case. From the outset, the person who discovered the body is always on the table. That would be you. Then there are the people who would benefit from the victim's death. You again—"

"Except I didn't know that until after he died," Emmy broke in.

"Maybe. There was a letter you claim you never received, but if you had received it—"

"I didn't."

"Okay, you aside, next we have Madelyn and Ramona and by a slim margin, Victoria because she would get the bookshop, but that hardly seems worth killing someone over. Madelyn and Ramona have alibis. Ramona was with a group of women from the island and Madelyn stayed on the mainland that night. We have her registered at a hotel and about a hundred photographs on social media of her at an upscale party in Seattle."

Speaking of alibis made Emmy think about Jonathon's fake one. "What about Jonathon?"

Pierce leaned closer. "Jonathon?"

Emmy found she wasn't quite ready to tell Pierce about the holes in Jonathon's story. "I don't know, mysterious newcomer to town, someone could have hired him."

"Again, he has an alibi. I checked the ferry records and the surveillance video. He was on the mainland by the time the professor was killed."

Emmy sat back. Jonathon had lied about where he was after he left the island, but he had left. Maybe he really was just trying to impress her with the picture of his niece.

"I'll throw it back to you then, Ms. Amateur Detective. Who would you say is the prime suspect?"

Emmy thought for a minute. "I think I'm the logical choice. I had motive and opportunity, but since I know I'm innocent. I think maybe the small town police officer might be my prime suspect."

"Me?" Pierce looked shocked. "How do you figure that?"

Emmy studied him for a second. She wasn't sure if she should go down this path, but it might lead to something. "You lured what you would call the prime suspect to the island with the offer of a date—"

"Wait. I lured you here? What could possibly be my mot—"

"Don't interrupt, I'm hypothesizing." Emmy leaned back, tented her fingers under her chin and continued, "You obviously don't want to be here. You're looking for the opportunity to advance your career." Emmy was straying dangerously close to what she and Ramona had overheard the chief telling him. She didn't want him to guess that the office had been bugged, but she pushed on anyway. "A high-profile murder might be just the thing."

"What kind of cop would commit a murder to advance his career?" Pierce asked.

"I've read a couple of books that had a similar plot," Emmy said

"You're back to your books. Remember this is real life."

"I'm sure it's happened."

"So I lured you here to frame you for murder. You've given me the motive, what about opportunity?"

"That one's easy. You spiked my drink with watermelon, knowing it would make me sick. When I was in the bathroom, you stole my purse, planted the drugs and then went to the patisserie to drug the cakes with the same medication."

"Motive and opportunity I'll give you. But where's your proof?"

"You lied." Emmy hadn't meant for that part to come out, but it had.

"I lied? About what?" Pierce was defensive, so defensive that Emmy realized she'd hit on something.

"You lied about having to leave our dinner to go out on a call that night. You told Jonathon that you had police business, but there was no police business that night." Emmy hadn't meant to show her hand so quickly. She didn't have any proof that he'd lied about the reason he left dinner early except for what Jonathon had said about the police scanner. The look on Pierce's face told her she was right. Her stomach twisted in knots. She didn't really believe Pierce was a murderer. If he'd lied it was because she wasn't what he'd expected. He wanted to get out of the date so he made up a fake police call.

"I didn't...I mean...I..." Pierce was floundering. His phone buzzed and he seemed grateful for the distraction. He focused on whatever text had come in. After a few minutes he tapped the screen as if he were zooming in on an image. Whatever it was, it looked important. Emmy guessed it had something to do with the case. She needed to see what he was looking at.

She bumped the table, spilling her tea on purpose. The hot liquid spattered on Pierce's hand and he dropped his phone. It bounced off his lap and onto the floor. "Oh, I'm so sorry." Emmy ducked under the table to retrieve the phone.

It was undamaged from the fall, but she could see the photo he'd received. It was an autopsy photo, a closeup of her uncle's chest wound. She swallowed hard, but there was no blood so she forced herself to look.

Pierce realized what she was doing and ducked under the table too. He took his phone back. "You aren't supposed to see these."

But she had seen. Her mind went back to her pathology courses. "Really thin blade, and extremely sharp. It had to go in quickly and with a lot of force because of how deep the cut is and the bruising around the wound."

Pierce stared at her dumbfounded. "That's exactly what the coroner said. How did you..."

Emmy didn't want to get into her long list of failed majors, so she asked, "Did you ever find the murder weapon?"

"No. But he believed it was some kind of specialized knife, like one you'd use for sport or—" He cut off abruptly.

"Or what?"

Pierce shook his head. "I can't share that information with you."

"Why not? If I'm the murderer, I already know what kind of knife was used."

"Nice try." He put the phone back in his pocket. "I need to get going. I have a meeting with the coroner."

"Can I come?"

"No. Despite what the will said, I can't have you looking over my shoulder during this investigation."

"But as the next of kin, I will get the autopsy report, right?" Emmy said.

"We'll see." Pierce turned toward the door, hesitated, and then turned back around. "For the record. I wasn't the one who chose the drink and I had no idea you were allergic to watermelon."

Chapter 36

History

"How do you like your tea?" Instead of screaming this time, Victoria was standing beside the green chair, setting down another platter laid out with cinnamon buns and steaming hot tea.

Emmy stretched. Waking up in the bookstore was becoming a habit. She'd been perusing the history section. Even though Pierce was sure the text message wasn't from her uncle, Emmy was hoping that there was still some kind of clue there.

Victoria nodded at a leather-bound volume of Sharp Island history. "Did you know Sharp Island was an important fort during the Westward expansion? The US government used it as one of its Westernmost outposts, to stake a claim to this part of the West Coast."

"I read that." Emmy yawned and reached for a cinnamon bun. She was too hungry to be worried about what might possibly be in the pastry.

Victoria poured them both a cup of tea. "Can I ask why you're suddenly interested in the history of Sharp Island?"

Emmy shook her head. "My uncle left me a message. He said I needed to explore history, to solve the mystery."

"That sounds like him." Victoria sipped the tea. She looked across the bookstore sadly. "He was fascinated by history." She gave a quick snort. "As long as it involved him or his family in some way." She looked at the pile of books beside Emmy. "I don't suppose you've looked in his reserve history collection."

"Reserve history collection?" Emmy asked.

Victoria hesitated like she still wasn't sure if she trusted Emmy. Finally she set down her teacup and stood up. "If he said history, he could only mean the kind he collected." She walked across the bookstore. "I guess I can't get in trouble for showing someone his collection now."

Emmy followed Victoria to the history section tucked under the staircase that led upstairs. Emmy watched as Victoria pushed aside a couple of books, as if she were searching for something. "He showed it to me once, but he never trusted me with the right title. He only brought me here when he wanted to talk about something important. He was always worried someone was listening."

Emmy scanned the shelves, realizing Victoria was looking for a lever like the one that unlatched the other secret door in the library. A book caught her eye, *A Muckraker's History*. "Muckrakers spread false news right?" She tugged on the book—it was fake. Tilting it released another lever. Slowly the shelf slid sideways into a panel in the thick wall. Behind it was a little room with a small table. Another shelf was built into the back. It was full of notebooks, journals, and photo albums—a complete Sharp family history.

"How far back do you think he meant?" Emmy murmured to herself as she pushed through the books. They had handwritten titles like *Edward Sharp: the College Years, Early Childhood Memories of Edward P. Sharp,* and *Ed Sharp: Son of Sharp Island.*

Victoria eyed the shelf reverently, but Emmy could only see her uncle's inflated ego. She wasn't sure how his personal historical fiction would help her find her mother's killer.

Next to the desk there was a pile of books waiting to be repaired—a very old copy of *Grimm's Fairy Tales* with the pages falling out, a faded red book with a torn leather cover. The title was in Spanish, *Las Paredes Oyen.* On top of it was an almost new copy of *A Wrinkle in Time* turned face down, marking a page. Because it seemed so out of place, Emmy turned it over. A phrase inside was highlighted. She read it out loud. "*As paredes tem ouvidos.* What does that mean?"

"The walls have ears," Victoria said absently, pushing through the shelves.

"You understood that?" Emmy asked.

"Edward used to say it all the time. I'm afraid he started getting a bit paranoid in his old age."

Emmy remembered thinking the same thing.

"Oh! I forgot about this," Victoria breathed. She lifted up a box from the back shelf. It had the word "Sharpopoly" printed across the side.

"What is Sharpopoly?" Emmy asked.

"A game based on the island." She pushed book repair supplies out of the way, and set it on the table in the little room. "Did you know our professor was an inventor as well as a scholar? He built the hidden rooms behind the bookshelves."

She lifted the lid, pulled out a map that served as the game board and unfolded it on the table. "Edward was going to manufacture this and sell it to the tourists. He had some brilliant ideas to bring extra revenue into the shops."

Emmy decided not to tell Victoria that almost any tourist town had a Monopoly version of itself. Still, a map of all the properties on Sharp Island could be useful. She studied the game board; it was laid out roughly like a Monopoly board, but with Sharp Island shops and properties creating a square in the middle. Unlike a Monopoly board, there were outlying properties that didn't seem to be part of the game.

"What are these?" she asked, pointing to squares at the perimeter of the game board.

"I'm not sure," Victoria said, "Maybe just places that aren't in the original town square."

Emmy read off the names of the businesses to herself. Redding Rentals, Cliffside Inn, Marian's Point lighthouse. She stopped. "Seaside Insurance?"

Victoria didn't answer. She was engrossed in another handwritten book, *Edward Sharp: A Short History.* "He was such a handsome young man," Victoria said, touching a picture taped to the page.

Emmy glanced at the page, her uncle in a graduation cap and gown. She disagreed with the *handsome* part, but didn't say so out loud. She put the board away and replaced the lid on the Sharpopoly box. She needed to stop getting distracted if she was ever going to figure out what the history clue meant.

She surveyed the shelves, utterly overwhelmed. Even in this small "reserve" collection, there was too much information. How could she ever sort through it?

A narrow book caught her eye. It was brighter than the other books around it. Instead of a stately black or brown, this one was ocean blue. She pulled it out to get a better look. In flowery handwriting it said,

"Maggie's Private diary, KEEP OUT!"

Her mother's diary. Emmy's breath caught. Maybe this is what her uncle had wanted her to find here. Emmy stared at the book for a few minutes, almost afraid to open it. She'd wondered so long what her mother had been like and right in front of her was a book filled with her deepest secrets. After a few minutes of hesitation, she sat on the floor with the book in her lap and opened it. As she flipped through the dates, she realized this diary was started when her mother was in high school and had been written sporadically from her freshman year of high school until she went to college.

A picture was stuck between the pages—the same picture that was attached to the text message on her phone. The entry was made on the night of her mother's senior prom.

> *Nancy will never forgive me and I'm not sure I'll ever forgive her. It was all her fault. I never meant to hurt either of them. She said I think I'm too good for Brighton, but she's wrong. I love him more than she ever could. Even if she's the one that can't stop blab-*

bing about how she's been in love with him since kindergarten. I didn't tell her he asked me to prom. Just me. I told him we should all go together...as friends. I thought it would be less awkward. Boy, was I wrong. Prom night is supposed to be the best night of our lives, right? Talk about a disaster. I walked in on them kissing and I lost it. I slapped her. Then I burst into tears and ran away like some deranged Cinderella. Nancy isn't speaking to me and I refuse to speak to Brighton. It's a good thing I'm leaving for college in a month. So much for friendship and loyalty, right? If she only knew how much I gave up because she's my best friend. If she only knew how much I wanted it to just be me and him tonight. It could have been, if I wasn't so damn loyal. Nancy wouldn't know loy-

al if it turned into a golden
retriever and bit her on the
butt.

Nancy? Emmy studied the picture again. Pierce had told her who one of the people in the group was, and he'd guessed the other one was her mom, but the third one he hadn't mentioned.

"Do you know who the people in this picture are?" she asked Victoria.

She lifted her head from the photographs she'd been fawning over. "I'm sorry, what did you say?"

Emmy pushed the picture toward her, covering one of her uncle lounging on the beach in a speedo (gross) and specifically pointed to the girl standing beside her mother, the one she hadn't identified yet.

"Hmm." Victoria shook her head. "I think it's Nancy Hamilton, but she looks a lot older now. I guess the kind of life she's led will make you old pretty fast."

Emmy's mind raced as she put the pieces together. Nancy Hamilton. Pierce's mom. The woman who had been put in jail for insurance fraud. No wonder he hadn't identified her with the others in the picture. "Are you sure this is her? When was the last time you saw her?"

"She was in the shop last week."

Emmy looked at Victoria for a second, realizing what she had said. "Wait. You saw Nancy Hamilton in person last week?"

"Yeah. She came by the bookshop on her way to see her mother."

Emmy's heart beat fast. "I thought she was in jail."

"She was. I think she just got paroled."

"And what was she doing in the bookshop?" Emmy asked.

Victoria looked thoughtful. "She said she had unfinished business with the professor."

Chapter 37
Sharpopoly

R amona stared incredulously at the box on Emmy's coffee table. "Where did you unearth that?" Emmy had invited Ramona to her apartment to ask her about her mother's diary. She'd brought the Sharpopoly box home to add to her pile of clues.

"I found it..." Emmy hesitated, she wasn't sure she should tell Ramona about the other secret room in the bookshop. Most likely she already knew about it, but just in case... "In Professor Sharp's things."

"Another of his brilliant marketing schemes." Ramona sat down heavily on the couch. "He was always trying to concoct one moneymaking scheme or another, but he didn't quite have the Sharp eye for business." She picked up one of the playing pieces, a jade dragon wrapped around a bookcase. "He must have had the pieces custom made."

"Victoria has a necklace like this," Emmy indicated the game piece. "She said the professor gave it to her."

"Figures." Ramona huffed out a disgusted breath. "He gave me one too. It's absolutely garish. He was pretty oblivious to what the women in his life might actually want. But he loved his games. I keep waiting for him to come back to tell us this whole murder mystery thing is just one of his elaborate games and he's still alive." A shadow passed over her face and Emmy wondered for the first time if Ramona actually missed her ex-husband.

She set the game piece back down. "You said you had questions?"

Emmy put the ocean-blue book on the table and turned to the page with the prom picture. "I found my mother's diary. She talked about her friends from high school, Nancy and Brighton."

Ramona leaned forward and nodded. "I remember those three were fairly inseparable—much to your grandfather's dismay. He didn't think they were good enough for your mother, especially Brighton. His family had a long-standing feud with the Sharps."

"Really? What was it over?" It wasn't the question she'd brought Ramona here to answer, but she was intrigued by the idea of a feud between families.

"The answer to that goes back to your great-grandfather, Franklin Sharp. When he bought the island he went into the venture with four other partners—the Rhineharts, the Hamiltons, the Waltmans, and the Reddings. Each took a corner of the island, but your grandfather took the lion's share in the middle. From what I understand the dispute over who owned which piece of the island began almost immediately and the partnership fell apart. Franklin Sharp spent his life trying to aquire the whole of the island. From what I understand the Waltman's were out almost immediately, but the Rhineharts still own the Bed and Breakfast, the Hamiltons are hanging on by a thread to Clara's little cottage, and the Reddings have their business on the bay. All still holding out against the—pardon the expression—'Sharpopoly.'"

"I didn't realize there were places on the island the Sharp family didn't own," Emmy said.

Ramona gestured to the game board in the middle of the table and the map drawn on it. "This is a pretty good illustration of what I'm talking about. See how most of the locations are in a square like on a regular Monopoly board, but in each of the four corners there are separate businesses?" Emmy nodded. "Like regular Monopoly, it's all about making money, but in this version you can't win unless you control those businesses."

"Why are they so important?" Emmy asked.

"Because those are the businesses that you'd need to get a monopoly on Sharp Island. Those are the only businesses that aren't controlled by the Sharp family."

Emmy looked over the businesses in the corners—Redding Rentals, Cliffside Inn, and Marian's Point lighthouse. She tapped the fourth business in the corner, Seaside Insurance. "I've never seen that one."

"That's because it doesn't exist anymore. Edward bought the property years ago. That whole side of the island used to be split between the Redding and the Hamilton families."

Emmy held her breath, remembering the little house where Pierce's grandmother lived. Was that all that was left of the Hamilton family land? And the insurance agency—Pierce's mom had been convicted of insurance fraud. "The insurance company was owned by Pierce's mom, right? But she lost it when she went to jail. Is that the reason his mom might have unfinished business with my uncle?"

Ramona looked at her shrewdly. "Nancy had unfinished business with Edward? Where did you hear that?"

"Victoria told me Pierce's mom was out of jail and that she was on the island looking for my uncle last week."

Ramona beamed at her. "Good girl! You've done some impressive sleuthing. I knew Nancy was out of jail, but part of her parole agreement was that she couldn't set foot on Sharp Island ever again. I didn't think she'd dare come back. I wonder if her fine upstanding police officer son knows she was here."

"You think Pierce would turn her in if he knew?" Emmy asked.

Ramona seemed to consider it. "At first thought, I'd say yes. Pierce was always a stickler for the rules. But maybe blood is thicker than duty, even if duty appears to be what runs in that man's veins."

"Do you think Pierce's mom is still upset that Professor Sharp bought out her family's land?"

"Upset would be an understatement, especially considering Edward was the reason she was put in jail and her family lost that land."

"My uncle put her in jail?" Emmy asked.

"Not directly, but he encouraged the insurance commission to investigate an inordinate amount of insurance claims stemming from accidents involving Sharp Island businesses." Ramona hesitated, reaching for another game piece, this one a tiny crown. She absently slipped it on and off the tip of her little finger "In particular, the accident that killed your mother."

Emmy stared at her for a long moment, but Ramona wouldn't meet her gaze. "Did Pierce's mother cause the accident that killed my mother?"

Ramona set the game piece down and finally looked her in the eye. "We couldn't prove one way or another. Nancy went to jail for another incident, years later, but I think Edward always suspected her."

"You said he suspected my dad," Emmy said.

Ramona sighed. "He suspected a lot of people. Losing your mom was hard on him. He was tormented by the idea that he had to solve her death, like he was Sherlock Holmes or something."

Emmy looked down at the diary, realizing she'd wrapped her hands around the edges so tightly that she'd squeezed all the blood out of her fingertips. She hadn't told Ramona that Professor Sharp had passed that burden onto her. "My mom wrote that the three of them—her, Brighton, and Nancy—had gotten in a fight at prom. Do you know if they ever made up?"

"Brighton and your mom did; that's how she ended up on his boat that night. But I'm not sure about Nancy. She ran off right after graduation, then came back a couple of years later, pregnant with Pierce—no explanation of who his father might be. She opened the insurance business and raised Pierce as a single mom. I think your mom tried to talk to her a few times, but apparently Nancy wasn't into mending old grudges. She did pretty well for herself, though. Folks around here saw her as a kind of folk hero—fighting the good fight against the Sharp family empire—until she got caught and her fortress of lies came crashing down. She went to jail and Edward bought out their land." Ramona traced a finger around one of the edges of the game board. "Except for this little piece around Mrs. Hamilton's cottage. Edward made a deal with her that she could keep it, until..."

"Until what?" Emmy sensed that Ramona had just remembered something important.

"Until his death, then it reverts back to his heir. Back to you."

Emmy didn't like the idea of taking away Mrs. Hamilton's little cottage. It felt like another way her uncle had made this whole thing harder. "So Nancy Hamilton might have had a grudge against my mom and my uncle," Emmy said. "Any idea how I could find her?"

Ramona smiled. "One of three people on the island might know where she is—her mother, her son, or her old friend Brighton. None of them are likely to talk to you about it."

"Mrs. Hamilton seemed nice enough," Emmy said.

"She appears that way, but don't underestimate her. Everyone in this game has their own objective. That house has been in her family for generations. She's not going to give it up easily." Ramona tapped on the boat rental shop. "And I wouldn't push your luck with Brighton Redding. He was your mother's friend, but that doesn't mean he has any love for the Sharp family."

"So that leaves Pierce," Emmy sighed.

"Appeal to his sense of duty," Ramona said. She picked up another game piece, this one a little dagger, like one you'd use to stab someone in the back. She handed it to Emmy. "And if that doesn't work, try a little of that Sharp ruthlessness. It's got to be in your blood somewhere."

Chapter 38
Sharp Tongues

"Refill on your meds, the rest of your clothes, and a replacement phone," Ginny said, setting down three reusable shopping bags on the floor at the front of the apartment. "Your policeman boyfriend hasn't given yours back yet?"

"Not my boyfriend and no." Emmy barely looked up from the gameboard in front of her. "Thanks for coming all the way out here."

Ginny sprawled on the couch. "So you've decided on the red-headed waiter?"

"Neither." Emmy mentally rearranged the pieces in front of her, trying to make them fit.

"You might want to be careful. Now that you're a multimillionaire, guys are going to be after you for your money."

Emmy looked up, annoyed at Ginny's disruption. "I don't have time to worry about my love life. I'm too busy trying to solve an impossible puzzle." She gestured to the piles of paperwork on the dining room table and the game set up on the coffee table.

"This is a mess." Ginny reached to straighten a pile of papers.

"Don't touch anything!" Emmy cried. "I have it all arranged."

Ginny shook her head. "There is absolutely no semblance of order in this disaster. How do you expect to figure anything out?"

Emmy sighed; Ginny was right. Everything around her was a mess even without the disaster in front of her. Jonathon had been MIA for the last couple of days and Pierce was off island meeting with the chief of police. Her thoughts were as scattered as the papers all around the room. There was no way she was going to solve this on her own.

Ginny knelt on the floor beside her. "Let me help. Remember how I helped you keep your assignments straight in college?"

"I need to do this by myself," Emmy said.

Ginny put her hand on Emmy's knee. "No, you need to surround yourself with the smartest people possible, and then when you've solved this, take credit for the whole thing."

Emmy laughed. She appreciated Ginny's humor and as usual, her friend was right. She sighed. "Okay, let's talk this out." She pointed to the game pieces and other assorted bits she'd found in the apartment and placed on the game board to represent people in the town—the dragon for the professor, a high-heeled shoe for Madelyn, the little dagger for Pierce's mom, a sailboat for Brighton Redding, her prescription bottle for the doctor, and a colorful button for Ramona.

"What about these people?" Ginny asked, surveying the pile of trinkets Emmy had pushed to the side—a teacup, a plastic cake, a coaster from the White Sails restaurant, and a little gray mouse, an old cat toy someone had left in the apartment.

"I've ruled them out for now. Mostly it's just too many people to think about, but I don't think they really benefit by having Professor Sharp dead. Yes, he was a horrible taskmaster, but he was a known evil. Without him, they ran the risk of their livelihood being sold out from under them."

Ginny picked up the little knife. "It looks to me like you've already decided on the killer. Who is this supposed to be?"

"Pierce's mom."

Ginny raised her eyebrows. "Golden boy has a dark secret?"

Emmy took the knife and put it on the Seaside Insurance square. "Yeah. His mom just got out of prison and violated her parole to try to track down my uncle. She said she had unfinished business with him. She's a convicted felon and the only person on this board who had a clear grudge against both my uncle and my mom. Unfortunately, no one seems to know where she is right now."

"Your mom?" Ginny looked at Emmy, her dark eyes were heavy with concern and pity. "This is about more than money and finding out who killed your uncle. It's about finding out what happened to your mom?"

"My uncle thought they were killed by the same person. If he's right then that just leaves the people on the board. They were all on the island at that time and they all had motives to kill both of them."

Ginny picked up the prescription bottle. "What about the doctor? What motive did he have to kill your mom?"

"He's obviously not over his daughter's death. Maybe he killed my mom to get back at my uncle."

Ginny set the prescription bottle to the side. "Strong motive to kill your uncle. Weak motive to kill your mom." She reached for the high heel. "Madelyn?"

"On paper she has the strongest motive. Everyone knows she's been hanging around waiting for my uncle to die so she can get her inheritance. She probably didn't know he'd changed his original will." Emmy reached for a piece of paper from the pile. "And I just found this in the pile of threats the professor supposedly was receiving."

Ginny took the paper. All the words on the page had been blacked out except for as, knife, the, sharp, of, wife, is, and tongue. "What does that mean?"

"I think it's supposed to say, 'The tongue of the wife is as sharp as a knife,'" Emmy said.

"The professor was killed by a knife," Ginny said. "But does it mean he was killed by his wife, or another wife?"

"I think it's a play on words, but it could be literal. The word sharp is significant. It's circled in red."

"Maybe it literally means one of the Sharp wives," Ginny said.

"I don't know if it means anything, but Ramona never took on the name Sharp," Emmy said. "She kept Beesley, even when they were married."

"Madelyn, then?"

"I don't know. It seems too obvious."

"What if you're overthinking things? You have a tendency to do that. Sometimes the most obvious person is the answer. If she was really the gold-digger Ramona says she is, maybe Madelyn wanted to get your mom out of the way so her husband would inherit more."

"Maybe?" Emmy wasn't sure that's what the paper was trying to say.

Ginny took the shoe and set it on the square that represented the Look Sharp clothing boutique. "At least we need to eliminate her as a suspect. She owns the clothing store, right? If I were you I'd do some shopping. Luckily, I'm an expert in that department."

Chapter 39
Look Sharp

"Hideous, overpriced, hideous and overpriced, hideous, overpriced and it will fall apart the first time you wash it," Ginny said as she flipped through the rack of clothes.

"Where is Madelyn?" Emmy asked. She was waiting on a bench in the town square in front of the tea shop. Ginny was on her cell phone, talking to Emmy through her earbuds. They'd both decided that Emmy going into the shop was a bad idea.

Ginny's voice got softer. "The LKO just came downstairs."

"What?" Emmy hissed. "What is that supposed to mean?"

"Louboutin knockoff. I'm using a code name, since I can't exactly say you-know-who's name right now. Louboutins are extremely expensive shoes. You chose the shoe in the game for her and she's the knockoff because she tries to come off classy, but—"

"Is there any possible way we can simplify this?" Emmy's head was spinning.

"I did. The LKO is dressed to the nines. Ten to one home girl has a date tonight."

"A date?" Emmy asked.

"I assume she's allowed to have a social life," Ginny said.

"I'm not sure she is," Emmy said. "Ramona said something about her not being able to get married again. That if she did she'd—"

"I believe talking to yourself is a sign of insanity." Jonathon sat on the bench beside her.

"I wasn't talking to myself," Emmy said. "I was—"

"Doing reconnaissance work?" He pointed to her earbud. "Don't tell me I've been replaced."

"No, I'm on the phone. Besides, you kind of disappeared off the face of the earth for a few days."

"I went to the mainland to visit my sister and my niece. Sorry I didn't let you know."

Jonathon mentioning his niece reminded Emmy that his alibi for the night the professor died was faulty. She hadn't asked him about it yet.

"Alert, alert, the LKO is on the move," Ginny said. "I believe she is coming your way."

"So who's on the other end?"

"It's just my—"

"What are you doing here?" Madelyn stood in front of them, her hand on her slender hip. Her period of mourning must be over because she was dressed in a hot pink party dress and matching high heels that looked like real Louboutins. Ginny was right. Madelyn's outfit screamed *date*.

Emmy opened her mouth to say something—she wasn't sure what—as Madelyn shot daggers at her with her eyes. "And with her?"

Emmy was confused. Madelyn was looking at her, but yelling at Jonathon.

Jonathon took a step back. He was trying to play things cool, but he seemed as rattled by Madelyn's anger as Emmy was.

His face broke into his signature charming grin. "Waiting for you milady. Your chariot awaits." He bowed and gestured to a dark blue convertible BMW parked on the side of the street.

"Good. We don't want to be late." Madelyn turned to Emmy. "Stay away from my shop and keep your bloody hands off my merchandise."

Emmy watched Jonathon open the door for Madelyn. He turned and shrugged at her before climbing into the driver's seat and speeding off. The whole interaction left her feeling like something was off. She'd never seen the car Jonathon drove for his Uber, but if it was the BMW, either the PI gig or one of his many side gigs was doing well.

There was something possessive in the way Madelyn looked at him. Emmy didn't think Madelyn had meant the clothes in her shop when she told her to keep her hands off her merchandise.

"Jackpot!" Ginny's voice in Emmy's ear made her jump.

"What?" Emmy said when she regained her composure—and her hearing.

"Madelyn's assistant just left. She forgot I was in the dressing room. Meet me at the back door in about ten minutes. It's time to search the lair. And don't forget that magic key. I can get you in the shop, but LKO's office is locked."

"She's planning a wedding," Emmy said once the skeleton key had gotten them into Madelyn's office. Strewn across the desk were bridal magazines, color swatches, even a brochure for a destination wedding venue in Italy.

"I guess you'd know," Ginny said.

"Right," Emmy said. She flipped through the magazines. They brought up a host of insecurities and bad memories. Wedding planning with Collin's mom had been excruciating.

She could almost hear Mrs. Jackson's voice dripping with honeyed sympathy. *Money is not an object, we'll take care of everything, choose whatever you want, we want this to be your dream wedding.* Every word, every interaction with Collin's mother was mingled with a strong undercurrent of *You're not good enough for our son, so you don't get a say in anything.*

"Who do you think she's planning to marry?" Ginny asked.

"Let's check the social media." Emmy moved to a pink laptop, set on the desk. "Madelyn seems like the kind of woman who is a wannabe influencer, or at least a serial poster."

"If we can figure out the password," Ginny said.

"Knowing Madelyn, it's probably something like 'password,'" Emmy said.

"Try it," Ginny said. "It can't hurt."

Emmy typed 'password' on the screen. To her surprise, the computer opened. "Maybe she doesn't know how to use a laptop." She was right about the social media posts. Emmy pulled up post after post from Madelyn. Some were advertisements for her shop or the island, but most showed her attending swanky parties or hanging out in high-end bars.

"She doesn't seem to be hurting for money or men." Ginny leaned over her shoulder. "Stop! She's wearing a ring in this one."

"She's wearing a ring in all of them," Emmy pointed out. "I just assumed she hadn't ever taken off her ring from her first marriage. Like it was her way of showing she was still in mourning maybe?"

"She doesn't look like a woman in mourning in this one," Ginny pointed to Madelyn in a red catsuit, holding a tall glass of champagne.

Emmy checked the date. "This was the night the professor died. Pierce said she was at a party."

"Is that who I think it is?" Ginny moved closer as Emmy zoomed in on a picture of a red-headed man.

"I can't tell for sure, but it looks like the back of Jonathon's head. At least it's the same hair color," Emmy said.

"That would explain why he lied about his niece's party." Ginny went through the pictures. "That looks like him too."

"Yeah," Emmy said. "But if they were together, why not use each other as an alibi?"

"Maybe they don't want anyone to know they're together. If that's true, she's not going to post anything where it's clearly Jonathon. But maybe there's something in her private photos."

"Good call." Emmy moved to the files on the computer and pulled up the photo directory. She clicked on one that showed a bare-chested man standing in front of a mirror. "This is definitely him," Emmy said.

"How can you tell?" Ginny leaned closer. "It still doesn't show his face."

Emmy zoomed in on the scar on his chest. "It's Jonathon, all right."

Ginny raised one eyebrow. "Do I want to know why you know what Jonathon's chest looks like?"

Emmy ignored the question. She was hyperfocused on the scar. "I'm not sure that's a bullet wound," she said almost to herself.

"What?" Ginny asked.

"Jonathon told me he'd been shot by a sniper and that's where that scar came from, but it doesn't look right."

"And you know this, how?" Ginny probed.

"From my stint as a pathology major. I had this weird obsession with scars and how they heal."

"This was after the pharmaceutical obsession, but before the blood thing, right?" Ginny said. Emmy made a noncommittal noise in her throat.

"So Jonathon is hanging out with a rich widow and lying about his scars. Sounds like a typical male."

"Yeah. But is he a typical male with a motive for murder?" Emmy asked. The whole thing made Emmy sick. She'd bought into Jonathon's act as much as Madelyn had. "Let's get out of here before we get caught." She reached to shut the laptop, but accidentally touched the screen and opened a search tab.

The last question Madelyn had searched was still on the screen.

How do you annul a marriage?

Chapter 40

Unfinished Business

"Why didn't you tell me your mother was out of jail?" Emmy took the chair across from Pierce at the tea shop. He was there at six o'clock, just as Ms. Lee had said he would be.

He nearly spit out his mouth full of coffee. He swallowed hard, his face went red, and he gasped as he reached for a glass of water at the edge of the table. The coffee must have been pretty fresh. She hadn't given him any warning because she wanted to get his honest reaction. She waited for him to say something.

"Where...how...what?" he finally choked out.

"Your mother has been in jail for insurance fraud. I hear she just got paroled."

"Who told you—"

Emmy held up her hand. If she let him start talking she might lose her nerve. "It doesn't matter how I know. What I need to know is where she is now and what unfinished business she might have had with my uncle. Also, have you told your police chief about this? And if so, why are you still on this case? It seems like a pretty obvious conflict of interest."

"I haven't seen my mother." Pierce was trying to regain his cool demeanor. "If I had I would have—"

"Would have what?" a woman called from the corner booth. The woman was wearing sunglasses and a hat that mostly covered her long dark hair. She'd obviously been listening even though Emmy hadn't noticed her until now. The woman stood. She was both taller and older than she originally appeared. When she took off her sunglasses Emmy recognized the piercing blue eyes she'd passed on to her son. "I think that's a question we'd all like answered."

Nancy Hamilton stood in front of her son. "Hello, Pierce. Are you going to arrest me? Throw me back in jail?"

Pierce sat gaping like fresh-caught fish. The expression on his face made Emmy sure he hadn't known his mother was here. She must have decided he wasn't going to answer because she turned to Emmy. "You're Mags's daughter."

It wasn't a question, but Emmy replied, "Yes," anyway.

"Mom, what are you doing here?" Pierce finally recovered. "You're not supposed to be—"

"You don't look much like her," Nancy said to Emmy, cocking her head like she was trying to get the right angle for some resemblance. "But there's something about you that reminds me of her anyway."

Emmy wasn't sure how to take that statement or Nancy's steely gaze that held more questions than answers. Finally she broke eye contact and turned back to her son. "No welcome back gift?" She indicated the handcuffs on his belt. "A shiny new bracelet or two maybe?"

"Mom, I—"

In a quick movement, Nancy pulled her son against her chest. "I've missed you, baby," she murmured into his hair.

Something melted in both of them as he slowly returned her embrace. Pierce's stiffness relaxed. Nancy's hard edge softened. Emmy watched them, growing more and more uncomfortable.

Finally he pulled away, saying, "Mom I can't let you—"

She held up her hand. "Before you say anything, I'm not staying long. I just—"

"Had unfinished business with my uncle. Like maybe the business of finishing him off," Emmy said. Their closeness pricked at her heart and caused it to harden. She hadn't been able to hug her dad for the last five years and she couldn't ever remember being held by her mom.

Nancy's blue eyes flashed. "There's not a person on this island who didn't benefit from Edward Sharp's death, except for my mother. She's the reason I needed to talk to him. I heard a rumor he was sick, dying even. He'd made a deal with her that allowed her to keep her house and the garden around it as long as he was alive. Once he died, she'd have to hand the house over to his heir, whoever that might be. I wanted to convince him to leave the house to her outright in his will." She turned back to her son. "That's why I violated my parole to come back here."

"What made you think you could convince him to let her hold onto the house?" Pierce asked.

"Because I have information that's worth more to him than our rocky little chunk of his precious island." Nancy's jaw was set with a confidence that reminded Emmy of the expression her dad wore when he was about to make a business deal—probably because both of them were con artists.

Emmy took the bait even though she was sure that woman was bluffing. "What information is that?"

Nancy's blue eyes turned on Emmy. "Proof that the accident that killed your mother was not an accident."

Chapter 41

The Patisserie

"I've heard these sausage rolls were to die for," Emmy said as Anjuli herself wrapped them up. Emmy was finally going on the tour of the island with Jonathon.

"Interesting way to put that." Anjuli handed back the wrapped rolls. "Considering I heard that my tea cakes were almost literally 'to die for' at the bookshop the other night."

"Actually," Emmy paused, considering the theory that was forming in her mind. "I think the point of drugging the cakes might have been to keep me alive. My uncle wanted me to be there, but he didn't want me to get hurt, so he drugged me and then moved me out of the way. Maybe he wanted me to be a witness, only I was too drugged to remember much of anything."

"That's a pretty big risk to take with your life," Anjuli said.

Emmy stared at the rows of colorful cakes with delicately piped icing in every flavor imaginable. "Who picked up the cakes for the bookshop that night?"

"Vicky. The professor's assistant always picked up his orders herself."

"That's what she told me," Emmy pointed to a lemon-flavored petit four like the one she'd had the night of the murder. "Can I have a couple of those?"

"Of course." Anjuli picked up a little box to package the cakes.

"Who else ordered cakes that night?"

Anjuli set the cakes down and moved to an order book. "I've already told Pierce this, but the shop was packed that night. I only kept track of the phone orders. The professor had a standing order and a couple of delivery boys had pickups that night."

"Jonathon?" Emmy asked.

"Jonathon always had an order or two coming in." She consulted her list. "Interesting. That night he didn't pick anything up."

"He was already on the ferry back to the mainland by then," Emmy said. *With Madelyn*, she added to herself.

"I see you've been asking some questions," Anjuli said. "Got any leads?"

Emmy shook her head. "Nothing concrete."

"You'll get this, you're a Sharp, which is almost equivalent to a shark on this island. Sharps don't back down." Anjuli handed Emmy her order, and nodded to the person behind her. "You two have a nice picnic."

"I'm not...I mean she's not, I mean...we're not going on a picnic." Emmy turned around to see Pierce stumbling through explanations. He looked more tired than she'd ever seen him. Despite everything, she felt sorry for him. She knew what it was like to have a parent in jail and it must be worse for Pierce, since his whole job was the law.

"How did things go with the chief and with your mom?" Emmy asked gently. The last time she'd seen Pierce he'd been leading his mother away in the silver bracelets she'd pointed out, reading her her rights, with an emphasis on the right to remain silent.

Emmy understood that Pierce needed to protect his mom, but she wished he'd let her talk. She wanted to know what Nancy Hamilton thought she knew about her mother's accident.

"She's staying on-island for now, in the old city lockup behind the courthouse. The DA is sending over their own team to question her." Pierce sat down at the nearest table and stared at his hands.

"Does this mean you're off the case?" Emmy sat down next to him.

"All but officially," he said.

"I'm sorry," Emmy said. He looked so miserable that she pushed one of the neatly wrapped sausage rolls toward him.

"No, I'm sorry." Pierce unwrapped the sausage; apparently his appetite wasn't affected by the loss of the case. "I can't imagine how horrible it was to hear what my mom said last night. Did you have any idea that your mother might have been murdered?"

"Yeah, I actually found that out fairly recently." She looked up at Pierce, her eyes pleading with him. "I would really like to hear what proof your mom thinks she has about what happened to my mom."

"I couldn't let her incriminate herself," Pierce said.

"So you think she did it? You think the accident was her fault?" Emmy said.

Pierce shook his head firmly. "No. My mom's not a murderer. No one was ever hurt in any of her accidents. But whatever she thinks she knows can't be good for her case."

"But it might help mine," Emmy pleaded. "It might help me know what happened to my mom and to my uncle and—"

"Clear your dad's name too?" He looked down at her. "Yeah. I've done my research. I know that your dad was the last person to see your mom alive and that she died under questionable circumstances." He set his hand on the table, but stopped short of touching her. "We're a lot the same, Emmy. We're both trying to protect a parent who pretended to have our best interests at heart, but who was really only taking care of themselves."

"My dad isn't like your mom," Emmy surprised herself by coming to her dad's defense when she still wasn't sure he was innocent. "He would never have..." But again, Emmy wasn't sure whether she really knew what he would or wouldn't have done.

"Sorry. You're right. I shouldn't have assumed anything." He moved his hands off the table. "If I thought she'd tell you the truth, I'd let you talk to my mom, but my mom never gives anything away without getting something back. Right now her only aim is to keep my grandma from losing her house. She's not going to speak to you until she knows you'll inherit the island, and right now you can't guarantee that."

"I still think Emmy's chances of solving this are significantly better than yours." Jonathon slid into the third seat at their table. "Sorry I'm late. I got an order for the other side of the island, one I couldn't refuse. This one's a big tipper." He looked at Emmy meaningfully before he turned to Pierce. "Are you joining us for the grand tour?"

"No." Pierce stood up. "I have bales of paperwork to fill out."

Jonathon watched him go. "Poor guy, after this, he'll be lucky to be a desk jockey." He said it loud enough for Pierce to hear.

He stood and reached for Emmy's hand. "Ready to check out your island?"

Emmy took his hand and let him help her up, but as the bell over the door clanged Pierce's exit, she couldn't help but wonder if she was taking her tour with the wrong guide.

Chapter 42
Big Tip

"Big tipper on the other side of the island?" Emmy asked as soon as they were out of the patisserie. After everything she'd learned, she didn't trust Jonathon, but something about the way he'd said it made her think he wasn't talking about delivering food and getting money.

"Yeah, I heard some things." He looked around. "Things I'd rather not discuss in town."

"Where, then?" Emmy asked. She was leery of going anywhere alone with him, but even if he was a liar, he couldn't have been a murderer. She'd seen photographic proof of his alibi.

"Are you up for a hike?" He reached out his hand.

She hesitated, but two could play the deception game. "Absolutely." She took Jonathon's hand and followed him out of the shop and to a trail that led into the woods.

The weather was bright and fresh, not too hot, but not too cold. It felt like summer was just beginning instead of just ending. The scenery reminded Emmy of a fairytale forest. It was strange and new and at the same time vaguely familiar.

The more time she spent on the island, the more she remembered. They weren't concrete memories, just images and feelings. Even this path felt like somewhere she'd been before. If she closed her eyes she could almost go back there. They had walked together up this path, the three of them. Her mother had been laughing. Her dad had swung her up on his shoulders because her legs had been too short to keep up with them.

"...we were pinned down and we knew the ambush was coming. We were too far away to call in any kind of support..." Jonathon was chest deep in a story that was most likely another lie. Emmy considered calling him on it, but she needed him to think she trusted him. So far he'd proved a pretty reliable source of information, as long as he wasn't talking about himself.

He stopped in front of her so fast that she almost ran into him. He turned to face her. "Once I thought my life was over, not just because of the bullet, but because I had to retire from the military." He reached up and brushed a hair off Emmy's cheek. "Turns out life as a PI suits me a lot better. I'm too independent to be tied down by something like the Army." He leaned in closer. "Although the thought of settling down and building a life with the right—"

"You said you had a tip?" Emmy interrupted him. She didn't have time for whatever he was about to say.

He looked around, like he was making sure they were alone. "I made a delivery to the boat rental place on the other side of the island. While I was waiting to be paid I overheard another customer talking to Brighton Redding, the owner. The customer was obviously an old friend. I found their conversation interesting, so I recorded it."

Emmy stopped. "You recorded them? Is that legal?"

"Does the will stipulate that you have to find your uncle's killer according to the law?"

"N-o-o..." Emmy hesitated.

"If you're going to do this, you might have to learn to play dirty pool. Leave the legalities to the Boy Scout."

Emmy still felt unsure, but maybe Jonathon was right. Pierce sticking to the law last night had kept her from finding out what Nancy Hamilton had to say. "What did you hear?"

Jonathon looked around again, then pulled his phone out of his pocket. The sound was garbled, but after a second she could make out two men's voices.

"...does it feel to have the old man out of the way?" the first man said.

"What are you talking about, Stan?" the second man said.

"I'm guessing you're feeling relieved."

"What happened to Professor Sharp is none of my business. Unlike you, he holds nothing over me," the second man said. "I'm an independent business man."

"Yeah, but it's how you got that way that raised some eyebrows," the other man said. "Any questions about the accident would probably die with ..." the recording became garbled again. Jonathon swore as he worked to turn it up.

When the sound finally became clear again, the second man sounded angry, "I don't ever want to hear her name again, especially in that context. What happened to Mags—"

A bell rang in the background and the man's voice changed as if he had just noticed Jonathon there. "You have a delivery for me?"

The rest was a conversation between Jonathon and Brighton Redding. Jonathon turned the recording off. "So what do you think? From what I gathered, they were talking about a boating accident that happened years ago. It seems like the payout from that set Brighton

Redding up to be independent of your uncle. We need to find out who this Mags is. If we could talk to her…"

Emmy stood in stunned silence. Her mind was piecing together everything she'd heard. "I know who Mags is," Emmy said quietly. "And we can't talk to her, she's dead. Mags was my mother."

"I'm sorry." Jonathon reached over and pulled her into an embrace.

Emmy closed her eyes and her stomach churned like an angry ocean. Her mother's friends. A storm. An accident that wasn't an accident. An insurance payout. If she couldn't talk to Pierce's mom there was only one place on the island she might find the answers about what happened to her mom. She pulled away from Jonathon. "How do you feel about sailing?"

Chapter 43

A Stab in the Dark

Emmy listened to the recording Jonathon had shared with her again. She couldn't shake the feeling she was missing something, something big. She closed her eyes. She needed to focus on something else for a while. She put her slippers on, headed for the door, and slipped down the stairs and to the bookshop.

Everything was quiet. Emmy moved to the shelf, already looking for *A Muckraker's History,* then she realized the sliding door was already open.

She moved inside, cautiously. Would Victoria have just forgotten to close the secret door? Emmy doubted it. Something felt off. Something was missing. She went to the desk and turned on the lamp, trying to figure out what it was. The books on the shelves seemed in order. The book repair supplies were arranged neatly on the desk. The *Grimm's Fairy Tales* book was on the floor next to the desk. The two other books were missing.

Emmy tried to remember what they were. One book was in Spanish and the other was *A Wrinkle in Time.* A passage had been marked in the book. "The walls have ears," she said out loud. She still wasn't sure what it meant.

A bell tinkled faintly.

She stopped. It sounded like someone had come in the front door. She strained to listen, but everything was silent. After a few minutes of quiet, her heartbeat slowed. It must have come from another shop. Maybe one of the shopkeepers had been working late and was just leaving. Almost every shop in town had a bell like the one in the bookshop.

That was it.

That was what was off about the recording. She pulled out her phone and played the recording again. The men were talking before the bell in the front of the shop rang, before Brighton Redding acknowledged that Jonathon was there. Did the bell mean he had just come in? How had he recorded their conversation before he walked in?

She shook her head. Maybe the men were so engrossed in their conversation that they hadn't noticed Jonathon. Maybe the bell just meant that someone else had come in.

The walls have ears.

Her uncle had thought that phrase was important. She thought of the room next to Ramona's office. She'd flipped a switch and they were able to listen to the conversation between Pierce and Chief Howe. Were there other places on the island that had been bugged?

A faint thump came from somewhere in the bookshop, like someone had unshelved a book. She turned off the lamp and stepped out from under the stairs. She stared into the shop. She didn't remember it being this dark when she walked in. Had the moon gone behind a cloud or... She froze, realizing that someone had pulled the drapes over the window that looked out toward the ocean. Emmy was sure they had been open when she came in.

Emmy slipped a thick book from the shelf, the only thing she could find for protection. She held it in front of her as she walked around the corner. "Hello? Is someone—"

Something sliced through the air. Instinctively, she raised the book. *Thwack!*

A knife pierced the book, sinking deep into the pages. Emmy screamed and fell backward.

Rapid footsteps sounded on the wooden floor. The door flung open and a figure in a dark cape fled into the night. Emmy stayed on the floor, cradling the book that had saved her life against her chest.

Chapter 44

Between the Pages

E mmy gripped the book like her life depended on it, and maybe it did. Her assailant didn't come back. The dark figure had disappeared out the door and down the street. She was just coming out of some kind of daze when two more figures appeared at the door to the bookshop.

Emmy looked down at her cell phone; she'd only had time for one number. She wasn't even sure which one she'd called, but somehow they were both here.

"Are you okay?" Jonathon was breathless when he reached her.

Pierce wasn't far behind. "What happened?"

"Someone...in the bookshop." Emmy held up the book. A knife was buried up to the jade dragon on the hilt.

Pierce leaned forward. "Did you see who it was?"

Emmy shook her head, blood pounding in her ears. She was fighting to stay conscious. "It was dark. I heard a noise and when I went around the corner—" She couldn't finish that sentence.

"And?" Pierce prodded.

"Someone was here, I think I surprised them. They threw—" She indicated the knife.

"Was it a man or a woman?" Pierce continued.

"I...I couldn't tell." Emmy's voice shook.

"Any idea which way they were going or where they went?"

Jonathon stepped forward. "Show some compassion for five seconds. She just got attacked and she's bleeding."

"I am?" Emmy put her hand to her neck. A trickle of blood ran from her breastbone where the tip of the knife had grazed her. She swallowed hard. "I...I don't..." She swayed on her feet. Jonathon reached to steady her, but Pierce got there first. He put his arm behind her back and guided her to a chair.

"Lean forward, put your head between your knees. Jonathon, get something to clean the blood away. I want to see how deep the cut is." Pierce was ordering everyone around as usual, but for the first time Emmy was grateful for his calm in the face of an insane situation.

Jonathon came back bare-chested, his T-shirt damp from the sink in the bathroom.

"Seriously?" Pierce said. "You couldn't have used a paper towel?"

"The dispenser was empty," Jonathon said.

"Hopefully you don't get a raging infection from this," Pierce said as he used Jonathon's T-shirt to gingerly sponge at the cut. "You're damn lucky. If that knife had been any longer or the book any thinner..."

"We need to get her to a doctor," Jonathon said.

"It's fine, I'm just—" But Emmy's head started to swim as soon as she looked up.

"He's right," Pierce said. "It's too late to take you to the mainland. We'll have to go to Dr. Gregory's."

The name brought Emmy around. Her first visit with the doctor had been disastrous. "Is he the only doctor on the island?" she asked.

"Right now, yes. Unless you'd like to go to the vet," Pierce said. "The cut is still bleeding. I think you might need stitches."

Emmy nodded. She didn't have a choice.

She lay still on the floor while Pierce bandaged the cut with supplies from his patrol car. He stood and threw Jonathon's bloody T-shirt back to him. "I called in some backup. We're going to canvas the streets."

"I'll take her to the clinic," Jonathon said. "You go chase down the bad guy. That's your job, isn't it? If you were better at it, then maybe Emmy wouldn't have been attacked."

Pierce glowered at Jonathon. He knelt down in front of Emmy. "I'm sorry this happened. Go get checked out, I'll start knocking doors to see if anyone saw anything. I'll be back to check on you later. If you remember anything—"

Jonathon leaned down and picked Emmy up. "She knows the drill. Don't worry. I'll take care of her."

Chapter 45
Stitches

D r. Gregory's house was adjacent to the clinic. The lights were all off, but a sign gave a number for emergencies. Before Emmy could protest that this wasn't an emergency, Jonathon had his phone out and was dialing the number.

After three rings a deep voice answered. Jonathon explained the situation and the doctor said something that was either "I'll be right there" or "I don't care." Since Jonathon said, "He's coming," Emmy assumed it was the first one.

"I'm coming into the exam room with you this time. I don't care what he says," Jonathon said while they were waiting for the doctor to come to the door.

"I'm not sure…"

"Look, he hates all Sharps. Since he'll be in close proximity to your throat with lots of different kinds of needles and other sharp objects—no pun intended—I don't want you to be in there alone."

Emmy wasn't sure whether that was a good idea or not. Before she could make up her mind, the door opened.

Despite the time of night, Dr. Gregory looked wide awake and alert. He stared down at Emmy. She was too intimidated to say anything.

"What do we have here?" He looked at the still bare-chested Jonathon. "It looks like everything has healed nicely, I don't see any..."

"Not me." Jonathon stepped back. "She's the one who's hurt."

Dr. Gregory leaned in and moved aside the gauze Pierce had used to bandage the cut. "It looks like you were stabbed." He narrowed his eyes toward Jonathon. "How did this happen?"

"I was attacked." Emmy swallowed to try to get her voice even. "In the bookshop."

Dr. Gregory looked from her to Jonathon like he didn't believe her. After a few tense moments he shook his head and directed Emmy back to the examination room.

"I'm coming with her," Jonathon said.

"I don't allow—" the doctor began.

Jonathon pulled out a badge. "I'm a police officer. I need to be there when you examine the victim."

Emmy stared at the badge in disbelief. Jonathon had never mentioned that he was a cop. She wasn't sure if the badge was real. The doctor considered it for a long moment.

"Okay." He led them to a dark hall, turning on the lights as he led them back into the same exam room where Emmy had been before. When they got to the room, Jonathon helped Emmy onto the table.

"Just lie back and let me take a look." The doctor moved a bright overhead light above her and gently pressed the edges of the cut together. Emmy flinched. "This definitely needs stitches." He pushed the light back to the corner. "I'll need to get the rest of my medical supplies. Give me a second. I'm lost without my nurse."

As soon as Dr. Gregory was out of earshot Emmy hissed at him, "You're a cop?"

"No. It's just a badge I keep on hand for emergencies."

"You shouldn't have lied. He saw right through it last time, when I was here, and it made him really mad. If I want people to trust me enough to listen and answer my questions, I have to be honest with them. Especially if I'm going to stay here. This island is too small for—"

"For lies and secrets?" Jonathon snorted. "I thought you'd already figured out there's enough room for plenty of those here."

"Like the secret you have with Madelyn?"

"Madelyn?" he scoffed, but the quick look of horror that had passed over his face told Emmy she was right. He backpedaled. "So what if I'm spending time with Madelyn? I'm supposed to be doing this investigation with you, right? Isn't she your top suspect?"

"I never told you I thought she was my top suspect," Emmy said.

"But you're investigating her. That's why you were outside her shop the other day," Jonathon said.

"Why were you outside of her shop the other day?" Emmy asked.

Again, there was a flash of fear in his eyes. "I was her Uber to the ferry. She was going to some party."

"Party? That reminds me. Where were you the nigh—"

The doctor came back before Emmy could finish. He looked between them, seeming to sense the tension in the room. He set down a syringe and a little bottle. Then he started rummaging through a cupboard above the sink. He shook his head and muttered under his breath. "Must be in the other room." He turned to Jonathon. "I have a storage room in the back. Somewhere inside it there's a suture kit."

"I wouldn't know what—"

"You're a cop who doesn't know what a suture is?" Dr. Gregory narrowed his eyes at him. "It's in a green and white package that says sutures. You can't miss it."

Jonathon looked at Emmy like he was hoping she'd tell the doctor he had to stay. But Emmy was too annoyed with Jonathon to want him around. He turned back to the doctor. "I don't think, I could—"

"You can and you will," Dr. Gregory said. Jonathon looked helpless for a minute, but headed for the door. "Oh, you'll need my keys. They're in the desk drawer, second drawer down." The request was made as if there was no question that Jonathon would follow his instructions. "There are extra scrub tops in the cupboard as well. I suggest you put one on."

"That should give us a few minutes," Dr. Gregory said as soon as Jonathon was down the hall. He filled the syringe attached to the needle with a clear liquid.

"A few minutes for what?" Emmy suddenly wished Jonathon hadn't left and that she knew what was in the little bottle.

"For you and me to have a chat. Lie back."

Emmy lay down on the exam table. The doctor sponged around the wound with alcohol. It stung and Emmy's eyes watered. "A chat about what?"

He stood above her with the syringe in one hand. Silhouetted against the overhead light, Dr. Gregory reminded her of a mad scientist. "A chat about the truth."

He put his hand on her forehead, restraining her. Before she could move, the needle pressed into her chest.

The world around her swam into darkness.

Chapter 46
Old Wounds

W hen Emmy opened her eyes there was a bright light above her.

"You didn't tell me you were sensitive to needles," the doctor said. He pulled out a little light and shone it in her eyes. "How are you feeling now?"

"Woozy," she admitted.

"Go ahead and lie still for a minute. I didn't get the chance to take care of your cut while you were out. I made a couple of calls instead."

"Where is Jonathon?" Emmy asked.

"Your friend who was impersonating a cop?"

"Yeah," Emmy admitted.

"Being detained in the front. Officer Hamilton arrived while you were out. I asked him to take care of your friend while I took care of you." For the first time Dr. Gregory looked at her kindly. "I was hoping if he was out of the way you could tell me what really happened."

Emmy spoke cautiously. "What do you mean what really happened?"

He sat back, his face was both tired and serious. "This is the second time you've come into my clinic with the same young man and a knife wound. If someone is hurting you. If that boyfriend of yours—"

Emmy was confused for a second, then she realized what Dr. Gregory was implying. "Oh. Oh. No, it wasn't Jonathon. He wasn't the one who threw the knife. I was in the bookshop and someone was there waiting for me."

He nodded. "That's what Officer Hamilton said. I just wanted to be sure. He did mention that Jonathon was the first one on the scene, that he got there almost too quickly."

Emmy hadn't thought of that. She'd called Pierce, not Jonathon. She was sure of that now, but he had come anyway. How had he known? She tried to remember how tall the person in the cloak was. The figure seemed too short to have been Jonathon.

"If it's in Officer Hamilton's hands. If nothing else, he's thorough." Dr. Gregory shook his head. "Although your Jonathon appears to be a slippery character. I imagine he told you he acquired that scar on his chest through some kind of heroics?"

"He said he was shot by a sniper," Emmy said.

Dr. Gregory nodded. "Doctor-patient confidentiality aside, I'd say the scar was from some kind of open heart surgery. He likely had a significant heart condition when he was a teenager or young adult."

"Oh," Emmy said. Even though she'd guessed what the doctor just confirmed, she felt like an idiot to have been taken in by Jonathon.

"I think we got off on the wrong foot last time. I'm Thomas Gregory."

She took a deep breath. "Emmy, I mean, Emerson. Emerson Fox."

Dr. Gregory reached into the cupboard and pulled out a white box with green lettering, the exact box he'd sent Jonathon to find. "Yes, I know. We've met before, but I'm sure you were too small to remember. Your mother brought you in because you had stomach issues related to certain foods. Watermelon, I believe it was. I told her you might grow out of it. Did you?"

"No," Emmy said.

"Pity. It's such a delicious fruit."

Emmy closed her eyes as he began sewing up the cut. She needed to talk to him. She was never going to get any further with this case if she didn't ask the hard questions. "How well do you know my family?"

He continued his work. "I knew your mother and your uncle when they were both children, though at different times. I knew your grandparents. Tragic what happened to your uncle."

She tried to feel out his tone. Did he really think it was tragic? He sounded more matter-of-fact than upset or consoling. But he didn't say it like he was bitter.

Emmy worked up the courage to ask the hard question. "I heard you didn't like my uncle very much." She opened her eyes to face him. "That there was an incident with your daughter. A lawsuit, even."

Dr. Gregory tied off the suture and snipped it in a quick motion. His face had crumpled into wrinkles of pain. "It took me a long time to forgive your uncle for what happened to Bethany. I foolishly blamed him instead of the drugs and the mental illness she'd suffered with for so long."

"But you did forgive him?" Emmy said.

"We didn't go out and play bridge together, if that's what you mean." Dr. Gregory sat on the stool beside the table. "But I don't harbor anything like a blood vendetta against him, if that's what you're fishing for."

"I didn't..."

"I've heard what you're trying to do, but you can cross my name off whatever suspect list you have going. What Professor Sharp did seemed cruel at the time, but I later learned he had good reasons for giving my daughter a bad recommendation."

"What reason could he possibly have had?" Emmy asked.

Dr. Gregory suddenly looked very tired. "She got the internship anyway, but quit after just a few months. We never found out why until after she was gone."

He stood. "Lie back and rest for a few minutes. There's something I want to show you."

He left the room while Emmy contemplated everything that had happened tonight. Someone had tried to kill her, but she wasn't sure if she'd actually been targeted, or if she'd just surprised whoever was in the bookshop. Were they looking for something important? If so, what were they looking for?

Before she could collect her thoughts the doctor was back. He helped her sit up and then handed her a file folder.

"We were in the middle of a wrongful death lawsuit with your uncle when these clippings showed up in my mailbox. I never figured out who sent them."

Emmy opened the file. It held a stack of articles about an editor from the *Seattle Times* who was accused of sexual harassment by a young intern. As the case continued, more and more young women came forward to accuse the man of sexual harassment. Then the charges got worse.

She looked up at the doctor as what the articles implied dawned on her. "This was the man your daughter had an internship with?"

"Her suicide note said *Professor Sharp was right* so we assumed it was the bad recommendation that had driven her to kill herself. He wouldn't come right out and tell us why he gave her that recommendation. My guess is he was trying to protect her privacy.

"The editor she worked with at the magazine wasn't interested in Bethany for her talent. He was a predator of the worst kind. Your uncle knew that. He tried to tell Bethany that. But she wouldn't listen. The abuse my daughter suffered at the hands of that man pushed her over the invisible edge she had been teetering on for a very long time. If there was someone to blame for her death—"

"How is she doing?" Pierce appeared at the door.

"She's sewn up, nearly as good as new." The doctor took the file from Emmy, set it on the table, and handed Pierce another one. "I'm sure your forensic guy will want to take a look at this." Emmy realized her name was printed on the file the doctor handed to Pierce. "If all three wounds weren't made with the same knife, they were very similar."

"What does that mean?" Emmy asked.

The doctor looked grim. "It means the knife that was thrown at you tonight was most likely the one that killed your uncle."

Chapter 47

Confession

Pierce finished his inspection of the apartment before circling back to Emmy. "It looks secure, but we didn't find the guy who did this. I don't think it's a good idea for you to be alone tonight."

Emmy nodded. She was too exhausted and too shattered to pretend to be tough.

Pierce sat down on the couch and pulled out a recorder. "I need you to tell me everything that happened in the bookshop before you were attacked."

Emmy stared at the device, remembering. "The walls have ears," she said.

"What?" Pierce looked at her like she was crazy.

"It's a message my uncle left for me. I didn't understand it, but now I think I do."

"What does it mean?" Pierce asked. He still acted like she'd lost her mind.

"Someone is listening." Emmy stood and circled the room. She didn't know what she was looking for, but she guessed her apartment was bugged. Maybe the whole island was bugged. But if it was, who was listening? Jonathon for sure. Maybe Ramona.

Pierce?

She turned to look at him. He looked as exhausted and lost as she felt, like he was the one who had been attacked. She sat down on the couch next to him. "Are you okay?"

"I have a confession to make," he said it so quietly that she almost didn't hear him.

"Let me guess, you killed the professor."

"No." He obviously wasn't in the mood to banter. "But I haven't been exactly honest with you."

For some reason that confession annoyed her. "There's a newsflash. It seems like everyone on this island is harboring some dirty little secret."

He lowered his head. "I didn't leave our date because I got a call."

She stood up. She didn't want to listen to him unburden his guilt right now. "I figured that out like the next day. It's okay. I get it. You weren't into me. You don't have to explain that to me now. I'm over it." Even as she said it, Emmy knew she was clearly not "over it." "In fact, I'm more than just over it. I'm over you, so unless you have something important to say about the case, I'm going to bed."

"I'm not," Pierce said quietly.

"Whatever. I don't care if you stay up all night." Emmy started walking to the bedroom.

"Not, not going to bed." He took a breath. "Not over you."

Emmy stopped. "Wait. What? You're not over...me?"

"I just"—he exhaled—"I just can't deal with vomit."

It took a minute for her to process what he'd just said. "You can't deal with vomit?" The whole thing was insane. She would have laughed, but he looked so miserable. "But all the blood after the professor died, and you're a cop, right? I assume you've seen worse."

"None of that bothers me. But puke?" He shook his head. "For some reason I can't handle that. Even now, just talking about it." He shivered.

"So when I got sick at the restaurant..."

"I had to bail. I felt terrible too, because everything up to the point had been awesome."

"You walked out because I got sick," Emmy repeated.

"Yeah, I'm sorry, I just..."

She stopped, staring at him for a second as the pieces fell into place. "Who else knows you can't handle someone throwing up?"

"I don't—"

"Someone spiked my drink, knowing I'd get sick. And I think that same someone knew that me throwing up would cause you to bail."

"You think this is some kind of conspiracy?" Pierce said.

"Yes. I told you. Someone is trying to frame me for my uncle's murder. More than that. I think that same someone also killed my mom."

After a few silent moments, Pierce spoke up. "I know I screwed things up, by deserting you and being a total wimp when you got sick, but..." He hesitated. "I'll get you in to talk to my mom. I don't know if she'll tell you anything, but..."

Emmy reached across the couch and took his hand. "Thanks. I think she's my only chance to find out the truth."

Chapter 48

Dangerous Engagement

"You've never been sailing before?" Jonathon said as they approached the boat dock in the dark blue BMW that was his. After everything that had happened, Emmy knew she shouldn't be going with him to the boat shop, but he'd made all the arrangements, and she needed to talk to Brighton Redding. Besides, it might give her the chance to ask Jonathon a few questions too.

"No. My dad always said he got too seasick, so he avoided water..." Emmy stopped as she realized what might be the real reason her dad had never taken her sailing on any of their trips to the coast. Was it too painful for him to relive the activity where he'd lost his beloved wife, or did he avoid boats out of guilt? She shook her head; she couldn't let those thoughts cloud her judgment today. "I've never been. What about you?"

Jonathon looked out on the ocean like he was looking at an old friend. "I grew up on the water, my parents loved sailing. We had a lake property with a ski boat and a sailboat. When the ski boat broke, it sat. When the sailboat broke, it was fixed immediately."

Emmy was surprised by the sincerity of this glimpse into his life. Everything she'd known of Jonathon up to this point had been about putting on a front or straight up lying. This story actually felt genuine.

Redding Rentals was a gray clapboard-sided building at the edge of the water. A large dock next to it held three small sailboats, five motorboats, and a fleet of Jet Skis. A rack next to the shop was full of kayaks, canoes, and paddle boards. Except for a teenage boy painting a canoe beside the rack, the shop was empty.

"Hello!" Jonathon called out. The boy came around to the front of the shop, wiping his hands on a paint rag. "Is your dad around?"

"He's out on *Poppy*," the teenager said. He pointed out toward the biggest boat by the dock. It was a kind of a mini-yacht with a cabin and big white sails fluttering above it. "He said he had to get it ready for an important customer."

"Thanks," Jonathon said. He took Emmy's hand and started toward the big boat.

"Where are we going?" Emmy asked.

"To rent our boat." He pointed to the beautiful sailing vessel.

"How can we..." She did some mental math. "I don't think either of us has enough money to rent that."

"I sure as hell don't, but I know you have a slush fund for the investigation and if everything goes well, you could own all this, that boat included."

She opened her mouth to tell him she wouldn't get Redding Rentals even if she did get the island, but he put his arm around her waist. "Besides, wouldn't you like to try out a boat like that, at least once?"

Emmy chewed her bottom lip. She'd always wanted to go sailing. She hadn't understood her dad's reluctance to go on the water. And as rich as he was, Collin thought recreation was a waste of time. When they were dating, anything fun had to serve some kind of networking purpose, and he didn't like any activity where he might end up wet or cold or dirty, so boats were out.

"It's a beautiful evening, and it's all in the name of the investigation," Jonathon said.

Emmy still hung back. "The kid at the boathouse said he was getting it ready for an important customer, and I don't know if he'd rent it to us anyway. I hear he's not a big fan of my family."

"He is getting it ready for a couple of important customers. Newlyweds Cameron and Kelsie Black."

"Who are—?"

When Emmy turned around, Jonathon was on one knee with a big fake diamond in his hand. "Kelsie Ann, will you pretend to be my new wife?"

"Get up!" Emmy smacked him on the shoulder and then looked around, embarrassed. The dock was empty and the teenage boy was on the other side of the shop and out of earshot.

Jonathon stood up and grinned mischievously. "Is that a yes or a no?"

"You set this up, didn't you?"

"I may or may not have told the shop owner that we were newlyweds and asked him to get that big boat ready," Jonathon said. "It seemed like the best excuse to talk to Mr. Redding. He doesn't let that boat out without him to captain it."

"But won't he recognize us?" Emmy said.

"He hasn't been to the restaurant since I've been on the island. He barely leaves his boat shop. The only place he's ever seen you was at the town meeting and he seemed too riled up to be paying that much attention to what you looked like. But just to be safe—" Jonathon unzipped a duffel bag he'd brought with him. He produced a long black wig, a big floppy hat, and a pair of gold sunglasses for Emmy, and another pair for himself. Then he smoothed a dark mustache over his upper lip. "How do I look?"

"I'm not sure I can be married to a man with such a horrible mustache," Emmy said, but she took the ring and slipped it on her finger. Then she put on the wig and the sunglasses. She didn't like being deceptive, and she didn't like Jonathon taking over, but she needed information. She was sure Mr. Redding wouldn't tell her anything if he knew she was a Sharp.

"You look gorgeous," Jonathon said.

"I'm not sure how to take that, considering the sunglasses cover most of my face."

"You have a beautiful face, but I wouldn't say it was your best feature," Jonathon reached for her hand.

Emmy pulled away. Jonathon grabbed her hand, gripping it in his. "You're going to have to play this up like we're newlyweds. If Mr. Redding finds out we lied to him, we're not going to get any information out of this at all."

"Right, darling," she drawled and let Jonathon wrap his arm around her waist. "Here goes nothing."

Chapter 49

Friends and Enemies

"Ready for us to come aboard?" Jonathon yelled as they got close enough to the boat. The man turned to face them. If it weren't for the map of wrinkles on his face, Emmy would have guessed he was closer to her age than her mother's. His arms and back bulged with muscles as he tightened the rigging on the ship and he moved like he was part of the boat.

The man pushed a ball cap back on his head and blinked into the sun at them. "Mr. and Mrs. Black?" he asked.

"Cameron and Kelsie," Jonathon said, stepping toward the ship.

The older man moved nimbly from the boat to the dock. "Pleasure to meet you." He reached his hand out and shook Jonathon's. "How long have you kids been married?"

"Two months, on Sunday," Jonathon said. He sounded confident. Emmy wished he'd filled her in on the plan, at least on the details of her supposed marriage, so they didn't get caught in a lie.

"Well congratulations. Are you on an extended honeymoon or...?"

Emmy let Jonathon answer the questions while she studied the ship and its captain. He seemed friendly enough, but friendly in that formal "I'm here to serve you" way she'd gotten from a lot of the people in town. It must come from catering to tourists for a few months every year. She wondered if she would ever fit in here, if she could get past the formality and really get to know the people of the town. Lying about who she was didn't feel like a step in the right direction.

"...it's important that you listen and answer for yourself."

Jonathon nudged her and Emmy realized for the first time that Mr. Redding had been talking to her. His friendly formality faded away. "I don't take safety lightly, Mrs. Black. If you can't listen to instructions and answer the questions yourself, you can't be on my boat, I don't care how much you're paying me. I haven't lost anyone in nearly twenty-three years, and I don't intend to start today."

Emmy felt her face grow hot beneath the wig. Mr. Redding was peering at her from bushy dark eyebrows that contrasted with salt and pepper hair. She got the feeling he saw right through her disguise. For a second she thought about just telling him who she was and asking the questions she'd come to ask outright. Most likely he wouldn't answer any of them and he'd throw both of them off the boat. She tried to sound sincere. "I'm sorry, I'll pay attention."

"My wife is a daydreamer." Jonathon put his hand on her shoulder. "I'm constantly bringing her back to reality. But you need to listen to him. I don't know what I'd do if anything bad happened to my little honeysuckle."

Jonathon was making everything an order of magnitude worse. He was a terrible actor and his condescending attitude brought back less than fond memories of her ex-fiancé.

"It's just such a beautiful boat, how can you not daydream on it?" Emmy ran her fingers along the rail. "You say you've never lost anyone?" She was baiting the captain, because she knew he'd owned the boat that went down with her mother.

His sharp blue eyes found hers. "It was a different boat, but that woman didn't know how to listen or pay attention either."

Emmy stared back at him, fighting the urge to defend her mother to him. "That's horrible! What happened?"

"Honey, we were in the middle of a safety lesson. If we want to actually get out on the water, I suggest you listen instead of asking so many questions."

Emmy gave Jonathon a dark look. It was like he forgot that the whole point of being on this boat was to ask questions.

"Your husband is a smart man," Mr. Redding said. "Let's get on with it."

Emmy paid close attention to the safety instructions along with the basic instructions on how to operate the boat, which Mr. Redding said was just in case something happened to him. Only after they both could complete all his instructions would he let them aboard. Emmy took a twinge of pleasure when she was able to finish the safety list before Jonathon.

As soon as they were on board, Jonathon picked up a bottle of champagne that had been left chilling on the deck. Emmy stood at the rail and watched the island shrink behind them as they pulled away. She couldn't help but wonder how much of her investigation fund was going toward this little excursion. Whatever the cost, so far it wasn't worth it in terms of the investigation. In terms of sheer beauty, however, it was priceless.

"To us, darling," Jonathon said, offering her a glass.

Emmy turned to face him. "No thanks. I've learned my lesson about drinking things other people leave for me."

"You have a good point. As for me"—he downed the glass—"I like to live dangerously."

She looked over her shoulder, but Brighton was at the helm and out of sight. "You can cut out the act. He can't see us anyway."

Jonathon set the glasses down and reached for her hand. "What if I'm not acting? What if I told you that ring you're wearing is real?"

Emmy looked down at the ring on her finger. The diamond sparkled in the sun. She wondered if he was telling the truth.

He stepped closer. "What if I can see a life where the two of us are together?" He put his arms around her and leaned into her ear. "What if I'm falling in love with you?"

Emmy pushed him away. Ginny's warning about men who'd only want her for her money rang in her mind. "Is that what you said to Madelyn?"

He stepped away. "Why would you think this has anything to do with Madelyn?"

She pushed forward. "You were together the night the professor died. That's why you lied about being at your niece's party. You couldn't exactly use her as an alibi, but I saw you in the background of one of her posts."

Jonathon's face was turning red, but he tried to play it off as cool. He reached for the other glass of champagne and downed it in a couple of gulps. "I don't know where you got that information, but it's not true."

"I know you've been lying to me, Jonathon," Emmy said. The clues started to line up in her mind. Jonathon was the one who had access to everything from the beginning. "You changed my drink at the restaurant that night, you stole my purse, sent that text, and you've been listening in on my conversations and the conversations of a lot of other people on the island. I don't think you were actually wounded in the Army and you probably aren't even a private investigator."

He stared at her for a long time. Finally a smile spread across his face. "You're a better sleuth than she gave you credit for." He poured another glass and hoisted it in apparent tribute to Emmy. "But I am a PI. One who's been watching you for a while now."

"Who is 'she'? Who hired you?" Emmy asked. "Madelyn? Ramona?"

"Your uncle, originally. He asked me to track you down, which I did, and then..."

"And then?" Emmy prodded.

"Let's just say, I got a better offer."

"From who?"

He laughed. "You're a smart girl, Emmy. Haven't you figured out who's pulling the strings in this little puppet show? I could tell you, but that would take all the fun out of the game."

"This isn't a game!" Emmy yelled. "My uncle is dead. My mom is dead. Someone tried to kill me too. If you know something—"

"I could tell you, for the right price." He pulled her close again, holding her in an iron grip. His breath on her cheek already reeked of alcohol. "You're not going to figure this out without my help and I'm always open to the next highest bidder."

"Let me go!" Emmy yelled. She pushed him away and he stumbled backward.

He lurched toward her. "You don't know who you're—"

The iron hand around Jonathon's neck appeared out of thin air. "Best let her be."

Emmy wasn't sure how long he'd been there or how much Brighton Redding had heard. After a few seconds he released his grip and Jonathon stumbled backward, coughing.

"This is none of your business, old man," Jonathon said.

"True. Your business is your business. Mine is sailing, and I say the wind's picking up and a storm's coming. We need to head for shore."

Jonathon sat back down on the deck chair, red-faced. He took another long drink of the champagne, this one straight from the bottle. He looked like he was ready to murder someone

Chapter 50

Captain's Log

"Are you cold?" Mr. Redding asked.

Emmy wrapped her arms around herself and nodded, even though her chill had more to do with what Jonathon had just told her than with the weather.

"Happens a lot out here. The spray off the waves and the wind makes the air chillier than most people expect." He nodded to the hold. "I keep a supply of blankets and sweaters in the closet downstairs. Help yourself to whatever you can find."

"Thank you." Emmy took the excuse to get away from Jonathon.

She caught her breath as she climbed down a dark wood staircase to the ship's hold. She hadn't expected things to escalate so quickly when she questioned Jonathon. She was right about his relationship with Madelyn, but did that mean she'd hired him, or was he playing her too? He said someone was pulling the strings on all this. What did that mean?

She came into a little cabin that consisted of a large bedroom, a bathroom, and a sitting and dining area. Mr. Redding had said the ship was available for overnight trips. Emmy wondered where or if he slept on those excursions.

She looked around the room. They were heading toward shore. This might be her only chance to do some investigating before Brighton threw them both off the boat, but she wasn't sure what she might find. The ship her mother had died on was long gone, and it wasn't likely there were going to be any clues on this one as to what happened to her, but maybe it was worth looking.

The table was bolted to the floor, as she guessed all the furniture was in case of rough seas. She opened the drawer of a bedside table and found a book inside. It was *Rebecca* by Daphne de Maurier. A book about a woman who dies in a shipwreck didn't seem like light reading for anyone spending time on a boat. She flipped through the pages and found a passage marked near the end.

"Men are simpler than you imagine, my sweet child. But what goes on in the twisted, tortuous minds of women would baffle anyone."

Emmy read the quote through three times, but she still wasn't sure what message it held for her. Finally she replaced the book and shut the drawer.

On the other side of the stairs was another door. She turned the knob, but it didn't budge. It was probably the room where Mr. Redding slept on overnight cruises. She doubted her skeleton key would open that door, even if she'd thought to bring it with her.

Another door opened to the closet Mr. Redding had told her about. There was a shelf of blankets and an assortment of different weights of outerwear. She pushed through the coats to the very back. Behind the waterproof parkas and soft cashmere sweaters was a dark jacket, lined with wool inside. It was both warm and waterproof, and smelled like the ocean. It wasn't as nice as the other jackets hanging next to it. From the size she guessed it was Mr. Redding's own coat.

She searched the pockets. At the bottom of one she found a little silver key that looked like it would fit the lock on the door of the other room. She hesitated, but it wasn't like Mr. Redding was going to leave the boat to steer itself and catch her snooping.

She fit the key into the lock and turned it. The click felt loud in the small space and she had to glance up the stairs to see if anyone had heard it. The door opened to another sleeping area, much smaller, with a bunk bed and a little table.

The table in the center of the room held a thick book. There was no title on the front and when Emmy opened it, she saw it was full of handwritten notes. It took her a second to see that it was a mix between a ship's log and a diary. The spine of the book had the name *Poppy* and a span of years written in black marker. She glanced around the room until she found a row of built-in cupboards. The second one was full of the same kinds of books. The very first one had a different title, instead of *Poppy* it was titled *Lady M*. The time frame only spanned three years—including the year her mother died.

She took the book to the table and opened it up to the beginning of the book. The first page had a brief entry.

> *Lady M's maiden voyage. Weather: fair. Wind: out of the west. Crew: 1. Passengers: 1. Beautiful sunset to match the beautiful girl beside me. Fitting that she was on the first trip out with me, since she's the one who convinced me this was a good idea. Spent a small fortune on*

this boat. Got a loan to cover it. Dad doesn't know where
it came from. He'd be furious if he knew I borrowed
money from a Sharp to keep his business afloat. Even
if that Sharp is Mags.

Emmy stopped. Her mother had convinced Mr. Redding to buy an expensive boat and then she died on it. She flipped through a few more pages. The dated entries in the beginning of the book were spaced weeks apart. Either he didn't record every voyage or the boat wasn't rented much in the beginning. She skimmed the entries. He sounded increasingly discouraged. Here and there he made a note of how much the boat was rented for with losses in dark red ink. Most of the entries were losses. One ended with, *will lose the boat and the business if something doesn't change.*

Emmy kept skimming for any entry that mentioned her mom.

Weather: fair. Wind: from the north. Crew: 1. Passen-
gers: 1. She always overpays me even though the boat is
basically hers. She keeps telling me not to worry about
the loan, everything will work out. Easy for her to say.

Weather: fair. Wind: from the north. Crew: 1. Passen-
ger: 1. Sunset run with Mags. Almost told her every-
thing tonight. Would have if I hadn't seen the ring.
What if I hadn't seen the ring? What if I'd said some-
thing earlier?

The next entry was over a year after the last one.

Weather: cloudy. Wind: from the north. Crew: 1. Passengers: 2.5. Mags brought her new husband on the boat. Already expecting their first. Never believed what they say about pregnant women, the thing about the glow. She had it. Even before the sunset was behind her. He didn't notice. Only wanted to talk business and remind me what I owed them. Doesn't deserve her or her money.

Weather: clouds gathering. Short trip. Crew:1. Passengers: 2. Mags brought the baby to try out the boat. Her husband didn't come. Apparently he had business in Seattle. His business seems to be spending Mags' money. Not that I have room to talk. I let her give me another loan, but it's that or kiss the whole operation goodbye.

Emmy found herself in the next entry.

Weather: fair. Wind: brisk and perfect. Crew:1. Passengers: 2. Mags and little Em. The little one loved the boat. Wanted to see everything. No fear in that one. So much like her mom. As usual her husband is MIA. Hard not to imagine them both as mine. If only there was a way to make them mine. But you can't sail back in time.

There's no mention of my mom again until I get to the end of the first log book.

> *Weather: gathering clouds. Wind: from the north.*
> *Crew: 0. Passengers: 2. Words with Mags' husband. He*
> *wants to take the boat out on his own. Said it's basically*
> *his boat now. His island too. He said he'd call the loan*
> *in right now if I didn't let him take the boat. I still*
> *wouldn't have let them if she hadn't asked. Mags is*
> *shattered. Taking her dad's death and everything else*
> *hard. Shouldn't have let them go alone. Bad feeling*
> *about all this. But she can handle the Lady M as well*
> *as I can. Praying this isn't a mistake.*

It was the last entry in that book. There were several blank pages before the end, but there was no mention of the accident. Emmy opened the next book with the title *Poppy*. The figures in the margin were all green. Either the ship business had a dramatic uptick in customers or Mr. Redding had benefited from her mother's death the way everyone said he had.

Emmy put the books away and reached to latch the cupboard closed. As she did the boat suddenly pitched sideways. A little bottle that had been tucked in the back of the cupboard rolled out. Emmy steadied herself against the bunk bed and then picked up the bottle. It was a prescription bottle.

She froze when she saw the label. It was for ketamine.

Chapter 51

Stormy Seas

"Where are you?" Mr. Redding was yelling from the top of the stairs.

She shoved the bottle back into the cupboard and latched it closed. She took a breath and called back to him. "I'm coming back up."

When she reached the top of the stairs the wind tore at the hat and the wig she was wearing. She took both off and let it take them. The boat rocked violently again. She steadied herself and made her way to the helm, fighting the storm and the lurching of the boat with every step. As she reached the deck, big pelting drops of rain started to fall.

"I need your help!" Mr. Redding yelled. "I need to trim the sails and I need you to keep her steady."

"Where is Jonathon?" Emmy yelled back.

"Who?" Mr. Redding answered.

"Jonathon." Emmy realized her mistake too late. "I mean, where is my husband?"

He gripped the steering wheel with both hands. "The last time I saw the man you came with, he was passed out on the back deck. If you think he would be more help than you, you're welcome to go find him as soon as I get the sails squared away. In the meantime, Emerson, I need you to hold the wheel steady while I trim the mainsail so we don't capsize."

He moved sideways so she could get her hands on the wheel, then stepped aside.

"You know who I—"

"Of course I know who you are. We can talk about that after we get back to the dock. Now I need you to focus and do everything I say."

Emmy nodded and gripped the wheel tight.

He stepped away. "Do you have it?"

"Yes!"

"Good. Hold it as steady as you can while I adjust the sails. Whatever you do, don't let go. If that sail swings around, one of us will end up overboard."

Emmy held the wheel with a death grip as Mr. Redding adjusted ropes and sails. The rain was coming down with a vengeance. She peered through strands of dripping hair to see if she could see Jonathon. The deck where he she'd last seen him was just below her line of sight.

The ship crested a wave and tilted sideways. For a moment she could see him, lying on the deck. Then the ship slid down the side of the wave. Emmy gripped the wheel. It felt like the ocean was trying to wrench it from her grasp. She held on, even when the rain made her fingers slippery. She held on even when Mr. Redding came up behind her and took the wheel. "I've got it now."

It took a few ragged breaths before she could relax her fingers enough to release the wheel into his hands.

"You did good," he said. "Your mother would have been proud."

Emmy looked away. She was ashamed of everything she'd done.

His voice softened. "We're through the worst of it, but keep your hand on the rail and stay close to the center of the boat. You never know when a rogue wave might come up and take you over the edge."

Emmy forced herself to face him. "Is that what happened to my mom?"

He shook his head. "I don't know what happened to your mom. I have my theories, as we all do. Only one person knows the truth."

"I'd like to hear your theories. Up until a couple of weeks ago, I thought my mom had died in a car accident."

He shook his head, in disbelief or disgust, she wasn't sure. "Again, a discussion for another time. Right now I think you need to check on your husband or boyfriend or whoever the man you came with is."

Emmy nodded and moved toward the sunken stern of the boat, where she'd last seen Jonathon. The whole area was full of water. The deck chairs were intact but stripped of their cushions, the bottle of champagne was rolling along the floor of the deck, completely empty.

Jonathon was lying face down.

Emmy knelt by his body. She reached to feel for a pulse, but she already knew he was dead.

Chapter 52

The Body on the Boat

A n ambulance was waiting on the dock when *Poppy* arrived.
Emmy didn't recognize the stocky blond officer who was
standing next to Pierce on the dock. She assumed he was the detective
who'd come from the mainland to take over the investigation.

Ramona and Madelyn were waiting. Madelyn lunged for the ship
as soon as they docked. Her face was pale and streaked with tears. If
the grief she'd poured out over Professor Sharp's death had been an
act, this was the real thing.

"This is your fault." She pointed a long nail at Emmy. "Everyone around you dies. You killed him! He was only trying to help and you killed him!"

Instead of bothering with the gangplank, Mr. Redding reached out a hand to Emmy and helped her off the ship. Ramona stepped forward. "I brought some dry clothes. I figure you'll want to change before you face another round of questions."

Emmy could only stare back at her. She was exhausted and freezing. She'd been questioned by the Coast Guard for what felt like hours. She was numb and not just from the cold. "I already told the Coast Guard everything I know. What else could I possibly tell the police?"

"You could tell them why you're wearing my ring!" Madelyn reached for Emmy's hand and wrenched the diamond Jonathon had given her off her finger. "You could tell them how you killed my husband."

Ramona and Emmy looked at each other in disbelief. Ramona found her voice first. "Did you say husband?"

"Maybe they'll arrest you this time before you kill someone else!" Madelyn shrieked.

"Mrs. Sharp." A soft voice came from the direction of the boat shop. "Come inside and get warmed up. I just put on a pot of tea." An older woman with soft edges and gray-brown hair came forward. Emmy assumed she was Mr. Redding's wife.

Madelyn turned, her face streaked with tears. "It's Mrs. Moore. Mrs. Jonathon Moore."

"Come with me, Madelyn." The woman's voice was soothing. "You can wait in the shop. There's no reason for you to stay out in the cold. Let the officers do their job." She put her arm around Madelyn's shoulders and led her toward the boat shop.

Emmy watched them go, feeling like she was on an alien planet. Just a few hours ago Jonathon had convinced her to pretend to be his wife and now she learned he was already married—and to Madelyn, a woman who was at least ten years older than him.

Brighton watched the departing backs of his wife and the hysterical woman until they disappeared into the boat shop. He turned back to Emmy. "We need to talk. We can go back to my office while the police remove the body and finish their investigation."

Ramona began to follow them, but he held up his hand. "Not you, Mona. Emmy and I have some things to talk about that only concern the two of us."

Brighton filled a mug and set it in front of her. Emmy was surprised by the gesture and by the fact that the cup was filled with black coffee, not the tea the rest of the town was addicted to. "This isn't from Ms. Lee's," she said, wrapping her hands around the warm cup. It did little to chase away the numbness in her chest.

"Never touch the stuff myself, but my wife might have something inside if you want me to—"

"No, it's perfect." Emmy took a sip. When she looked up, Brighton was studying her, like she was something completely unique, but at the same time familiar. Emmy took another drink of coffee before she spoke up. "Was it like this the night my mother died?"

Brighton shook his head. "I've been wondering when you might circle back to that."

Emmy blew the steam off the mug. "I'm sorry we lied to you. Jonathon said—" His name made her swallow hard. "It was a stupid thing to do."

He nodded like he understood and took a sip from his own mug. "It was a lot like this night, yes. The calm after the storm. The dread-awful fear in the pit of your stomach. The haunting feeling that there was something you should have done."

"So you were there the night she died?" Emmy asked.

"Not on the boat with her, if that's what you mean. If I could do one thing over in my life…" He took a long drink that had to burn all the way down. "I should have never let her take the boat out without me that night. I should have never let her go out alone with him."

"By him you mean my dad," Emmy said.

Mr. Redding looked away. "Guess so." He silently watched the waves through the window for a few breaths. "I thought you'd look more like her, that you'd come back as a ghost to haunt me with her face, but instead I see him. I don't know which is worse."

"I look a lot like my dad," Emmy said. "People have told me that for my whole life." She hesitated, because his eyes were full of pain. "I never knew my mother."

"But Mags is there too. More in mannerisms than appearances. Funny, I didn't imagine that could be inherited."

Emmy glanced around the little room. Without being decorated in any kind of fashion, it screamed "sea dog." Tide tables, maps and miscellaneous pieces of riggings were strewn everywhere. It was all strangely familiar, even the smell of brine, seaweed, and wood.

"I've been here before," Emmy said.

Mr. Redding looked surprised. "You have. When you were very young, you and your mom used to go out on the boats with me."

"I thought Santa Claus lived on a boat. When my preschool teacher told me Santa had a sleigh, I told her she was wrong. I knew Santa had a boat."

"You meant my dad. He was an ornery old cuss, didn't care much for the Sharps, but he had a long white beard and a soft spot for kids."

He took another drink from his coffee mug. "Wish he'd lived long enough to meet mine."

"Your son is pretty young," Emmy said.

"I got married later than most in life. For a long time I didn't think it would happen. For a long time I didn't want it to happen."

"Because you were in love with my mom." Emmy hadn't meant for it to come out that way, but she didn't have the energy left for any kind of impulse control.

Brighton looked taken aback, then he laughed. "You are like Mags. She was a sweet little thing, but always said what was on her mind."

Emmy waited for him to get serious again. "It's the truth, isn't it?"

He looked at her from under his eyebrows. "You got into my ship's logs."

There was no way for her to deny it. "I did."

He nodded and then kind of bowed his head. "Mags was out of my league in every possible way—looks, social status, intelligence, temperament. But somehow my adolescent brain couldn't wrap itself around that fact, and like a fool I fell in love with her."

"But you didn't think much of my dad?" Emmy said.

"He didn't deserve her," Mr. Redding said. "He didn't like me hanging around her, or you. He was furious when he found out she'd lent me money for my new ship. But she was too good a person to turn me down."

"When the Lady M sank, you came into a lot of money," Emmy said.

"I had good insurance on it. I wanted to make sure if anything happened I could pay your mother back."

"But you didn't use the insurance money to pay her back. You used it to buy another boat and expand your business. You didn't ever pay the money back."

He narrowed his eyes. "After she died I found out Mags had signed the note back to me that morning. She'd just inherited more money than she knew what to do with. She didn't want me to pay her back."

"Convenient that she did that just before she died," Emmy said.

A wariness came back into his eyes. "What are you getting at?"

"I looked up the report on the accident. The ship had a defect in it that caused it to sink. The police never determined whether the defect was caused by sabotage or just poor workmanship. It was your ship. What do you think happened to it?"

"The bastard killed her," Mr. Redding spat out.

"You mean my father," Emmy said.

"Yes."

"But it could have been you. You had the opportunity. You had access to the ship, more access than anyone, especially my dad, who knew next to nothing about ships. You sent my parents out on the boat, something you never did for anyone. You had a motive. You owed my mother a big chunk of money, a debt she conveniently excused just hours before she died. You admitted to being in love with her, so maybe jealousy paid a part in it too."

His face had gone purple with rage. He slammed a fist on the table so hard that the coffee mugs shook. "If you were anyone else's daughter, I wouldn't sit still for this."

Emmy stood her ground. She needed to talk this through, to get it straight in her mind and study his reaction. "And then I'm on board your boat today and another accident happens. And there was a bottle of ketamine in your private quarters. What motive would you have for getting Jonathon out of the way, or my uncle? Did they know what really happened that night?"

"None, for either of them. If you're about finished—"

"She is." Pierce and the detective from the dock, Detective Harris, had come in sometime while they were talking.

Detective Harris walked over, pulling a pair of handcuffs from his belt. "I'll take it from here, Mr. Redding. Ms. Fox is done asking you questions. It's time for her to answer some of mine."

Chapter 53

Arrested

"Hasn't she had enough tonight?" Ramona asked as they led Emmy out of the office in handcuffs.

"If by enough, you mean getting involved with another murder, then I'd say so." Pierce was all business. The words were clipped and Emmy sensed he was fed up. With her or the case? Probably both.

"Murder?" Ramona said. "I just talked to the Coast Guard medical examiner. He said the cause of death was most likely due to a mix of alcohol, drugs, and Jonathon's pre-existing heart condition."

"That may be true, but they found an unknown substance in the champagne bottle. It looks like someone deliberately drugged or poisoned Mr. Moore," Detective Harris answered.

Ramona shook her head and then turned to Pierce. "Shouldn't you be questioning Madelyn right now? She just dropped a bombshell. She was married to the man who died."

"We'll get to that, if Madelyn Sharp's marital status has any bearing on our investigation," Detective Harris answered.

"But it does." Ramona was trotting along beside them as they marched Emmy toward a waiting patrol car. "Her prenuptial agreement says she gets nothing from Professor Sharp's estate if she remarries."

Emmy looked at Ramona. "So marrying Jonathon means she's written out of the will?"

"Yes," Ramona answered.

"And if her husband dies?" Detective Harris asked.

"It doesn't change anything. Once she's married she loses all claim to an inheritance," Ramona said.

"I wonder if Jonathon knew that," Emmy said.

"That sounds like her revelation gives her less motive for murder, not more," Pierce said.

"Oh." Ramona stopped for a second. Then she hurried to catch up. "Emmy is not going anywhere without her lawyer present."

"You said you couldn't be my lawyer. That it was a conflict of interest," Emmy said.

"So I did. I guess all this will have to wait until tomorrow when we can get someone here from the mainland. Until then, Emmy needs a hot meal, a hot bath, and a good night's sleep."

Pierce stood in front of the patrol car while Detective Harris opened the door and put Emmy inside. "We'll make sure she has access to her lawyer. Tomorrow. She's spending tonight in jail."

"On what charges?" Ramona asked.

"Murder one," Pierce answered.

Chapter 54

Insurance Fraud

"When do I get my academy award?" Detective Harris said as they left the harbor and headed into town. "Before or after I lose my badge?"

"That depends on how tight you made those handcuffs." Pierce turned around to look at Emmy. "Are they hurting your wrists?"

"What's going on here?" She wasn't sure who was on her side anymore.

The officer in the driver's seat nodded at her in the rearview mirror. "I'm Nick Harris, Detective Nick Harris. I just got assigned to this case."

"Luckily, he also happens to be an old friend of mine from the police academy," Pierce added. "I told him everything you've found out and he agreed that we need to keep you safe."

"So where are we going now?" Emmy asked. Her shoulders hurt more than her wrists and she had this sudden need to scratch her nose, impossible with handcuffs on. Worse though, her head was crammed full of a million different thoughts. It felt like it might explode.

"I guess you could say I'm taking you into protective custody," Pierce said. "Based on what my mother told me, I'm convinced one of the people we just left at the boat shop is a murderer and I wasn't about to let them get a second shot at you."

"So where are you taking me? Some kind of safe house?"

"Kind of," Pierce said.

"The safest kind of house there is," Detective Harris said as they turned toward the city building.

Pierce looked uncomfortable. "We actually are taking you to jail, but only for your own protection, and so I can keep my promise. My mom is ready to talk, and I think you'll be interested in what she has to say."

***

"What made you decide it was okay to talk to me?" Emmy sat at a small table outside the jail cell across from Pierce's mom. Sharp island's answer to a police station was a little office and sitting area adjacent to two small jail cells at the back of the town hall. The cells each had a cot, a tiny sink, and a less-than-private bathroom.

Nancy took a sip of tea. Apparently the shopkeepers had been bringing her food since she'd been arrested. "Pierce told me what you said to him the night you were attacked. About who might know he has an aversion to people throwing up, who knew you were allergic to watermelon, and who had a motive to kill your mom and your uncle. In my book that narrows the suspects down to just three—Ramona, Brighton, and Madelyn.

"All three of them have known you and Pierce since you were kids. All three of them have had occasion to learn that Emmy is allergic to watermelon and Pierce can't deal with people puking. Ramona used to take care of Emmy when her parents went away. Brighton had both of you on his ship at different times." She looked at Pierce. "He had to keep you from jumping overboard when another passenger on the ship got seasick."

"And Madelyn made the mistake of serving watermelon at her wedding reception." Nancy shook her head. "That may have been your first reaction to the stuff. It was terrible what happened to your flower girl dress."

"I was a flower girl at Madelyn's wedding?" Emmy couldn't imagine a scenario where Madelyn liked her enough to have her as part of her wedding.

"A lot of things were different then," Nancy said. "Madelyn was actually nice and for the most part happy, and you were a pretty cute kid."

Emmy needed the conversation to get back to what was important. "You said you had proof my mother's accident wasn't an accident."

Nancy looked down at her hands. "I'm ashamed of myself for that. I shouldn't have used your mother's death to try to get your uncle to release my mom's land, but I was desperate."

Emmy's heart fell. "So you don't really have proof."

Nancy hesitated. "Actually I do, if you're up for it."

Emmy looked up at her. "After everything that's happened, I feel like I'm up for anything."

Nancy exchanged a look with her son who was sitting watch outside the cell. He nodded and went into another room. He came back with an old tape recorder.

"What is this for?" Emmy asked.

Nancy smiled. "What would you say if I told you everything I know about insurance fraud I learned from your mom?"

Chapter 55

The Walls Have Ears

"A re you sure about this?" Pierce had come back from the office with an old cassette player.

"I need to know," Emmy pleaded with him. "Even if I don't inherit the island or find out what happened to my uncle. I need to know what happened to my mom."

"Okay." Nancy set the cassette player in the middle of the table and pushed play. "But this might be hard to hear."

After a few seconds two voices crackled across the old recording. The first one she recognized as a younger version of her father's voice.

"You want to sabotage his boat and let him collect the insurance money? That's completely insane, not to mention dangerous. What if you get caught? That's called insurance fraud. You could go to prison. You have a kid to think about."

"I owe it to Brighton," a female voice Emmy guessed was her mother's replied.

"It's always about Brighton! Maybe you should have married him." Her father was angry, gearing up for a fight.

"Let me do this one thing for him, and then I don't have to see him ever again. He won't be tied to me by money anymore. I'll accept the inheritance. You can spend the money any way you want." Her mother's voice was pleading, but at the same time soothing. Emmy could almost remember her mom speaking to her that way.

"Why don't just tell him the debt is paid, that you don't want him to pay you back?" her dad's voice answered. "Why go through this whole insane plan?"

"He won't accept that. And besides, it's not enough. The boat he bought isn't good enough. His business is failing and he isn't going to let me just give him more money. He has too much pride. He's as stubborn as his father was. I have to find a way to do it so he won't know it was me."

There was a long pause and then her dad said, "You still love him." His voice cracked with pain.

"Yes," her mother said softly. Emmy held her breath as she continued, "But not in the way you think. I love you. I love our daughter. I love the life we're building together. But we're bound to this island now. If we're going to build a life here, I need to take care of Brighton and cut his ties to me at the same time. He needs to have his own life, but he won't do it as long as he feels like he owes me."

"If you're sure you can do this without getting hurt, I'll help you." Her father sounded resigned. "You know I'd do anything for you. But if it's even a little bit dangerous..."

"I'll be careful, I promise. I know how to make it look like an accident. The hard part might be getting Brighton to let us take his boat out without him," her mom said.

"If anyone can convince him, it's you. I don't know what power you have over men, but you definitely have it over me."

"Mommy, look at what I found." A child's voice broke into the recording. "Will you read it to me?"

"Mama's busy, baby," her mother said.

Another voice came on, faint, like it was far away. "Come with me. Mystery will read it to you."

Emmy pressed the stop button. She couldn't listen to herself as a child talking to the mother she would never know. She was hurt and confused, but mostly angry. Angry with her mom for taking the risk, angry with her dad for letting her do it, angry at Brighton for being so stubborn and so needy.

"Why would she do something so stupid?" Emmy said.

"I shouldn't have let her do it," Nancy said softly. "We came up with the plan together. I sold him an inflated insurance policy and Maggie figured out how to sabotage the boat to make it look like an accident." She looked at Emmy, her eyes misty with regret. "She was my best friend. Brighton Redding was the only person who ever came between us. Ultimately, he was the one that brought us back together. Neither of us wanted to see him lose his family's business." She looked down at her hands. "We didn't know our plan would end up costing Mags her life."

When she finally found her voice, Emmy asked, "Where did you get this recording? Who made it?"

"I'm not sure. Someone mailed it to me when I was in jail. It took a while to find a recorder that would play it…"

"The walls have ears," Emmy said.

"What?" Nancy and Pierce said at the same time.

"My parents had that conversation in the bookshop. That means all the buildings in this town are bugged and have been for a long time, but by who?"

"I believe your grandfather started it," Nancy said. "He was paranoid about anyone in the town getting out from under his thumb. Your mom must have known, or at least suspected. She always wanted to talk outside. I don't know who continued to listen after he died."

"Jonathon said *she* was pulling all the strings," Emmy said, "but I don't know who *she* is.

"I think I do," Pierce said. "There's more to the recording. If you're okay listening."

Nancy looked at Emmy, her finger poised over the play button. Emmy nodded.

"Make sure the champagne makes it on the boat—the best we have. Those two should be celebrating. Hell, I would be if I'd inherited this place." The tape was garbled, so they couldn't hear whoever the second person in the conversation was.

The first voice came back again. "...like an accident. Maybe I'll get the chance to show them how a place like this should be run after all."

The child's voice came back again. "Mystery, you said you'd—"

The tape player clicked off.
Emmy recognized the voice on the tape.
It was Ramona.

Chapter 56

Tenacity

"The champagne on the boat," Emmy said. "It was drugged tonight and back then. That's why my mom couldn't make it off the boat in time. Her plan was dangerous, but someone else made sure it was fatal. That someone had to be Ramona."

"She's wanted to be in charge of the island for as long as I've known her," Nancy said. "She always believed she could run things better than your grandfather or your uncle."

Emmy sat for a second, letting the pieces fit together. Ramona killed her mother, thinking she'd get the chance to own the island. Maybe her uncle suspected something and that's why he divorced her. She came back after their son died and...Something Victoria had said over and over ran through Emmy's mind, *he wasn't the man everyone thought he was.*

"Ramona was the one pulling the strings. She took over running the island after her son Weston died and my uncle couldn't, or wouldn't, do it anymore. Ms. Lee said my uncle changed the way he ran things then. He became more of a tyrant. They thought it was because he was devastated by his son's death. But it was because he wasn't managing the island, she was."

She stood, pacing. "My uncle hired Jonathon to find me, but Ramona paid him more to follow me and to drug me that night. She might have even convinced him to seduce and marry Madelyn so she'd be disinherited and then everything would go to her."

She grew more angry as every conversation she'd had with Ramona played over in her mind. "And she's been pulling the strings on my investigation. She's the one that told me about Dr. Gregory's daughter, and Brighton and Nancy, and all the shopkeepers hating my uncle. She pretended to help me. Even put her own name on the suspect's list. Then when I got too close, she tried to kill me too."

Pierce stopped her. "The knife in the bookshop and then the champagne on the boat. Who's to say it was only meant for Jonathon?"

Nancy stood. "You need to arrest her, tonight, now."

"We don't have enough evidence to get a warrant," Detective Harris said. "If you're right, she just killed the one person who could implicate her, so unless there's someone else, or some kind of confession..."

"We could set a trap." Emmy's mind was working overtime. "If everything is bugged, I could get her to confess and the whole thing would be recorded."

"How are you going to do that?" Nancy asked.

Emmy thought for a minute about Ramona and her ego and what it would take to get her to confess. "She thinks she's the smartest person on the island. We have to find some way to appeal to her vanity. If I'm right, she's not going to want anyone else to take credit for her genius. That's where we'll get her. The problem is she's the only one who knows where all the recording equipment is. She's not going to confess in a room she knows is bugged."

"Why don't you just put your phone on record when you walk in to talk to her?" Nancy suggested.

"No." Pierce's blue eyes flashed. "If we're going to go through with any kind of a scheme that puts Emmy in danger, I want it to be where I can hear what's going on and monitor the situation. I want to be close in case something goes wrong."

"Maybe she could wear a wire," Detective Harris said. "But if we do that we're back to trying to get a warrant."

Pierce shook his head. "And I'm not exactly in the chief's good graces right now."

Emmy held up her phone. "We've all got recording and listening devices. There has to be some way to make this work."

Nancy leaned forward. "If I were you, I'd check in with Madelyn, now that we know she's not a murderer."

"Madelyn?" Emmy looked at her in disbelief.

"She's pretty techy. At least she once was. She and Weston owned a high-end tech company in Seattle before he died."

"Then why is she running a clothing store?" Pierce was obviously as surprised as Emmy was by this revelation.

"I think it's what Edward wanted her to do," Nancy said. "And she wanted to keep him happy. He probably never asked her what she was good at or what kind of shop she might want to run. She was a woman, she wore clothes, so obviously she should have a clothing store."

Emmy looked at her skeptically. "I don't think she'd be willing to help me, especially now. She blames me for Jonathon's death."

Nancy picked up another cookie. "Might be worth a shot. She has no love for Ramona."

"No. Way." Pierce said. "This is way too dangerous. We'll have to find the evidence another way."

"Until then, what? You keep me in jail?" Emmy said.

"If that's what it takes to keep you safe." Pierce crossed his arms over his chest.

"I believe that's called false imprisonment," Nancy said.

"Better than death," Pierce said.

"Is it?" Emmy asked.

"You need to back off, son," Nancy said. "You won't win this. Better to go along and help Emmy with her plan and do what you can to keep her safe. If she's anything like her mother, she won't back down. Tenacity runs in their veins."

Chapter 57

Disaster

E mmy got up from the little cot in the corner of the cell quietly. The tape player was still sitting on the table in the sitting room outside her unlocked cell. She turned the volume down as low as it would go and replayed the taped conversation. She still had the nagging thought that she was missing something. Maybe it was just that everything had come crashing down on her so quickly, or that she wasn't sure she had the courage to go through with their plan.

Was she just like her mother in both the good ways and the bad? Her mother had caused her own death. Obviously someone had helped her, but she'd taken the risk, knowing that she had a little girl who needed her. Even on the recording, her mother had dismissed Emmy. Instead of spending time with her she was trying to take care of someone else. She couldn't even be bothered to read a story to the daughter she'd be deserting. Someone else, another voice had promised to read to Emmy.

Mystery? Who was that?

"Can't sleep either?" Pierce said. Emmy stifled a scream. She hadn't heard him come up behind her. Detective Harris had said he'd keep watch. He was snoring from a little couch in the office. Emmy thought Pierce had gone back to his grandma's house to sleep.

"Sorry," he said and took the seat across from her. "You don't have to go through this, you know."

"What other choice do I have?" Emmy asked.

"Let Detective Harris and me figure out how to arrest Ramona and bring her in according to the law," Pierce said. "It might take time, but you'll be safe."

"I'm down to a week," Emmy pointed out. "If I don't solve this, Ramona gets everything."

"Not if she's arrested for murdering your uncle or your mother."

"You think you can make that happen in a week?" Emmy asked.

"Not likely," he admitted. "You said the money doesn't matter anyway. That this was all about finding out who killed your mom."

"It does and it doesn't matter. If I don't solve the case and Ramona goes to jail, then the island is still split up and sold."

"Better than you being dead." Pierce covered her hands with his. "Please, just let me take care of this."

She pulled her hands away. "That's the problem. People have been taking care of me my whole life—Dad, Collin, even Ginny." Emmy closed her eyes. She wasn't sure how to explain what she was feeling to Pierce. They were so different. He'd always known what he wanted. He set goals and achieved them. He took care of everyone around him. Emmy was a failure at pretty much everything she'd tried. She could barely take care of herself. "I wanted something I did on my own. If I could solve the mystery, if I could catch a killer...maybe it would mean my life hasn't been a complete waste. Maybe it would mean that I wasn't a complete disaster."

Pierce reached across the table and took her hand again. "Why would you think that?"

"Because the only thing I've accomplished in life is a mountain of debt and a do-nothing college degree. My mom died trying to save someone else. The stepmom who raised me doesn't want anything to do with me and my dad is a felon who's been lying to me my whole life."

"We have a lot in common," Pierce said. "Only my mom was the one lying and my dad doesn't want anything to do with me."

"But look at all you've accomplished. You're a police officer, you're on your way to being a detective. You're smart and driven and honest and"—she caught his eye—"and kind of devastatingly handsome."

A smile brightened Pierce's face. "You think I'm devastatingly handsome?"

"Kind of." Emmy looked away, embarrassed. "It's one of many reasons you're out of my league and should run. Like I said, I'm a disaster."

"But you're a beautiful disaster."

Emmy made a face at him. "That doesn't help."

"You're not a waste and you're not a disaster. You're intelligent and brave, and honestly, one of the strongest and most independent women I've ever met."

She shook her head. "I continually screw things up. Look at all the majors I tried in college. Look at everything I've failed at."

"But you never gave up and in the process you've learned a lot. You're like some kind of freaky walking search engine. And now you've solved an impossible mystery. My mom is right, tenacity runs in your veins."

He looked down at her hand, gripping it tightly for a long moment. Finally he faced her again. "I'll do what I can to help you, only...only promise me you'll be careful."

Emmy met his piercing blue eyes. For the first time she saw something in the way he looked at her. There was a tenderness that wasn't pity and something else—respect. Respect for her. Collin had never looked at her that way in all the time they'd been together.

"Thank you for saying that," Emmy said.

"It's all true," Pierce leaned over the table.

Emmy moved closer, waiting for his lips to meet hers.

"Will you two shut up and go to bed already?" Detective Harris stood up from the couch in the office just outside the cell where Emmy thought he had been sleeping. "Look, I'll take the cot in the other cell. You two can have the couch. Get whatever is going on between you two out of your system so we can all get some sleep. I have a feeling the next few days are only going to get crazier."

Emmy woke up on the couch outside the little jail cell. Her head was on Pierce's chest, his arm around her waist. She couldn't quite remember how they'd gotten in that position. His mother was in the cell on the little cot, the door wide open. Officer Harris's large form was hanging off the cot in the other cell.

She needed to find the restroom. She moved slowly, trying not to wake up Pierce, but only got more tangled in his arms. A buzzer sounded and Pierce jumped up, knocking Emmy to the floor.

"Oh, shoot, sorry." He reached a hand to help her up. The buzzer sounded again.

"What's that?" Emmy asked.

"Someone's at the door." Pierce walked over to the computer and pulled up a camera on the front door. He swore.

Emmy joined him and saw Ramona standing in front of the door with Chief Howe and the lawyer she'd tried to get Emmy to hire.

"She's persistent, I'll give her that," Emmy said. She looked up at Pierce. "You're going to be in big trouble, right?"

"I'm already off the case. I don't know what else she's going to do to me. I guess she could throw me out of the department." He looked at Emmy's expression. "I'll be okay. You'd better go back to your cell. Get Detective Harris out and don't forget to pull the door shut behind you. I'll go see what they want."

Detective Harris stood up and made his way into the men's room, while Pierce ran his fingers through his hair and pulled his shoes on. The buzzer started up again and didn't stop. Ramona was obviously holding the button down.

"Coming, coming," Pierce said. He glanced over his shoulder at Emmy. "I don't know if I'm going to be able to keep her from taking you with her."

"It's okay," Emmy said, even though her heart was pounding. "This is all part of the plan."

Chapter 58

Sharp Women

"I cannot believe they locked you up all night. They don't even have enough evidence to prove Jonathon was murdered, much less that you did it. I hope they both lose their badges. When all this is over I'm going to help you file a lawsuit against the police department." Ramona stopped to catch her breath as they reached the door to Emmy's apartment. "Take a long hot bath, get yourself a nice breakfast, and I'll see you in my office when you're ready. And Kenneth is on retainer now. Call him anytime."

"Thanks for bailing me out." Emmy slid her key into the lock.

"Anything, anytime," Ramona gave her a quick hug. "There are only a couple of us left. We Sharp women have to stick together."

Emmy pulled away. It made her skin crawl to have Ramona hug her. Inside she seethed. She wanted to scream at Ramona that she knew she'd killed her mother and her uncle and now Jonathon. But she kept it all inside. Instead she said, "Speaking of Sharp women, do you know what happened to Madelyn?"

"Last I'd heard she locked herself in her apartment. Poor stupid Madelyn. She should have checked her prenup before she lost everything by marrying that con artist."

"Maybe she knew what she was doing. Maybe she loved him enough that it didn't matter if she lost her inheritance." Emmy wasn't sure why she was defending Madelyn, but she had the idea that she had misjudged her.

"Maybe." But Ramona didn't sound very sympathetic. "Call before you come, please. I might want to take a nap myself."

Emmy guessed Ramona just didn't want her to come unannounced. She hoped that didn't mean she knew what Emmy had figured out.

Emmy stood in front of the door and hesitated. None of her interactions with Madelyn Sharp had been pleasant, and she didn't expect this one to go any better. She gripped the photo album in her hand. It would probably only serve to dredge up more painful memories, but she was running out of time and maybe a trip down memory lane would soften Madelyn toward her.

Madelyn came to the door, no makeup, blotchy eyes. "You!" She started to close the door in Emmy's face.

Emmy put her foot between the door and the frame. "I know you hate me, but we need to work together."

"Why should I care if you solve Edward's murder and inherit the island?" Madelyn asked.

Emmy pushed harder. "Because whoever killed my uncle killed Jonathon, and I think I know who that is."

Madelyn hesitated and then tightened her grip on the doorknob. "And what if I still think the person who killed Jonathon was you?"

"I know it's going to be hard for you to trust me or believe me, but I need you."

Madelyn didn't move.

"I don't believe you married Weston for his money. I don't think this was ever about the money."

Madelyn let her push the door open a couple of inches.

"And I just found out, there was a time when we didn't hate each other." Emmy opened the album to the page with her as Madelyn's flower girl.

Madelyn pushed the door all the way open. "Who do you think killed Edward and Jonathon?"

Emmy looked around the room. "Not here."

Madelyn looked confused for a minute. Then she rolled her eyes. "I fixed that ages ago." She pointed to a device stuck to the window.

"So you knew someone was listening to everyone on the island?"

"You mean Ramona? Yeah, I knew that. Why do you think I hate her so much?"

Emmy shook her head. "Why didn't I come to you earlier?"

"Because you thought I was stupid, like everyone else, and probably because you didn't think I'd help you, and you'd have been right." She sat on a chair in the living room. "So who killed Jonathon?"

"Ramona." Emmy sat on the couch. She looked around the apartment. It wasn't at all what she'd imagined Madelyn's apartment to look like. The couch was comfortable, but kind of spartan compared to the luxury she assumed Madelyn would have surrounded herself with. The walls were bare except for a large canvas picture of her and Weston on their wedding day. The plain black coffee table only held a half-eaten bag of chips and an empty pint of chocolate ice cream. Against the wall was a desk full of computer components. Madelyn herself was dressed in what looked like men's sweats with no makeup and her hair up in a sloppy ponytail.

"Are you sure?" Madelyn asked. "What proof do you have?"

"None, yet. That's what I need your help for."

"You want me to help you find proof that Ramona is a murderer?" A smile lit up Madelyn's face. "Now that's the kind of project I can get behind."

"First tell me one thing," Emmy said. "Why did you let me get into the laptop in your office and see those pictures and your search history?"

"You know about that, huh?"

Emmy gestured to the window. "Someone who is smart enough to know her apartment is bugged and then find a way to circumvent it isn't going to use 'password' as the password to get into her computer."

Madelyn sat back. "I was tired of being alone. I was tired of trying to please Edward, and I was tired of running the damn clothing shop that I hate. Jonathon caught me at a very vulnerable time. He convinced me he was in love with me, and I convinced myself that I was in love with him, or maybe that he was my only way to escape a life I'd grown to hate."

"But by marrying him you forfeited your inheritance," Emmy said.

"Yeah. He wasn't very happy when he figured that out. Turns out he just married me for the money. I'm pretty sure he was working on annulling our marriage. When I saw him going after you..." Madelyn gestured to the photo album. "Maybe I remembered the cute little girl we all tried to protect, especially after your mom died. I couldn't let him scam you the way he scammed me."

Emmy thought about what Madelyn had said. "What do you remember about me as a little girl?"

"You were kind of adorable. We all doted on you, even me. At one point I thought I'd have a little girl of my own someday." She shook her head. "It wasn't in the cards for me." She stood up. Her eyes had clouded over, "Would you like tea or something to eat? If you spent the night in jail you couldn't have—"

Emmy's mind drifted back to the recording. "Who used to read to me at the bookshop when I was a little girl?"

Madelyn put a tea kettle on the stove and a couple of English muffins in the toaster, even though Emmy hadn't said she wanted anything. "I'm not sure. Edward maybe. He used to take you with him to the bookshop. Torri was obsessed with you. Your mom used to say if you ever disappeared, she'd know who to look for."

"Torri?" Emmy asked. There was something familiar about that name.

Madelyn pulled a jar of jam out of the fridge. "Edward's assistant. She's a quiet little thing. She was at the reading of the will, but you may not have noticed her. She has a tendency to blend into the walls."

"Victoria?"

"Yeah, you couldn't say her full name, so we all started calling her Torri. Well, everyone but Edward."

Madelyn poured the tea—this one smelled like chamomile—and set the English muffins on a plate in front of Emmy. Then she grabbed a plain gray laptop from the desk and sat back down on the couch. "So tell me about your plan to trap Ramona. I've been waiting almost thirty years for this."

Chapter 59

Tech Support

E ven though it had worked twice before, the click of the lock
and the door to Ramona's office swinging open still surprised
Emmy.

"Nifty little gadget," Madelyn said. "Is that what you used to break
into my office too?"

"Yeah," Emmy said. She shined her tiny penlight around Ramona's
office. They were looking for wires that connected the "definitely
bugged" office where Pierce and Chief Howe had been talking with
the "probably more secure" office where Ramona did all her business.
She took a couple of steps and then tripped over one of the smaller
poufs, knocked into a lamp, and pulled a pile of paperwork off the
desk.

Madelyn stood over Emmy with her hands on her hips. "Perfect. Now if you'll just release the herd of angry orangutans, our incognito mission will be just about complete."

"Sorry," Emmy said. She took advantage of where she was and looked for the switch that Ramona had used to eavesdrop. She shined her light on it. "I found the switch."

Madelyn walked over and knelt down by the desk. "This is all pretty low-tech stuff, probably left over from your grandpa's days as the tyrant of Sharp Island." She pulled out an electronic device and used it to follow a length of wire that ran up the shelves. "Because it's old, the recording won't be as clear. I'll add new wires where she won't see them and I'll switch the setup so the recording end will be on this end and the listening will be in the other room."

"What about the other places with listening devices, like the boat rental place? Those can't be wired like this one," Emmy said.

"My guess is there's a more high-tech device there. Something with a radio signal. Maybe Jonathon took care of that one for her." As she said his name, a tired sadness washed over Madelyn's face. "I'm not sure why Ramona never upgraded this part. Doesn't matter, her office is the best bet we have of catching her saying something incriminating."

While Madelyn worked, Emmy restacked the paperwork that had fallen. One piece caught her eye. It was a proposal from Khonico for Ramona to sell the bulk of the island. "I can't believe it," Emmy said. "All her talk about trying to save the island and she was planning to sell it as soon as she was the only heir."

"I wouldn't put anything past her." Madelyn tapped on the wall. "This one feels solid."

"Why would you say that?" Emmy asked. "Aren't all the walls solid?"

"Not around here, they aren't. There are all sorts of passages built into these old buildings. Great-Grandpa Sharp was as nosy and paranoid as the rest of them. He couldn't exactly use electronic surveillance to spy on his tenants back then, so he had passages built into the walls. Weston showed me some of them that he'd found when he was a kid."

Emmy tapped on another wall tentatively. She couldn't tell if it was solid or not. She sighed. The more she learned about her crazy family, the more she understood why her parents hadn't wanted her to be raised here.

She went back to the desk and stacked the papers as close to the original order as she could guess they went in. Then she sat down on one of the poufs and watched Madelyn work. She was impressed; the pretend-ditzy blonde knew her way around all sorts of tools and technical equipment. Watching her brought up a bunch of questions about who Madelyn really was.

"Where did you learn to do that?" Emmy asked. "I thought you were a business major."

"I was. I learned all this from my dad," Madelyn replied. "He could fix anything."

"Where is he now?" Emmy asked.

"He died when I was sixteen from a massive heart attack."

"I'm sorry," Emmy said.

"It was a long time ago." Madelyn stood and pulled a small drill from the black bag of tools she'd brought with her.

"You've lost a lot of people in your life," Emmy observed.

"Yeah." Madelyn was focused on the drill.

"You seemed pretty upset when Professor Sharp died," Emmy said. "Were you close to him?" She didn't mention that she'd thought Madelyn's grief over the professor's death was manufactured to create an effect.

"I haven't spoken to my mom or my sister in years. Not since they figured out I didn't have the money they thought I did, so I wasn't lying when I said Edward was all the family I had left, but really no one was close to the professor. At least not for the last ten years since Weston died. He retreated into his books and his bookshop and his other pet obsessions. I tried to take care of him for Westy's sake." She paused. "I'd be lying if the money part of this whole equation didn't play into it. We lost our business and then I lost my husband. It was just easier to let Edward take care of things." She put the drill back into the bag of tools and pulled out a roll of wire.

"Even if that meant running a business and living a life you hated?"

"Yeah." Madelyn looked down at the roll of wire. "When Edward was found dead, all I could think was I'd be blamed. My only reaction was to go numb. I didn't feel bad or sad or even horrified over what happened. I couldn't even muster tears. I've watched enough true crime shows to know that police officers get suspicions when someone isn't grieving properly, whatever that is. I did my best, but I'm guessing it backfired. I'm sure you thought I was an overdramatic gold-digging trophy wife." "I didn't—" Emmy started.

"Yeah, you did." Madelyn stood. "Enough interrogation, Sherlock. We need to get this finished before Ramona decides she needs to check on something in her office. She's a classic workaholic. I need you to feed the wires through the wall to me, when I say to. Can you handle that?"

"Sure," Emmy nodded.

Madelyn picked up the bag and stood at the door. "I've played the dramatic, money-grubbing, weeping widow for so long that I don't know who I am anymore. Watch out for that if you decide to stay on the island. You kind of fall into the role people expect you to play around here."

Chapter 60
The Trap

"Emmy, what a surprise." Ramona stood in the doorway to her office. Despite Ramona's request that she call first, Emmy had gambled on showing up unannounced for the element of surprise. She could tell that Ramona wasn't expecting her or anyone else. Ramona's dog Belle, walked over, sniffing Emmy like she knew something was up.

Emmy casually pushed her way past the dog. "I'm running out of time and I wanted to talk through everything with you. Not the legal stuff, just what the mystery looks like. Everything I've figured out. I need your opinion."

"Of course." Ramona stepped aside.

Emmy tried to think of a way to casually walk behind Ramona's desk so she could flip the switch and turn on the speaker. Pierce was waiting in the other office and would be recording and listening to their conversation in case something went wrong. Emmy recognized the risk he was taking for her. Their method of getting Ramona's confession wasn't exactly legal.

Ramona walked back to her desk and sat behind it before Emmy could get ahead of her. "I'm sorry everything is such a mess." She pulled out her colorful notebook and set it on the pile of papers Emmy had looked through the night before. She obviously didn't want Emmy to see them. "What do we know?"

Emmy looked at the jar of half-eaten chocolates on Ramona's desk. She reached for it. "Could I have one? I skipped breakfast."

"Of course." Ramona reached for the cap, but before she could open the jar, Emmy lunged for it. The jar tipped over on the desk, spilling chocolates everywhere.

Emmy caught it just before it rolled off the desk and shattered. "I'm so sorry," she said.

"Get them before Belle eats one!" Ramona yelled. She held the dog back as Emmy crawled under the desk and gathered up the chocolates. As she stood, she flipped the switch under the desk to turn on the microphone. She only hoped Madelyn's reverse wiring worked.

"Sorry about that." Emmy stood and replaced the chocolates in the jar. Belle looked at Emmy as if she'd cheated her out of a treat.

"So what have you found out?" Ramona asked.

Emmy resisted the urge to say something along the lines of "I found out you killed my mother and my uncle and that you've been cheating the people of Sharp Island for the last ten years." Instead she started slowly. "It looks like someone else has been managing Sharp Island. Someone who wasn't Professor Sharp." Emmy studied Ramona's reaction, but her face didn't change. "Ms. Lee said he'd changed that way he ran things, that he got to be more tyrannical, but"—Emmy swallowed; she needed to appeal to the part of Ramona that liked being in charge, the side that was dying to take credit for taking care of the island—"but she said it was better. The shops were doing more business, and more tourists were coming in."

"Interesting." Ramona leaned forward, like she was intrigued. "And who do you think was running things if Edward wasn't?"

Emmy casually scratched Belle behind her soft ears. "I was thinking maybe Madelyn. I mean, she does have a degree in business management maybe—"

"Madelyn?" Ramona let out a snort. "Madelyn couldn't manage her way out of a paper bag. Look Sharp is the one business in town that is falling apart, maybe because I haven— Maybe because Edward left that one all up to her."

"I guess that makes sense," Emmy caught Ramona's slip, but decided not to exploit it...yet. "If it wasn't Edward managing the island, I'd like to know who it was, for a couple of reasons. One, because I might be the next one who has to manage this place and two, because I think whoever was managing the island was the one who killed him."

Ramona looked at Emmy for a long moment. "Why would you say that?"

Emmy held her gaze. "Why go to the trouble of making the island profitable, if there's no way you can profit from it?"

Ramona nodded vigorously. "That's a very good point. What we need to figure out is who profits from the island?" She poised a stylus over her tablet, like she was getting ready to make another list.

Emmy took a deep breath. "The way I see it, with Madelyn out of things, there are only two people left who have anything to gain by my uncle's death. Me, and you."

"Unless," Ramona countered, "Madelyn didn't know she'd be written out of the will by remarrying."

"Madelyn isn't as stupid as people think. I think she knew exactly what would happen if she married Jonathon, and even if she didn't, what motive would she have for killing him?"

"So no one would know she was married?" Ramona tried.

"Then why blurt it out as soon as he was dead?" Emmy said. "You saw her at the dock. She was shattered. I don't believe Madelyn killed Jonathon. Whoever killed Jonathon did it because he knew too much, because he was playing both sides."

"What would make you think that?" Ramona sounded wary.

"He told me. Before he died he told me he was willing to sell his secrets to the highest bidder. He laughed at me because I hadn't figured out who was pulling the strings yet." Emmy leaned in, watching Ramona's reaction carefully. "But now I think I've figured it out. That person is you."

Chapter 61

Speechless

There was silence for a long moment. Belle let out a low growl, but didn't move from her bed.

"I don't know what you're talking about." Ramona backed away from Emmy, her hands up as if she wanted to defend herself.

Emmy moved closer. "You've been controlling everything that happens on this island, from the businesses, to Jonathon, to my investigation. You are the only one left who had anything to gain by the professor's death."

Ramona was shaking her head. "I admit I've been running things on the island for the last ten years. Maybe I was a bit harsh, but I kept everything afloat. I mitigated all the bad loans Edward had made, and borrowed against some of the land. The interest from the extra debts

I acquired made it so I had to raise some rents, but things are looking up. The businesses on the island are all turning a profit."

Belle was on her feet now, her low growl building within her throat.

"Turning a profit so you could sell it at a higher price." Emmy indicated the paperwork on the desk. "You've been talking to Khonico about selling the island, once you're in control of it."

"Selling the island?" Ramona appeared shocked. "That paperwork is nothing but an offer Kirsten sent me. I wasn't planning on taking it. I'm sure they've drawn one up for you too. Emmy, I don't know what you think you've figured out, but you're wrong."

Emmy was getting frustrated. This wasn't where she'd planned on this going at all. She'd gotten ahead of herself and maybe ruined any chance of a confession. Belle started to bark. She was probably upset by the tension in the room. Emmy was trying to stay calm and think through the noise.

"I know, Ramona. I know that you killed my mom. You found that she was going to try to sabotage Brighton's boat so he could get the insurance money. You saw it as a way to get her out of the way so Edward would inherit the island."

"Your mom was trying to sabotage Brighton's boat? Are you sure? That seems completely out of character for her." Ramona looked genuinely confused. She was a better actor than Emmy thought.

"Don't pretend you didn't know. I heard you, on the tape. I heard you making sure there was going to be champagne on the boat. Champagne that was drugged. I think you meant to kill them both, but my dad managed to escape."

"The champagne?" Ramona finally seemed to understand. She nodded. "I did ask that there be champagne on the boat, but only because I wanted them to relax. They were both so stressed about everything. Their marriage was falling apart, but I thought maybe they could work it out. I..." She stopped. "How did you hear me ordering champagne twenty-three years ago?"

Belle bayed at the wall in front of her.

Emmy raised her voice. "It was on the tape that my uncle sent to Nancy. One of your bugged rooms came back to bite you. Edward knew you killed my mom, but he couldn't bring himself to accuse you in person until he was gone." She took in a breath to collect her courage. "But I will. I know you killed my mom, I know you killed my uncle, and I know you killed Jonathon."

Ramona stared at her. Emmy waited for the explosion of anger, for the denials, for the confession, for anything. Slowly a light dawned in Ramona's eyes. "You couldn't have heard that conversation. It couldn't have been recorded. The bookshop wasn't part of the record-ing system. That was Edward's domain. My father-in-law didn't wire the bookshop like he wired everything else. That was the one thing he let Edward have. It was all he ever wanted."

Emmy felt unsure for the first time. "So maybe Edward recorded it. Maybe he learned that particular trick from his father."

Ramona looked thoughtful. "That could be true, but if he did, he misunderstood me. I didn't drug your parent's champagne and I wasn't the one who put it on the boat." She took a couple of steps forward like she was thinking. "It was my voice on the recording, but only because I asked—"

Air whooshed past Emmy's ear. Red bloomed from a slice across Ramona's neck. She fell backward, her hands clutching at her throat. A knife embedded in the wall behind her. She opened her mouth. No sound came out.

Emmy caught her as she fell.

Chapter 62

Of Knives and Men

P ierce gripped Emmy's hand as they sat outside the hospital room. After what seemed like an eternity Dr. Gregory came out. "She's damn lucky, but I think she'll pull through. The knife missed her carotid artery by a hair. She won't be able to talk for a few weeks. That will make her crazy, but at least she'll be alive."

"Thanks, Doctor." Emmy slumped in her chair. She was exhausted.

"Can we see her?" Pierce said. "Can she write or draw a picture or...I think she was about to say something important and that's why she was targeted."

Dr. Gregory shook his head. "Not for a while. She's in a medically induced coma to keep her from moving. She'll stay that way until there's no danger of her doing any further damage."

"Keep us posted. Let me know as soon as she's well enough to be questioned," Pierce said.

"Of course." Dr. Gregory turned and walked out the door.

"This is all my fault." Emmy buried her face in her hands. "I was so sure Ramona did this. She almost died because I was wrong."

"It wasn't just you." Pierce stroked her hair. "We all thought she was the killer."

Emmy pulled away and then stood up. She didn't deserve his sympathy. "I'm giving up. The island isn't worth it. Too many people have been hurt. Too many people have died. Let Ramona take it, or Madelyn. Or sell it all to Khonico to build their resort. I'm done with Sharp Island. I'm going back to the mainland, my mountain of student debt, and Ginny's uncomfortable pull-out couch."

Pierce stood beside her. "That might not be your only option anymore. You've made friends here. A lot of people on the island would be willing to help you, whether you own the place or not."

Emmy shook her head. "I failed all of them: the people on the island, my parents, you. I especially failed myself."

"Give yourself some time and space." Pierce put his hands on her shoulders. "You did the best you could. You got pulled into an impossible and dangerous game of cat and mouse. Forget solving the case. You're lucky to be alive."

Emmy pulled away from him. "None of it matters anyway. My time is up. The month ends tomorrow."

Emmy walked into her apartment for what she knew would be the last time. She looked at the Sharpopoly set still set up on the coffee table, and the piles of paperwork covering every flat surface. All monuments to her monumental failure. She walked into her bedroom and threw her clothes into her suitcase. She replaced the key in the *Skeleton Key* book and packed up everything she'd brought with her into one small suitcase and the two reusable shopping bags Ginny had brought her.

She'd intended to leave the disaster that represented her failed investigation in the living room, but at the last minute she pulled a garbage bag out from under the sink and swept the whole thing into it. It wasn't fair to make someone else clean up her mess.

Emmy held up the little gray mouse that had been a toy for some unknown cat. She thought about what she'd told Pierce about winning a game of cat and mouse by becoming a cat. She'd failed at that, just like everything else. She threw it into the garbage bag and tied it closed.

She only kept the little crown which she knew her uncle meant to represent her mother, the island princess. As she was walking to throw the bag down the chute in the hall, she stepped on something sharp. She bent down to pick it up. It was the little dagger from the game, perfect for stabbing someone in the back. She looked at it closer. It had the same dragon shape as the knife that had stabbed her uncle and the knife that had been thrown at her.

A throwing knife.

Something wedged itself in her mind, deeper than the knife that had penetrated the book and nearly her chest. She left the bag on the floor, put on her shoes and walked out the door. She had one destination in mind.

The little bell signaled her entrance into the tea shop. The tables were mostly empty, but the room was filled with the scent of mint and licorice and lavender.

"Emmy," Ms. Lee greeted her. "I heard you were leaving us. You don't know how sad that makes me. Can I offer you one last cup of tea, in hopes it will persuade you to stay?"

Emmy shook her head. "I don't have time for tea right now. I came to ask you a question. You once said you could tell me which of the women on this island would survive a zombie apocalypse and what would be their weapon of choice. I need to know who would choose a throwing knife."

Chapter 63

In Case of Emergency

The gas lights had just started to cut through the mist rolling off the ocean when Emmy stood outside the bookshop. The evening reminded her of her first walk to the bookshop with Professor Sharp nearly a month ago. She hoped it wouldn't be her last.

Unlike the last time she'd thought she was confronting a killer, she didn't have a plan or backup in place. It was just her and the little bit of knowledge she'd gained over the last month and the desire to win her uncle's game by becoming a cat.

The bell in the bookshop rang as she walked in. "I'm sorry, we're closed," Victoria called. "I must have forgotten to change the sign."

"It's just me," Emmy called back. "I came to say goodbye."

Victoria came around the bookshelf. She'd obviously been rearranging things, making the bookshop her own in anticipation of becoming its owner. "I'm sorry to see you go," she said. Emmy guessed that she wasn't really sorry.

Emmy plastered a smile on her face. "I'm sorry to leave, but at least I know the bookshop will be in good hands." She ran her fingers over the shelves. "You really do love this place, don't you?"

Victoria straightened one of the books Emmy had displaced. "It's always been my space on the island, even when I was a little girl."

Emmy forced a nostalgic smile. "I came here as a little girl too, didn't I?"

Victoria stopped, her face clouded over. "You remember?"

"A little. You used to read to me. I called you Miss Torri…Mystery." Emmy looked at the shelf behind Victoria, the Mystery Shelf. "You showed me the little room there. I thought that's where you lived. And that was why it was called the Miss Torri shelf."

Victoria shook her head, "Edward never liked the name Torri, or Vicky. I was always Victoria to him. He liked things to be called by their proper names."

"Like the bookshop and the patisserie."

"Yes." Victoria chuckled.

"You took care of me when I was a little girl. You read to me when my mother was too busy to pay attention."

Victoria nodded, a mist of memory covering her eyes. "And I would have kept taking care of you. If both your parents had died on that boat, I would have raised you as my own. Edward and I together. The bookshop could have been our kingdom. But your father took you away, and when you came back you didn't even remember me."

"I'm sorry I didn't remember. I was just a little girl."

"But you're all grown up now, grown up, but I hear you're leaving the island." Victoria looked hopeful.

"I failed to solve the mystery. The island goes to Ramona tomorrow and the bookshop to you. Did you have any idea that my uncle had left it to you in his original will?""No, I..." Victoria's hands fluttered nervously. "Edward didn't talk to me much about his personal affairs."

"Did that bother you? You were my uncle's assistant for almost thirty years and he didn't tell you anything. In fact, he barely noticed you."

"He was a very busy, very important man." Victoria said. Her eyes darted around the room like she was looking for something—an escape, maybe? "And none of it was my business anyway."

"But the bookshop was your business. It was your place. And I think you were listening, even if he wasn't talking to you. One of the benefits of being the bookstore mouse. No one knew you were in the room. Not even Edward."

Emmy stepped to the Mystery shelf and ran her hand along it. "And if you really wanted to be invisible, you hid in the little rooms behind the shelves. There you could watch everything, the way you were watching the night he brought me here." Emmy paused at the green wingback chair where she had sat with the professor that first night.

"Who else came to the bookshop that night?" Emmy asked the question she should have asked the first time she saw Victoria.

Victoria took a deep breath. "You came, and you ate the cakes and then...then you fell asleep. After you were asleep *she* came."

"She? You mean Ramona. You can say her name. She's somewhere that she can't hurt you anymore."

Victoria laughed nervously. "I've always been kind of afraid of her. She was always in a hurry and so loud. And I knew she didn't like me very much."

"But Edward loved her, despite all that, didn't he?" Emmy said.

Victoria shook her head. "She wasn't even pretty and she wasn't very nice to him. They were always fighting. She didn't like the bookshop and she never read anything but her horrible, huge law books."

"I don't know what he saw in her." Emmy worked to appear sympathetic. "Do you know why she was here the night the professor died?"

"I'm not sure. She came with another man. They talked to the professor. I think there was a piece of paper."

Emmy kept her eyes on Victoria's hands. One was in front of her, but the other was feeling behind her, tracing the book spines with her fingers.

Emmy picked up a book from the table, a thick volume of Sherlock Holmes stories, and pretended to flip through it. She scanned the shelf behind Victoria. Casually she said, "They came to sign the professor's new will. The one that named me as his only heir. The one that would have given me the bookshop if I choose. Whether I solved the murder or not."

She looked up from the book, meeting Victoria's eyes. For a second they were narrowed and beady, more like a rat's eyes than a mouse's eyes. "You knew what was in that will because you'd helped him videotape himself reading it. You'd even helped him prepare the clues and the 'threats' he said he'd received. You may have even added a few of your own clues, like the ketamine in my purse and the picture and message left on my phone. Edward didn't believe in technology. You added other things that kept me chasing red herrings, but every little piece helped me put the puzzle together, even your misdirections."

"I d-don't know what you're talking about." Victoria's voice trembled, but her hands remained steady.

"You didn't care about the money or the island or any of it, but you were furious that he was changing the will and that I would be inheriting the bookshop. You'd done everything for him. You'd even killed his sister when she inherited the island instead of him. You drugged the champagne Ramona had asked you to deliver to the ship. He wasn't grateful at all. He continued to ignore you. All you wanted was the bookshop. You didn't care if I got everything else. But he didn't see that.

"When you found out that he'd signed the papers and officially changed the will that night, you got angry. Angry enough that in a fit of rage you threw a knife and killed him."

"You don't have any proof of any of this," Victoria hissed, her hand still behind her back, feeling for the right book.

"Don't I?"

Emmy kept moving forward, scanning the shelves for her own escape. She had to keep Victoria talking and distracted. Victoria was searching for one of the knives she'd hidden in the books, like the one Emmy had cut her hand on after the professor was killed. It was only a matter of time before she reached one. Emmy knew how deadly her aim could be. She wouldn't have time to get away or even scream, but if she kept her talking, maybe there would at least be a recording of Victoria's confession.

"You didn't think this room had the same kind of recording system that the rest of the island had, but I know it does. My uncle sent a tape to Pierce's mom. I bet Madelyn could find it, or Pierce. They might have to tear apart the room and all the shelves, but—"

Victoria's eyes lit up. A book thumped to the floor. She gripped the jade handle. Emmy lunged for *The Mousetrap*. She unshelved it and jumped back. The bookshelf groaned. Victoria spun around. The shelf tipped forward. Victoria dropped the knife and raised her hands to protect herself from the cascade. Her scream faded as she was buried in a pile of books.

Chapter 64

Watermelon Patisserie

R amona gestured wildly as she sat in one of the green wingback chairs in the bookshop. Emmy was doing her best to decipher what the gestures meant, but there was so much going on, she was having a hard time focusing on just one thing.

Madelyn strode by, a cocktail in her hand. She nodded toward the mute Ramona, her neck sporting a white bandage, still under doctor's orders to not speak. "I could get used to this."

Ramona's face turned red, and her hands clenched into fists, but she couldn't make a sound.

Emmy looked around the crowded shop. She felt more at home here than she had anywhere on earth. Almost the whole town had turned out to celebrate her officially inheriting the island. She'd already made a few changes. Ginny was taking over Look Sharp and Madelyn had opened her own tech boutique a few doors down.

Pierce had been made a detective. It meant he would be spending less time in an official capacity on the island, but Emmy had convinced him to take one of the vacant apartments near hers even though his grandmother insisted she'd always have room for him in the cottage with the million-dollar view. It now fully belonged to the Hamilton family. Even though she couldn't talk, Ramona had found a loophole that made it possible for Nancy to stay on the island, as long as she wore a monitoring bracelet.

Brighton Redding wasn't here. Emmy knew she hadn't exactly won him over with her accusations, but she hoped that someday he would forgive her. Her mother had considered him a friend, and Emmy knew she'd need all the friends she could get on this island.

Victoria had survived her encounter with the professor's *only in case of an emergency* bookshelf mousetrap. She was awaiting trial in a prison on the mainland and there were rumors that she had become the caretaker of the prison library.

"Looks like you're running low on pastry and petit fours," Andrew, the new waiter from the White Sails said. The whole party had been catered by the various businesses on the island and the food was to die for.

Ginny watched him refill the trays. "He's the perfect tall, dark and handsome stranger—like someone from one of your books. I wonder how long he'll stick around."

"What do you think, Emmy?" Pierce put one arm around her waist and reached for a little pastry on the tray in front of them with his other hand. "Is he devastatingly handsome?"

"I've seen better," Emmy said leaning against his shoulder. A frantic movement from across the room caught her eye. "What do you think is wrong with Ramona now?"

"No idea," Pierce said.

The older woman gave up gesturing and started writing on the colorful white board she'd started carrying with her everywhere.

Emmy picked up a wedge-shaped pastry and popped it in her mouth just as Ramona raised her sign.

It had one word:

Watermelon!

The flavor hit Emmy's tongue the minute she comprehended the sign. It was too late. She covered her mouth and made a mad dash to the bathroom. She leaned over the toilet as everything she'd eaten from the party was evacuated from her stomach.

When she sat up, she was shocked to see a very pale-looking Pierce. He was holding back her hair.

The End

Turn the page to get started on Emerson Fox's next adventure in "The Haunting in the Hall"

Chapter 1: The Haunting in the Hall

E mmy settled into her favorite chair in the library. For all the bad things that happened in the book shop—being drugged, her uncle's murder, and then catching his killer here—it was still her favorite place on the Island. It had become her after-hours refuge. Here she could forget about the problems and responsibilities she had inherited and be transported somewhere else.

The autumn chill had settled over the island. Emmy liked to lock the doors, close the curtains, build a fire in the brick fireplace, and read for hours. It was a luxury she hadn't allowed herself for a long time.

Even now, she knew she didn't have time for this indulgence. Running the Island had become a full-time job. Sharp Island was an entity in and of itself. The power, the water, and even the roads were all owned by Sharp Enterprises—in other words, her. This meant that the community had to pay for upkeep on almost everything. The state managed small bits, like the island-hopping police officer, the small office/jail cell Emmy had become intimately acquainted with, and maintenance of a small fire station with two trucks, a rescue boat, and an all-island volunteer fire department. In some ways, the Island was less of a city and more of a huge housing development with an overarching HOA and her at the helm.

Her uncle's ex-wife Ramona chuckled as she handed over the reins. "What this Island really needs is a benevolent dictator," she said. "But as I learned, the problem with being a dictator of any kind is that there is always someone waiting in the wings to overthrow you. I'm glad you were the person who overthrew my uncredited reign."

Her friend Ginny's advice was always the same; surround yourself with the smartest people possible, and then take all the credit when things go well.

Emmy sighed. Tomorrow was the town hall meeting where she would break the news that she wouldn't be able to reduce any of the rents or fees that her uncle had imposed on the Island's shopkeepers. There just wasn't enough revenue coming in to cover the costs of running and maintaining the Island, especially now that the tourist season was over.

She tried to go back to her book. She'd been going through her uncle's collected histories of Sharp Island, hoping to find some advice on how to run things, but it seemed the members of her family who had been in charge before her had been all but benevolent dictators. At least they had managed to keep things running and profitable.

She stared into the flames. Her imagination ran wild and the flames became faces of the people who had inhabited Sharp Island before her. She wished she could ask them how they did it. Somehow her eyes closed, and the warmth of the fire lulled her into sleep.

The chill was the first thing she noticed. It took a few seconds to get her bearings. The bookshop was cold, freezing actually. The fire had burned itself out, but the room still shouldn't be this cold.

She stood up, stiff from sleeping in the chair. She needed to go up to her apartment and her real bed. She leaned over to turn off the light when she saw her. A woman in white stood next to the open compartment behind the history bookcase. She had a scarf draped over her head and a lantern in one hand. Emmy opened her mouth to ask her what she was doing there, but stopped when the woman moved. She had an iridescent, almost transparent appearance.

Emmy blinked a few times. She had to be dreaming or seeing things. But although the woman appeared ethereal and not exactly solid, she also seemed very real. She glided along the shelves as if she were searching for something. A book, maybe? She stopped, hovering for a moment before she slid into the bookshelf and disappeared.

Something hit the floor behind Emmy with a loud thud. She whirled around. A thick black book had fallen out of one of the shelves.

Emmy picked it up. It was an old leather-bound notebook. The title on the front said, *Sharp Island History and Legends*.

She stared back at the place where the woman had vanished. Was she some sort of Sharp Island phantom? Was she leaving the book behind as a warning for Emmy?

Continue reading "The Haunting in the Hall"

For my Write Club. Follow your dreams.

Also by Jennifer Shaw Wolf

The Second Kiss

Jess never told anyone about her first kiss, her crush on the too-old-for-her boy next door, or what his departing gift meant to her.

Jacob has been gone for six years, and a lot has changed. The shy, awkward little girl he left behind has grown up. Jess is a high school senior with plans, popularity, and a football star boyfriend. Just as everything she's worked for falls apart, Jacob is back—assigned to the Army base near her home. Is this her second chance at love, or will Jacob only see the little girl he left behind?

The Extra

Desperate for cash, a starving student takes a job as an extra on a B-list horror movie and finds herself in a fight for survival.

To get your free copy of "The Extra," subscribe to my mailing list, and get access to free content, visit my website at:

jennifershawwolf.com

The Body in the Bookshop

Inheriting a bookshop and the island that comes with it could be the solution to all of Emmy's problems, or it could be the last thing she ever does.

Emerson Fox's ADHD has left her with a do-nothing degree, a jilted ex-fiancé, mounds of student debt, and a knack for forgetting important things while focusing on obscure details. When a disastrous blind date leaves her stranded in a quaint bookshop on a tiny island in Washington's Puget Sound, the last thing she expects is to find the bookshop's owner has been murdered. Even more shocking, he's left a will that names her as his long-lost niece and sole heir to his bookshop and the entire island. Emmy can't claim her inheritance until she unearths a long-buried family secret, convinces the only police officer in town (and the other half of her disastrous date) that she's innocent, and finds the focus she needs to solve her uncle's murder.

Dead Girls Don't Lie

Jaycee and Rachel were best friends. But that was before. . .before that terrible night at the old house. Before Rachel shut Jaycee out. Before Jaycee chose Skyler over Rachel. Then Rachel is found dead. The police blame a growing gang problem in their small town, but Jaycee is sure it has to do with that night at the old house. Rachel's text is the first clue-starting Jaycee on a search that leads to a shocking secret. Rachel's death was no random crime, and Jaycee must figure out who to trust before she can expose the truth.

Breaking Beautiful

Allie lost everything the night her boyfriend, Trip, died in a horrible car accident - including her memory of the event. As their small town mourns his death, Allie is afraid to remember because doing so means delving into what she's kept hidden for so long: the horrible reality of their abusive relationship.

When the police reopen the investigation, it casts suspicion on Allie and her best friend, Blake, especially as their budding romance raises eyebrows around town. Allie knows she must tell the truth. Can she reach deep enough to remember that night so she can finally break free?

Meant to Die

Ever since her twin sister died at birth, Miranda has walked with the dead. But what she knows about death has kept her from living life. Then she meets Remy, a little girl with a different view of life and death. Remy sees people on the brink of a violent end, people who were never meant to die. When Remy shares her visions with her, Miranda has to decide whether to team up with this fearless girl and a restless spirit to solve a string of decades-old murders. But can someone who's spent her life in fear find the courage to catch a killer, even if it means she might be the next to die?

Acknowledgements

First thanks to my husband and kids including my kids by marriage for standing by me and supporting the long hours and never ending craziness that writing brings. Thanks to my parents and siblings for teaching me to follow my dreams. Thanks to my North Thurston Write Club for being my inspiration in the world of words, wonder, writing, and all things weird. Whenever someone brings up Donald Trump, time machines, hidden treasure, and oddly-flavored Cheetos, I'll think of you. (Sorry I deserted you, not my idea.) Thanks to the real Emmerson Fox for the loan of her awesome name. Thanks to super-fan Orissa for her hand written letters and drawings that continually encourage me to keep moving forward. Thanks to my ANWA sisters and (now) brothers from our Rainy Day Writers group for making me feel slightly less insane (or at least in good company). Thanks to Christie for begging me to have something ready for her to read on vacation and then for actually reading it. Thanks to Zach and Cady for their mad beta reading and editing skills. Thanks to my awesome cover designer Angelica at Purposes on Paper for putting up with endless rounds of indecision. Thanks to Lynda at Easy Reader Editing for being understanding with my ever shifting timeline and the moving targets that are my "deadlines." Also, thanks for making it look like I actually know how to punctuate. Thanks to Agatha Christie my absolute favorite mystery writer, for her brilliance, perseverance, and inspiration.

Thanks to the Great Creator for this life, this beautiful world, and all the wonder and mystery that surrounds it.

About the Author

Jennifer Shaw Wolf was that kid you see hiding behind a stack of books from the public library—most of them mysteries. She read her way through life, learning the who, the what, the where, the why, and the how dunnit, from some of the best—Agatha Christie, Arthur Conan Doyle, Edgar Allen Poe, and Daphne du Maurier. She looked up from her books long enough to meet a guy, fall in love, get married, and have four amazing kids (all of whom have betrayed her by becoming adults.) She lives with her Prince Charming and an incredibly spoiled (but also very charming) dog in the mysterious green forests of the Pacific Northwest. Her favorite things are reading, writing, and spending time with her family which now includes three wonderful in-law kids and a beautiful granddaughter.